The Proposal
at Siesta Key

The Proposal at Siesta Key

Amish Brides of Pinecraft, Book Two

Shelley Shepard Gray

AVON

INSPIRE

An Imprint of HarperCollinsPublishers

P.S.™ is a trademark of HarperCollins Publishers.

HarperCollins books may be purchased for educational, business, or sales promotional use. For information please e-mail the Special Markets Department at SPsales@harpercollins.com.

FIRST EDITION

Designed by Rhea Braunstein

Illustrated map copyright © by Laura Hartman Maestro
Photographs courtesy of Katie Troyer, Sarasota, Florida

Library of Congress Cataloging-in-Publication Data has been applied for.

ISBN 978-0-06-233772-6

15 16 17 18 19   OV/RRD   10 9 8 7 6 5 4 3 2 1

To the members of the Buggy Bunch. You ladies have inspired me more than you will ever know! Thank you for everything you do.

The author is grateful for being allowed to reprint the Chocolate Pecan Pie recipe from *Our Family's Favorite Recipes* by Clara Coblentz.
The Shrock's Homestead
9943 Copperhead Rd. N.W.
Sugarcreek, OH 44681

Open my eyes to see the wonderful truths in your instructions.

PSALM 119:18

Growing old is easy—the hard part is growing up.

AMISH PROVERB

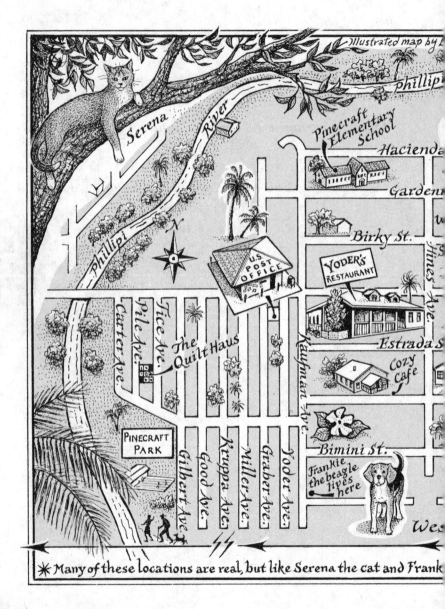

Illustrated map by L

Phillip

Serena River

Pinecraft Elementary School

Hacienda

Garden

Birky St.

YODER'S RESTAURANT

Phillipi

N

U.S. POST OFFICE

Kaufman Ave.

Estrada S

Cozy Cafe

Carter Ave.

Pile Ave.

Tice Ave.

The Quilt Haus

Bimini St.

Frankie the beagle lives here

PINECRAFT PARK

Gilbert Ave.

Good Ave.

Kruppa Ave.

Miller Ave.

Graber Ave.

Yoder Ave.

Hines Ave.

Wes

✳ Many of these locations are real, but like Serena the cat and Frank

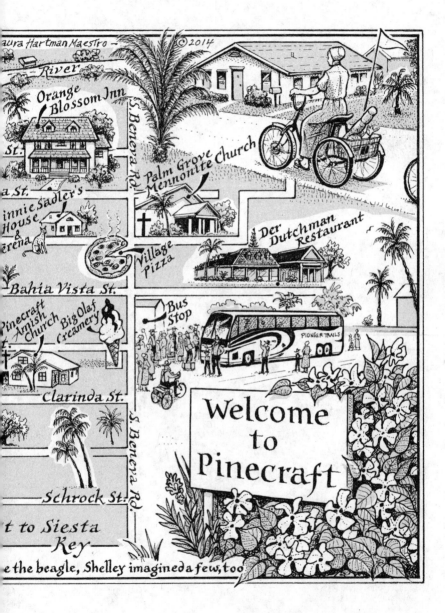

Laura Hartman Maestro — ©2014

River

Orange
Blossom Inn

St.

a St.

S. Beneva Rd.

Palm Grove
Mennonite Church

innie Sadler's
House
rena

Village
Pizza

Der
Dutchman Restaurant

Bahia Vista St.

Pinecraft
Amish Church

Big Olaf
Creamery

Bus
Stop

PIONEER TRAILS

Clarinda St.

S. Beneva Rd.

Welcome
to
Pinecraft

Schrock St.

t to Siesta
Key

e the beagle, Shelley imagined a few, too

*T*he moment Penny Troyer turned the dead bolt on the front door, she knew it was a big mistake.

No matter what her mother was doing, or where she was, she always, *always* heard the distinctive *snap* of the front door dead bolt disengaging.

Penny froze, feeling vaguely like a burglar caught red-handed, and mentally began to count to five.

She barely made it to three.

With all the fanfare of a trio of trumpeter swans, her mother's high-pitched call echoed down the hall. "Penny? Penny, what are you doing?"

Penny bit back an irritated retort—something she'd been doing more and more lately. "Nothing."

"It must have been something. I am fairly positive I heard you at the door."

God had really blessed her mother with hearing that was just *too* good. "I'm simply going to sit on the front porch."

Practically before Penny had time to take another breath, her mother appeared in the entryway. Her hands clutched the sides of her apron, and concern shone in her truly beautiful periwinkle-colored eyes. "Why?"

The question was so, so unnecessary, Penny almost smiled. But that would've been the wrong thing to do. Instead, she kept her voice even and respectful. "No real reason. I simply wanted to sit outside."

"But you'll go no further?"

The correct answer was the one she'd given for the last twelve of her twenty-four years. No, she would not. She would stay close. Free from harm.

But she simply wasn't sure if she could do that anymore. "I don't plan to go anywhere. But I might."

Her mother froze mid-nod. "What in the world does that mean?"

"It means that I'm far too old to be forced to promise to stay on my parents' front porch," she replied, almost patiently.

Immediately, hurt filled her mother's expression. "You know I like you close because I care about you, dear."

Penny knew that. She really did.

But of course, she knew that her mother asked for other reasons, too. They both knew those reasons. And they both knew that her mother would do just about anything to avoid speaking of them.

But today, Penny had finally had enough.

Fortifying herself for the drama that was about to ensue, she gestured toward the open doorway. "Mamm, why don't you come out on the porch, too? I think we need to talk."

"Penny, you know I don't have time to lollygag. Your grandparents are coming over for supper."

"Yes, and I know that everything is ready. I helped you set the table, make the casseroles, and marinate the chicken."

For a moment, Penny was sure her mother was about to argue, but then at last, she followed Penny out to the swing situated exactly in the middle of the wide front porch. Surrounding them were her mother's carefully tended pink roses and a quartet of blooming pansies. Daisies, snapdragons, and begonias lined the footpath of their tidy, one-story home in Pinecraft, Florida—a small Amish community in the heart of Sarasota.

Once they were seated side by side, the fabric of her mother's blue dress overlapping with Penny's own teal-colored one, Penny tried to think of the best way to say what was on her mind. But as she mentally tried out different approaches, she knew there wasn't a single explanation that would be accepted.

Sometimes there really was no way to deliver bad news, even if that news was only going to be regarded as bad by one of them.

Steeling her spine, she decided to go for the direct approach. "Mother, it has now been twelve years since Lissy died. She's been gone for half my life."

Her mother flinched. "We don't need to talk about your sister."

"*Jah*, we do," Penny said gently, though taking care to weave resolve into her tone. "Mamm, everything we do is a result of what happened to Lissy." Before her mother could get up and walk away, Penny wrapped her fingers around her mother's wrist and held on tight. "Mamm, what happened to Lissy was a terrible thing. I know that."

Before her eyes, her mother aged another ten years—as she always did when she thought about what happened to Lissy. "It was worse than terrible."

Yes. Yes, it was. One winter's day twelve years ago, back when they'd lived in Ohio, Penny's older sister Elizabeth—Lissy to all who'd known her—had been lured away by a very, very bad man. He'd raped her. He'd beaten her. And then he'd left her in a field. She'd died alone and in pain.

The event had sent shockwaves through the whole community, both English and Amish. Everyone in the area had attended the memorial service and contributed to funds set up in Lissy's name. Some had even begun neighborhood watch groups. Within a week, the police caught the man who later confessed to the attack. A week after that, the man died in his jail cell without having stood trial.

Many members in the community had written editorials in the paper about how happy they were that justice had been served, but for the three remaining members of the Troyer family, the man's death hardly mattered. Nothing mattered except their loss. They were nestled in a dark fog of grief, oblivious of everything but the passing of each never-ending, painful day. But as the weeks passed, it became obvious that nothing was ever going to ease their pain, and nothing was ever going to bring Lissy back.

Two years later, her parents decided to move to Sarasota, claiming they needed a change of scenery. Someplace fresh to start anew. Somewhere that would never be cold and snowy. Where there were no reminders of that horrible day.

Penny had been eager for the move, too.

But though they now lived in a place where the sun always shone and nobody knew about their hardships unless they were told, the grief and worry in her family hadn't changed.

If anything, it began to affect everything in their lives.

Over the years, instead of venturing out into their new world, her parents had become more reclusive. Their fears had begun to center on Penny, and their restrictions on her had become more and more pronounced. At first, Penny had been glad for all the rules. She'd been afraid of strangers, and most of her nights had been haunted by memories of her sister and visions of what must have happened at the kidnapper's hands.

Eventually, however, the nightmares faded. As she became accustomed to their new life, Penny's heart had begun to ease. She'd started to think about Lissy in terms of her life instead of her death—she remembered the way Lissy had loved to can vegetables and how she could eat a whole jar of pickles in a single day. Penny recalled Lissy's infectious laugh and the way she'd hated to get up in the morning. In fact, she'd been almost insufferable until she'd had a cup of coffee. And as these memories flourished, Penny had realized that Lissy would have hated for her little sister to do nothing but mourn for the rest of her life.

And, deep down, she'd known Lissy would have been right.

Penny began to feel the pinch of her circumstances. Her parents' refusal to see her as a grown woman instead of a susceptible child was aggravating. Still, she'd kept silent out of respect, but there was no denying that their rules and fears had begun to chafe. After a while, it had festered, but now it pained her.

And when she'd woken up this morning, Penny knew she couldn't take it another day.

Not for one more hour.

"Mamm, you and Daed are going to have to give me more freedom." Truly, she was proud of her firm tone of voice.

But even that didn't make an impression. "Don't be silly. You have freedom, Penny."

"Not really. You haven't let me take a job. You don't even like me walking anywhere alone."

"That's because it's not safe."

"Mamm, if I was still a child, I would agree with you. But I am a grown woman. Of course it's safe."

The skin around her mother's lips tightened. "Things can happen."

"That is true, but I will be careful." She ached to point out that she always tried her best to avoid eye contact with strangers. She even fought with her blond curls every morning, taming them as best she could so they would stay neatly confined under her *kapp*.

"Bad things can happen even when one is careful."

"I know that. But I can't live like this any longer. I have a feeling if you let yourself actually see me as I am, you would see that, too." As she felt her mother's blue eyes skim over her tan arms, loose teal dress, and blue rubber flipflops, Penny waited patiently. She knew she was dressed exactly like every other twenty-four-year-old Amish woman in Sarasota. "Why, many women my age are married and have their own children."

"Is that what this is about? You are wanting a husband?"

"Nee!" How could her mother have jumped from her needing to be able to walk down the street by herself to wanting a husband?

Her mother's expression gentled. "Don't worry, dear. We'll all go to more gatherings. You'll meet a man."

"You don't understand. I am not simply looking for a husband. I am looking for friends, activities." Around a sigh, Penny added, "I am looking for a life."

"You have a life. And a good, safe one, too. Daughter, everything we've done has been to protect you."

"Jah. But it's also been to protect you and Daed, too. Mamm, you and Daed must loosen your hold on me."

"I'll speak to your father. Perhaps we can come up with a plan. . . ."

"I don't want to wait for a plan. Tonight, there is a gathering at Pinecraft Park. A missionary group, the Knoxx Family, is speaking. I'm meeting Violet Kaufmann at the pavilion to hear them."

"Violet?" More worry lines appeared around her mother's eyes, illuminated by the setting sun. "But she's not Amish anymore."

"I know. But she is a nice girl from a nice family." She was also one of Penny's few friends. "I'm going to go with her."

"Your father is going to be upset when he hears about this."

"I know and I'm sorry about that. But I can't live my life trying to make him happy with me." Especially since she knew that nothing was going to ever truly make her father happy again. "Please try to understand my point of view, Mamm. I feel like I'm trapped. No one wants to feel like they are living in confinement."

"I'm sorry, child. But you know I cannot support this . . . this whim of yours." She paused, looking as if she was about to add something more, but then merely stood up and walked back inside.

Penny slumped against the back of the wooden swing. In that moment she knew she had two choices. She could either back down so she wouldn't hurt her parents . . . or she could finally do what Lissy would've wanted and live her life.

And suddenly, her decision was so very easy. Everyone at some point in their life had to stop being someone's child and start being their own person.

It seemed that it was finally time to do that.

With a new resolve in her heart, Penny stood up and started walking down the street toward town. It was time.

Chapter 2

$\mathcal{T}$hank you, Michael Knoxx, for your wonderful and truly inspiring testimony!" Amos Nolt boomed into the microphone. As everyone in the pavilion clapped politely, he continued. "You and your family's presence have been a blessing to us all. Now, let's give the Knoxx Family another round of applause!"

While the audience clapped, Michael nodded his thanks to their sponsor, smiled at the crowd, and then stepped down from the platform with a feeling of relief. He hadn't known how much longer he was going to be able to last up there. The skin around his prosthesis was feeling pretty bad. Either he'd managed to get a scrape along his scar or he needed to get the top of his prosthesis readjusted. The skin that had healed long ago currently felt as raw as it ever had.

There was not a minute to dwell on his aches and pains, however, because he was immediately surrounded by well-wishers who had been listening to him from all corners of Pinecraft Park.

"*Danke*, Michael," a man about his father's age said as he clasped his hand in an iron grip. "Your words were what I needed to hear today."

"I'm glad my story meant something to ya," Michael said.

"It meant more than something," the gentleman said quietly as more men and even some children edged their way closer. "It meant the world."

Michael took in the man's fierce expression, wondering what had made his story of survival resonate so much. Surely being stuck in a ravine and losing half a leg was a bad thing—but meaning the world? He wasn't so sure about that.

But of course, that wasn't the correct response. "I'm grateful you came. *Danke.*" As circumspectly as he could, he glanced toward the horizon. It was after seven o'clock now. Shadows were appearing around the citrus trees and on the shuffleboard court. The day was almost done.

He still had more hands to shake and people to talk to, however. Including one small towheaded boy who was gazing up at him with shining eyes.

"I was in an accident three years ago," he blurted. "But I didn't have to have my leg cut off like you did."

The child's expression was so earnest, it eased some of Michael's tension. Actually, he was suddenly finding it hard to keep from smiling. His amputated leg never failed to interest young boys. "That is something to be thankful for. Ain't so?"

The boy nodded solemnly. "Do you ever miss your right foot?"

Michael's lips twitched. Leave it to a child to get to the heart of things. *"Jah."*

"Does it hurt where they cut it off?"

"Not usually."

"But sometimes it does?"

Michael nodded. *"Jah.* Sometimes it does." It was a struggle to keep his expression easy and kind. His leg had begun to throb something awful. In a few minutes, he feared he wasn't going to be able to concentrate on anything but how much he wanted to sit down and remove his prosthesis. It was as if that centralized pain was intent on eating away at every bit of goodness inside him.

The boy tugged at one of his pant legs. "Want to see my hurt?"

Good manners said he should nod. He should kneel down and give the child the attention he deserved. However, Michael had a very strong feeling that if he even tried to kneel there was a very good chance he wouldn't be able to get up on his own.

"Maybe you can show me later," he said. "After I sit down for a bit."

Disappointment filled the boy's gaze. "Oh."

"Sorry, son," he muttered. "We can talk later." When the boy turned away, Michael scanned the area. The sun had continued its way down the horizon, and with it, most of the men and women were either walking down the street or pedaling away. The thinning crowds made it easy to locate his sister and brother. They were standing a good five feet away grinning at him like fools. They also weren't doing one single, solitary thing to help.

He didn't blame them. They had no idea he was feeling like someone was slowly, steadily driving a nail into his knee. And even after all this time, he knew they still enjoyed the way the audience crowded around him after he spoke. They were proud of him. Proud of his story. Proud of the way he'd survived for twenty-four hours at the bottom of a ravine after a bicycle accident.

And, because none of them took one another too seriously, they also enjoyed watching Michael squirm under all the attention he received.

Evan always said Michael's celebrity status was his cross to bear.

Because his testimony was always the main focus of their family's events, his brother and sister did most everything behind the scenes. Evan dragged most of their luggage around, as Michael's condition made holding even a duffel bag difficult.

For most of the year, he and his family toured, speaking to anyone and everyone interested in hearing them. When they'd first started these events, their parents had simply referred to them as the Knoxx Family, because they wanted their message of evangelism to be the focus, not the name of their group.

Wherever they went, they were well received. They visited prisons, Amish and Mennonite churches, community auctions, and all manner of Gospel revivals and gatherings. They spoke to crowds, offering a few songs, a wealth of experiences, and shared stories about their belief in the Almighty.

Sometimes his parents would talk and sometimes their time on stage would consist of music. But most of the time, it was just him. And because he believed in the Lord's will so wholeheartedly, he did what was asked of him.

Again and again, he shared his story about being nearly sideswiped by a car in the mountains of Colorado, sliding into the road's gravel shoulder, then falling twenty feet into a narrow ravine. His leg had been badly injured. He'd waited for twenty-four hours to be found, with only the will to live and his belief in the power of prayer to keep him company.

After he'd been rescued, the doctors had done everything they could to save the lower part of his right leg but the damage was just too extensive. In the end, it had been futile. They'd talked to his parents and opted for amputation.

Some had thought he'd mourn the loss of his right calf and foot, but in truth, Michael didn't miss it all that much. When he'd been hurt and alone, afraid he was going to die, he'd spent a lot of time praying and making promises to the Lord if he survived.

Never once had he asked to survive without injuries.

While in the hospital, a couple of the doctors and nurses asked him to share his story. After hearing it, they'd asked him to speak to their churches. Before long, he'd begun speaking to even bigger crowds, and his family began participating as well.

Which, of course, brought him to the present. Except now he was tired, hiding how much pain he was in, and, not for the first time, wishing their schedule was not so tightly orchestrated.

After another five minutes or so, Evan walked to his side. "You okay? You look kind of pale."

"Stump's sore," he said with a smile, since it was just him and his brother. His mother hated him referring to his injury so bluntly. "I think I need to call it a night soon."

Evan's easy expression turned to concern. "It's that bad? Do you need anything?"

"Nah. Just a good night's sleep. We've been on the road for weeks now. My leg probably could use a rest."

"I bet you're right. Well, just so you know, I thought it was a real *gut* service tonight. There had to have been over a hundred people here."

Michael nodded. "I heard almost two hundred. A lot of donations came in, too." They always collected donations for CAM, Christian Aid Ministry, only taking enough to pay for their living and traveling expenses.

"Molly and I were thinking of taking the Kaufmanns up on their offer of a late supper. Want to come? You could camp out on their couch."

Michael knew the Kaufmanns from their other visits to Pinecraft. They were a nice family, easy to talk to and undemanding.

But even the thought of being around the Kaufmann family sounded like just another activity he'd have to push himself to get through. He simply couldn't do it.

"Tell them thanks, but I'm not up for it tonight. I'm going to walk back to the inn early."

"Sure about that?" His tone held a note of doubt. Though his brother liked to tease Michael about the crowds of people he attracted, he was still protective. Evan was two years older than Michael and took his role seriously. "How about I walk you back? Or I can tell someone you need a ride."

"*Nee*, don't do that." It was stupid, but even though Michael easily spent two hundred days a year talking to people about his accident, he still hated to be treated any differently. He would have had to be a whole lot worse off to accept his brother's escort. "I'll be fine. I just need to take a cool shower and lie down for a while." And hope his pain reliever would kick in quickly.

"I'll tell Molly. Mamm and Daed might stay awhile, but we'll head back to the inn within the hour."

"No need. I'll either be reading or asleep by then. Take your time."

After giving him another long, searching look, Evan finally nodded. "Okay, see you in the morning."

Five minutes later, Michael was able to slip out from the crowd and begin the four-block journey to the Orange Blossom Inn. But after two blocks, he was leaning against a fence, hoping and praying the shooting pain that was radiating from his knee would dull. He took one shaky breath after another, doing his best to control the pain.

He was an idiot. He should have accepted Evan's help. Pride really was his enemy. As the pain twisted through his leg again, Michael closed his eyes to fight the burning sensation.

"Excuse me? Mr. Knoxx—Michael—are you okay?"

He opened one eye to see a woman about his age staring at him with concern. She wore a teal dress, which served to highlight her blue eyes. He thought he'd noticed her in the crowd earlier, but he couldn't be sure.

"I'm fine," he said through clenched teeth. Usually he could fake his way through the worst of it. Tonight, however, it was a different story. It was as if his sore knee had decided it had finally had enough.

"Um, I'm sorry, but I have to tell you that you don't look fine. Not at all."

What was he supposed to say to that? "Listen, I appreciate your concern. However, there is no reason for it. You ought to get on your way."

But instead of listening, she stepped a little closer, even going so far as to bend over slightly so she could look him in the eye. For a moment, Michael was sure she was going to touch his arm or shoulder, but she didn't. "My name is Penny. Penny Troyer. I was in the crowd tonight. I heard you speak. You were really inspiring."

Michael appreciated her words, he truly did. But at the moment, he couldn't think of anything he wanted to do less than talk about his speech.

Though he knew surviving the accident and having the ability to talk about it were the Lord's work, sometimes he felt he spent too much time talking about his own personal trials and triumphs. There were plenty of people who had been through far more harrowing experiences yet never said a word about it. Plenty of people who didn't talk about their personal tragedies again and again and again.

Almost as soon as he thought that, Michael felt his insides burn with shame. Who was he to look down upon such a blessing?

"Thank you for saying that, uh, Penny," he replied through clenched teeth. "I am glad you enjoyed hearing my story."

Her eyes widened. "Oh, it was more than that! You have a true gift for storytelling. It's no wonder that everyone was so excited to see you."

"Danke."

"You're welcome. Seeing you truly made my day. *Nee*, my week." She smiled shyly. "Maybe even more than that."

With a sinking heart, he realized she was making him into something larger than life.

Every once in a while he met girls who looked at him with stars in their eyes, making him out to be something more than he was, just because he had a story to tell and an appealing way of telling it.

"Danke." He smiled, but he knew it was probably strained. He really needed to sit down for a while. Maybe a week.

"All that is why I wanted to check to see if you were all right. I could help you get to wherever you're going, if you'd like. May I help you?"

As much as he would like some help, experience had shown him that going anywhere alone with a female fan was a mistake. "I thank you for stopping, but there truly is no cause for concern. I'll be fine." He would. Eventually.

"Are you sure?"

Actually, he was not. The incision area burned like nothing he could remember in ages. The fear of finally succumbing to his doctors' warnings—that he might have to have another surgery, another round of recovery and therapy—petrified him. And that fear made his words a little harsher and his tone a little colder than he intended. "What I'm trying to tell you is that I don't need you to stand here with me."

As if stung, she stepped backward. "Oh. I'm sorry. I guess

you must get tired of people always trying to be around you. Wanting to talk to you and ask you questions."

He popped his chin up and gritted his teeth. Now he was beyond embarrassed. She was reading him all wrong. She thought he was acting like some spoiled rock star or celebrity, worn down by adoring fans. "It's not that. I, uh, do appreciate your concern."

"But you'd rather be alone." Hurt and disappointment glistened in her eyes.

Obviously, she was trying hard not to cry. Now he felt like a real jerk. "I'm the one who is sorry. I'm, ah, just not in the mood for conversation right now. It's been a long day, and I'm afraid it's gotten the best of me." He ached to tell her that he had serious concerns about his ability to make it back to the inn.

"Of course." She took another step backward. "Well, then. Good evening," she said before turning away and walking quickly in the opposite direction. Closing his eyes, Michael tried to tamp down the guilt he felt. He knew better than to be so ungrateful for her concern, knew better than to send her on her way alone. But he felt like he needed some time to himself. He needed to be selfish, at least for a few minutes.

"Lord," he murmured, "I'm sorry. I have a feeling I've disappointed You something awful, but I hope You'll understand. I'm only a man. And sometimes I'm afraid I'm as selfish as anyone."

He breathed in, exhaled, then at last felt the burn in his knee start to ease. Deciding to take advantage of that fact, he once again started limping toward the Orange Blossom Inn.

Chapter 3

$\mathscr{B}$everly Overholt didn't need a doctor's diagnosis to understand that her handsome guest was feeling poorly.

She could figure that out all on her own.

After watching Michael Knoxx painfully climb the first two front steps of her inn, grasping the wooden railing with all his might, then pulling himself up each step, she knew it was time to intervene. Seconds later, she was at his side, one arm securely wrapped around his waist.

"Just a few more steps, Michael," she said in her best no-nonsense way.

"I'll be fine."

"*Nee*, I think not." When he stiffened, she kept her voice sure and steady—and laced it with a thorough amount of salt and vinegar, too. "Don't even try to tell me that you don't need my help. You do."

After another second, he allowed more of his weight to press against her. "*Danke*," he muttered, his tone hoarse. "I'd be grateful for your assistance."

Though she was glad he gave in without further argument,

his easy acquiescence caused even more worry. From his previous visits, she knew that Michael Knoxx's pride was important to him. He toured the world, preaching God's word and sharing his stories about self-reliance. As far as she knew, Michael seldom depended on anyone for anything.

Never had she heard him complain, either—not even about things most people found annoying. Instead, he took everything in stride, whether it was the hot and humid weather, pouring rain, their incredibly busy schedule, or travel glitches. If he was not only struggling with a flight of stairs but also admitting he needed her assistance, he had to be in incredible pain.

And that concerned her very much.

After Beverly got him through the broad front door, she led him to the big overstuffed couch just off the entryway.

He collapsed against it with a sigh. "Thanks again. I was beginning to wonder how I was going to make it inside by myself."

Her concern was growing into real fear. "Where is your family?"

"Hmm?"

She leaned down, pressed her palm against his forehead. Was he feverish? She couldn't tell if he was perspiring from the heat, his effort to climb the stairs, or an infection. "Your family, Michael," she repeated. "Where are they?"

"Oh." His eyes focused. "They went to someone's *haus* after our meeting."

"Do you remember the family's name? I think it would be a good idea if I sent someone over there."

"No need."

"I think differently. Michael, whose house did they go to?"

As she'd hoped, her direct, firmly phrased question got results. "The Kaufmanns', I think?"

She relaxed. That was probably correct. She'd known the Kaufmann family for years. Frank Kaufmann had supervised much of the inn's renovations when she'd taken over the place. Just a few months ago, she'd become better acquainted with everyone in the family when one of her guests had fallen in love with their youngest son, Zack. "I bet it was the Kaufmanns. They're New Order Amish, so they have a phone. I'll give them a call and ask someone to let your parents know you're having some problems."

"Please don't."

"I think it would be best."

"It isn't. My brother said he wasn't going to stay there too long. Besides, there's nothing they can do except listen to me whine about the pain I'm experiencing."

"What is hurting you?"

"My knee." Running a hand over his face, he mumbled, "where it was amputated."

"I've never heard you complain about that before," she said slowly. "Is this pain something new?"

He hesitated before nodding. *"Jah."*

"What can I do? Do you need a pain reliever? Ice?"

Hazel eyes met hers, full of gratitude and relief. "Yes to both."

After ascertaining whether he wanted some Advil or some medicine of his own, she trotted off to the kitchen. "I'll be right back."

"I'll be here." He gave her a halfhearted smile.

By the time she returned with a Ziploc bag filled with ice and two tablets, he had taken off his prosthesis, placed his leg on the couch, and rolled up his pant leg.

She'd never seen an amputated limb before. When she saw the mottled, scarred skin that the surgeons had carefully reworked around his knee, she gasped. Not from the scars, but from the red lines extending from the area. At the very least, he had a bad infection and needed antibiotics.

"I know," he said around a grimace. "This leg of mine— what's left of it—it's not a pretty sight. Ain't so?"

"Actually, I was thinking that it looks very painful."

He shrugged. "Tonight it is."

"Here, then." She handed him a glass of water and two pills. After he'd swallowed them, she handed him the bag of ice. "How about a kitchen towel or something to put on your skin?"

"That would be *gut. Danke.*"

Ten minutes later, her guest was lying back against one of the armrests with his eyes closed. She walked to the kitchen in order to give him some privacy, but after a few minutes, she knew that was the wrong place to be. She was too antsy to sit in the back of the house.

All she could think was that his family was going to be concerned—and that was putting it mildly. Usually she tried not to interfere with her guests' wishes, even when they were sick or injured. But this time she knew she was going to have to make an exception. Michael needed medical attention, and it was becoming obvious that he had not been letting on just how badly he was hurting. She was going to have to tell his family everything she'd observed. In order not to disturb him in the front room, she walked out the back door and circled around the house to the front, planning to sit on the steps and wait for their return.

As minutes passed, she watched her porch lights and the solar-powered landscaping lanterns slowly illuminate like the fireflies she'd chased when she'd been a young Amish girl in Ohio. Several years ago, after a failed engagement, she'd decided not to join her order. Instead, she joined the local Mennonite church in Pinecraft and adopted their ways. Now, as she sat in the darkness and waited for the Knoxx Family to return, she closed her eyes and prayed for guidance. The air was fragrant with the scent of orange blossoms and lilacs. Lavender and roses. The scent was heavenly.

As she heard the laughter of children in the distance and the sound of the traffic on Beneva Rd., she found herself looking to the right, at another inn.

Where Eric Wagler stayed when he was in town.

Three months ago, she'd run into Eric by chance at the library and soon discovered that he'd come to Sarasota to claim ownership of *her* bed-and-breakfast. How it came to be his was a complicated story and they'd left things unresolved. All she knew was that she'd agreed to run the Orange Blossom Inn for another couple of months while he decided what he wanted to do.

Her girlfriends thought it was foolish to be so agreeable, and she supposed she didn't blame them. Part of her ached to rage at Eric, to cry and whine and remind him that she'd put her heart and soul into the bed-and-breakfast while he'd been occupied with his own life. But time had also taught her that crying and whining didn't solve anything. Most of the time, it was better to simply try to see the other person's point of view.

This was hard, because at the moment, Eric held all the cards. She was reduced to relying on his good nature. However, she kept hoping and praying that something would work out between them. But he was supposed to return to Pinecraft by the end of the week, and this time he was planning to take a room at *her* inn.

And she was going to have to let him.

Happy chatter interrupted her thoughts, and when she saw the Knoxx foursome approaching, she got to her feet. "Hello!" she called out.

They grinned and returned her greeting, but as they got closer, it was obvious that they saw her worry. Mrs. Knoxx's smile vanished. "Beverly, is there anything wrong?"

She descended the last three steps to greet them. "I'm not sure, but I'm afraid there might be. Michael is resting on the couch just off the entryway."

"What happened?"

"I don't want to alarm you, but he seems to be in a lot of pain. His, uh, knee is giving him trouble. Well, the part that attaches his prosthesis. We put some ice on it, and I gave him two pain relievers from my kitchen cabinet."

His parents exchanged worried looks.

"Thank you for looking after him, Beverly," Mrs. Knoxx said.

"It was no trouble and I wasn't waiting out here for thanks. Instead, I was hoping to give you some warning about how badly he was feeling."

"*Danke*," Mrs. Knoxx said. "Even when he was young Michael never did like to ask for help. It seems that some things never change." Looking determined, she strode inside, Evan and Molly on her heels.

When only she and Mr. Knoxx remained, he looked at Beverly with solemn eyes. "There's a chance we're going to have to get him to the hospital tonight. Would you help us arrange transportation?"

"Of course. One of my neighbors drives for the Amish. I'm sure he wouldn't mind taking you if that's what you decide you need to do."

"I hope I am wrong, but unfortunately his doctors have told

me that he might need surgery again. That time might have come."

When the door opened and Mrs. Knoxx peeked her head out, Beverly realized that he was probably right. The expression on Mrs. Knoxx's face told Beverly everything she needed to know.

To the rest of the world, Michael Knoxx might be a symbol of invincibility, capable of withstanding pain and all kinds of human frailties. Beverly now knew better, however. He put on a good face, but at the moment, he was just as susceptible to aches and pains as anyone. And actually, what he really needed now was someone who didn't see him as anything but a man in great need of a friendly, helping hand.

Thank the good Lord that she still had two good ones.

Chapter 4

$\mathcal{T}$welve hours later, Penny was still feeling the sting of Michael Knoxx's cool brush-off.

Oh, she hadn't expected him to want to chat with her for hours. Or even be especially excited to learn that he had a new fan in Sarasota.

Actually, if she was being completely honest, she'd never imagined that a man like him would feel like paying much attention to her anyway. After all, he was Michael Knoxx, the most famous member of the Knoxx Family, a mighty renowned group.

She, on the other hand? Well, she was Penny Troyer. A girl who was a bit mousey, a whole lot of an introvert, and until very recently, practically a prisoner in her own home.

But even taking all that into consideration, she had assumed he would have recognized her sincere attempt to help him, accepting that even girls in small towns like Pinecraft were capable of offering a helping hand.

At the very least, she'd thought he would be kind.

He definitely had not been.

Instead of thanking her for her stopping to ask about him, he'd hardly looked her in the eye. Instead of thanking her for her praises about his speech, he'd looked irritated. His tone of voice had been clipped and cool, nothing at all like the smooth, almost melodic words she'd heard floating down from the loudspeaker in the pavilion.

In short, meeting him had been a disappointment. And it would have been even if it hadn't been obvious that he'd thought she was some kind of creepy, adoring fan.

And while she had been a fan—and okay, for a few minutes, she'd been rather close to adoring him—she had *never* been creepy. Besides, pretty much every girl there had been gazing at him the same way she had.

Surely there was nothing wrong with admiring a man who was fit and healthy and sported dark blond hair and striking hazel eyes with golden flecks?

No doubt even the Lord himself would have admired His handiwork in Michael Knoxx.

Still, she had not stopped for him because she'd thought he was special. Instead, she'd been worried about him. He had looked like he was in pain. She'd stopped for him the way she would have for anyone, whether they'd recently been on a stage sharing their incredible story of survival or merely sitting in the audience.

She was still stewing over their brief conversation the next morning after she finished her chores and went into the kitchen to have breakfast with her parents.

As usual, her mother had made a platter of pancakes, scrambled eggs, sausage, and bacon accompanied by a big bowl of sliced fruit. It was always delicious and always too much for the three of them. Her mother just couldn't seem to prepare anything for less than four people, and her father still couldn't bear to invite anyone over. Neither seemed able to admit that they'd been a family of three for a long time now.

After they said grace silently, Penny dug in. Once again, her mother's pancakes were light and fluffy and the tropical syrup she made from scratch was the perfect combination of sweet citrus and tang.

"Mamm, everything is *wunderbaar*," she said, thinking once again that it really was a shame no one else ever got to try her mother's *wonderful-gut* pancakes.

"*Danke.* It is *gut* to see you eating. I'm glad you joined us."

Holding a forkful of sliced oranges, Penny paused. "What do you mean by that? I always enjoy your Saturday breakfasts." She was also always home.

Well, except for last night.

"We thought maybe you were going to change your mind about eating breakfast here."

"Why?"

"Because you seem so intent on getting away from us."

If she had been alone, Penny would have closed her eyes and groaned in frustration. Her mother's ability to heap on the guilt was alive and well. "Just because I went to the gathering with friends last night doesn't mean I've changed."

"Did you enjoy yourself?" her father asked with a pointed glare. "Did you like being out among so many strangers?"

Irritation rode up her spine. The way her *daed* was eyeing her was making her more than a little uneasy. "I did have a good time."

"And how was the Knoxx Family's latest performance? Did you get your fill of staring at the illustrious Michael Knoxx?"

Though her cheeks were no doubt turning red, she protested his description. "Daed, it wasn't a performance. You know the Knoxx Family would never describe their testimony like that."

"They sing."

"The daughter does. She sang 'Amazing Grace,' which many people in the audience sang along with. But mainly it was the men talking about their walk with the Lord. And Michael Knoxx told his tale about being stuck alone in a ravine for days."

Her father rolled his eyes. "Oh, I'm sure he told all about his adventure. In detail."

"It was hardly an adventure, Daed. Michael lost part of a leg."

"*Jah.* I know how he lost his leg. A person would have to be deaf not to hear about it." With a grunt, her father put down his fork. "They use one event that happened to them years ago for their own personal glory."

Penny hated how her father was reducing Michael's story to a mere publicity-seeking stunt. "Did you go to see them last night, too?"

"You know I did not."

"Have you heard them speak before?"

"Of course not. But I have heard accounts about the Knoxx Family and the way they promote themselves."

"If you had heard Michael Knoxx speak for yourself, I think you would feel differently about his message, Daed. At least I certainly hope you would!"

Her mother gasped at her raised voice, just as if Penny had stood up and yelled at them. "Penny, you will show your father respect."

Knowing that protesting would do no good, Penny simply cut another bite of pancake.

"Since we're discussing your behavior, I think I should mention that you came home later than expected," her father continued.

She was now completely miffed. "*Nee*, I came home earlier than I had thought I would," she corrected. "A lot of people were going to each other's houses to play cards or talk but I decided to come home instead."

Her parents exchanged looks. "Thank goodness you showed that little bit of sense at least," her mother said before taking a fortifying breath. "So, today I thought we would get a head start on some Christmas projects."

"Mamm, it is April."

"*Jah*, but with so many of your cousins having *bopplis*, we've got a lot of baby quilts to make."

The unintentional reminder of how the other girls in their extended family were living their lives dissolved the last of Penny's appetite.

And just like that, she knew she was going to have to keep pressing for more freedom and independence. It was becoming obvious that her parents intended to treat her evening out as a one-time thing. Since she'd not even had her *rumspringa*, Penny knew it was past time.

She was going to need to push a little harder for independence, and do it immediately.

Pushing her plate away, she said, "Mamm, I enjoy quilting with you, and I want to help you make Christmas presents. But I have other plans for today."

"What is that?" her father asked.

Penny took a breath, prayed for courage, and then blurted, "I'm going to go find a job."

"What?" Her mother gasped for at least the third time that morning. "Why in the world do you need a job? We give you everything you need."

No, they had given her everything they'd *thought* she needed. And while her material needs might have been met, Penny was certain that she needed more for herself. Getting out last night had made her realize just how sheltered she'd become. And after she got over the sting of Michael Knoxx's brush-off, Penny had come to realize that she not only needed to leave the house more, but she needed to get to know more people her age. She needed friends, men and women, with whom to try new experiences. And to fund those things, she was going to need money.

However, she wasn't quite ready to be completely honest and up-front. "I want to do something on my own," she said slowly. "I want to meet other people. I want to feel good about myself."

Her father glared. "All you are doing is setting yourself up for disappointment."

Though she'd imagined that they would do everything possible to dissuade her, the comment took her by surprise. "Why is that?"

"Jobs are hard to come by and you have no qualifications."

His harsh words felt like a slap in the face. More than that, really. "I was good in school," she pointed out. But even to her ears her statement seemed woefully inadequate.

"You have no experience. And at your age, people will expect that you should."

"At my age?" This was something new. She was twenty-four, not forty-four. Surely no one expected someone in their twenties to have loads of experience.

"Most girls your age have been doing all sorts of things," her father replied. "Amish girls leave school at fourteen. Most have had ten years' experience at something or another by now."

"I realize that." The years had passed in a haze of grief for her sister and the fear of the unknown. Though she'd been intent on obeying her parents, she'd also allowed herself to become a recluse. But at last, she'd summoned the courage to finally do something different. It was time to start stretching herself, to take responsibility for her life.

"Lissy would most likely have already done all sorts of things by now," her father added somewhat desperately.

Penny was so hurt, she could barely get out her next words. "Lissy would have?"

"Lissy was special."

Penny knew that. Penny had always known that.

But while she would never have her sister's beauty, independent nature, easy smile, or even her beautiful, oh-so-feminine name, Penny had thought her parents would one day notice her worth, too. Actually, a small part of her had felt sure her parents would agree it was time she spread her wings—once they got their heads around the idea of her being more independent.

But now, her parents' point of view was starting to look mighty clear. Her parents had been keeping her close to them on purpose. They hadn't wanted her to have lots of other options. They kept her nearby for their own selfish reasons, so that she would never get away. But it wasn't because they especially wanted her near. No, to them she would always be a poor substitute for her sister.

And while she still wasn't prepared to think the worst of them, she couldn't bear to imagine that they'd kept such a tight hold on her for any reason other than the fear of losing her. It was now plain, to her at least, that they'd hoped that she would always be dependent on them.

Which was terribly unfair.

A temper that she'd never known she possessed filled her just then. Suddenly, all she knew was that she couldn't stay in this kitchen, pretending to have a meaningful, caring conversation about her future for another minute.

"I need to leave." With a jerk, she stood up so abruptly that her chair scraped the floor.

Her mother blinked in confusion. "Penny, what in the world has gotten into you?"

"Everything," she said, thinking that just about summed it up. Everything had finally gotten into her. A backbone. Goals. Even the Lord's caring whispers that she wasn't leading the life He had given her. Instead, she'd merely been in some kind of holding pattern.

Lost without even knowing it.

Her mother was now staring at her as if she were a foundling who'd come calling unannounced and uninvited. " 'Everything' is certainly no kind of answer."

"I would explain myself, but I'm fairly sure you wouldn't like the answer."

Her father glowered. "Penny, you must apologize for your behavior."

"I will when you will," she retorted.

"What have I done?"

"What have you not? I am sorry for scraping the floor, but it is perfectly fine." Pointing to the tile underneath her feet, she realized that she was just like it. Far more durable than she looked, yet deceptively fragile. Hard to keep in perfect condition, but no worse for the wear even after a couple of hard scrapes.

"See? It is just fine," she repeated.

Her mother looked on the verge of tears. "Penny, what is wrong with you?"

"Not a thing." Not a thing, not anymore. As she carried her breakfast dishes to the counter, she knew that, at least, was the honest truth. For once she was becoming the type of person she used to dream she would be. She was making plans. If she made mistakes, they would be hers, too. "I'll help you with the breakfast dishes, and then I'll be on my way."

"If you're going to act like such an ungrateful girl, don't bother with the dishes," her father warned. "You just might as well leave."

His words sounded so final, she looked at him carefully. "I can go right now."

"Oh, Penny, why are you doing this to us? You can't go. Not like this," her mother pleaded. "This is your home."

After taking one last long look at her parents and seeing the combined dismay and anger lurking in their eyes, Penny realized that everything between them was now forever changed.

She'd refuted their decisions. Past events and hurts that they'd all carefully kept buried for years were now out in the open, and in some ways just as painful now as they had been then. She couldn't go back to how things were even if she'd wanted to. And she didn't want to do that. Not at all.

Therefore, she did the only thing she could do. She went upstairs to bide her time.

In two days, at a quarter to ten on Monday morning, she would open the front door and walk outside.

All in order to find herself—even if she wasn't exactly sure which road to take . . . or where it might lead.

Chapter 5

On Saturday night, Michael's parents insisted on holding a family meeting in his room at the Orange Blossom Inn. Michael had not supported this idea. Actually, he had argued against it. Forcefully. He was a grown man and could make his own decisions. The last thing he wanted was to have his life and health determined by his siblings and parents. Moreover, he really was in no hurry to have this discussion after being poked and prodded in the emergency room for the last twenty-four hours. He was tired, frustrated, and in considerable pain.

Dr. Barnes, the surgeon on call, had examined his knee when he'd arrived Friday night and recommended surgery as soon as possible. His knee was in sad shape—as if Michael needed to be told that. His prosthesis should have been adjusted months ago, and its increasingly poor fit had created a lot of irritation and a sizable infection. They'd tentatively scheduled the surgery for the following Friday.

Now, finally back in bed at the inn, surrounded by his family, he was crankier than ever. And while he was grateful for their love and concern, all he wanted to do at the moment was sleep. For the next two days. He'd even make do with the next eight hours.

"Michael," his father began, worry shining in his eyes, "there's something that needs to be said, and I fear it's going to be hard to hear."

"And what is that?"

"We've come to some decisions, you see."

Actually, he did *not* see. "About what?"

Looking just as pained, his mother continued. "Evan, Molly, your *daed*, and I had quite a bit of time to sit together in the waiting room." Shooting Michael a chiding look, she added, "Lots and lots of time, since you wouldn't allow any of us in the exam area with ya."

"I'm twenty-five years old, Mother. Far too old to be getting my hand held at a doctor's visit."

Besides, he'd been in a small room wearing only a thin cotton smock, which—no matter how hard he'd tried—he couldn't seem to tie tightly enough to completely cover him. It had been bad enough to sit there so exposed to doctors and nurses. No way had he been about to sit there like that in front of his family, too.

Evan grunted. "It was far more than a mere doctor's visit and you know it."

"We've been really worried," Molly grumbled as if he'd just pulled her hair. "Don't make light of it."

"Sorry."

"It's all right." She looked at their father again, obviously waiting for him to make his big announcement.

Which was obviously only a mystery to him.

His fight for patience ended. "Can we simply get to the point? What did you all talk about?"

"We discussed the rest of our tour," Evan blurted.

"I know the schedule," he said wearily. "What happened? Did someone cancel one of the bookings?"

"*Nee*, dear. Nothing like that. . . ." His mother's voice drifted off.

The back of his neck started tingling as he realized that they were struggling to tell him something important. Pressing his hands down on the bed, he worked to pull himself up. "What is it?"

"We didn't want to have this discussion without you, son. But when we got the news, we felt we had no choice."

The news. The news that something was wrong with his right leg. What was left of it. "What happened?"

"Nothing too terrible."

That was evasive maneuvering if he'd ever heard it.

"Just. Tell. Me."

"You have a fair bit of an infection, Michael. The skin is raw and in a bad way. After your surgery on Friday, Dr. Barnes says that you're going to need to stay off of it for at least two weeks."

Like that was going to happen. He knew how jam-packed their timetable was. Even if they juggled a couple of the dates, there was no way they could completely rearrange things to free up two solid weeks. "I won't need two weeks. I bet three days' recovery will be more than enough."

His mother sat on the edge of his bed. "*Nee*, Michael."

"Actually, we don't think even two weeks is going to be adequate time," his father added.

"Of course it will be. Besides, it's not like we have a choice." Mentally reviewing their itinerary, he said, "We're scheduled to speak in New York City on Monday. It's been planned for a year. We can't cancel."

Evan nodded. "I agree."

"Okay, then. So it's settled."

"It is settled, Michael," Daed announced. "But we've also de-cided that you are going to stay here and the four of us are going to continue on tour."

His stomach dropped. "Pardon?"

After exchanging glances with his father, his mother said, "Son, Evan called Jeremiah Miller. He's agreed to come with us in your place."

He blinked, hearing the words but not really processing them. "You asked Jeremiah to take my place?"

"He's a wonderful speaker," Molly said, a strong note of apol-ogy in her voice. "His stories about surviving that robbery al-ways gives everyone chills."

"He is inspiring, for sure." Michael liked Jeremiah a lot. He considered him a friend. But he wasn't thrilled about the man replacing him.

He was even less thrilled about being left behind.

His mother continued. "Your father and I spoke with Beverly this morning. She's going to give us a special rate while you stay here for the month."

A month? A whole month? "That's ridiculous! I will not need to stay here that long."

"The doctors seem to think differently."

"*Nee*, the doctors said two weeks."

"They said you need to rest for two weeks, preferably without your prosthesis. While you were getting your prescriptions filled and being discharged this morning, we talked to them about our tour schedule. Dr. Barnes took us into his office for a confer-ence call with Dr. Collins back in Denver."

Dr. Collins was the surgeon who had performed his amputa-tion. "You had this call without me?"

"You were hooked up to the IV," Evan said unhelpfully. "Remember, you were on some pretty strong pain relievers this morning."

Michael looked down at his hands clenched in his lap so he wouldn't be forced to admit that he didn't remember much about being at the hospital.

Too afraid to dwell on that, he bit out, "And what did Dr. Collins say?"

"Well, it was amazing, really," his mother said in a sweet, singsong voice. "They were able to send the pictures and scans they did of your leg right there on the computer."

"And?"

"And Dr. Collins was in complete agreement with what Dr. Barnes and his team recommended," his father said. "Of course we cannot schedule any of this without your approval, but we hope you will agree that this is the right choice to make. The surgery will help alleviate some of the pain of your scar tissue. But the plain and simple truth is that your knee has been under a lot of stress, son. It needs a good rest. Your prosthesis needs to be adjusted, maybe replaced. And if we don't do something to stop the damage that is happening now, there's a mighty good chance you're going to make things even worse."

Suddenly it seemed as if all the air had been pulled out of his lungs. "You all are acting as if I've already agreed to this."

After a moment, his father sat down next to Michael's hip. "I know this is difficult, son. I'm sorry for that, too."

It was on the tip of Michael's tongue to say that no, they had no earthly idea how difficult this news was to hear, but then something his mother had said caught his attention. "When are you all planning to leave?"

"Some of us will be leaving in a couple of hours."

"Some?"

His mother looked to his *daed* and Evan and Molly. "We thought one of us could stay behind with you."

Molly nodded her head. "All you have to do is say who you want."

"So one of you would volunteer to stay behind and look after me?" He couldn't think of anything worse.

"It wouldn't be a hardship," Evan said.

"*Jah*, none of us wants you to have to be here all alone," Molly added in a rush.

"I see." One of them had volunteered to be his babysitter.

That could not happen. He would rather go into surgery and recover by himself than be forced onto one of his siblings for a whole month. "I'll be fine. I don't want any of you to stay."

"Michael, think about what you're saying," his mother cautioned.

"I have, Mamm. I'll be fine. I promise, I will."

"You could always let us know if you change your mind," Molly said. "Then one of us could come back and be with you."

"That's a *gut* plan," Michael said, though he knew he wouldn't ask any of them to return.

"I know it feels like we're leaving you, but I'm afraid we can't cancel the tour completely," their father said. "Besides the fact that we need to honor our commitments, we need to raise money for the surgery and the hospital and the doctors."

He shook his head. "No. We preach and give witness for charity."

"This time we need to ask for some help."

He shook his head again. "I can pay for my surgery. I've saved quite a bit of money from some of the side jobs and speaking engagements I've taken over the years."

"This is true. But if you pay for the surgery by yourself it will drain all of your savings," his father replied. "There's no shame in asking for some donations, Michael."

"I'd really rather you didn't do this. It's not necessary. Remember how well that conference chair paid me last June?"

"That is your money, son," his mother said. "You earned it, and one day, when you start your own family, you'll need it."

"But—"

"We have no choice, Michael," his father said. "I'm just as uncomfortable with this as you are, but doctors need to be paid."

Michael couldn't even begin to imagine how much another surgery was going to cost. "I hate this."

"I know, but you mustn't dwell on it too much," his mother soothed. "We made this choice when we decided to preach and spread the word about our faith and experiences."

"In the grand scheme of things, you will be out only for a brief while," Evan added. "Then, when you've recovered and are feeling healthy again, we'll go back to how things have always been."

To how things have always been. Those words took the last bit of fight out of him. "Fine."

Molly raised a brow. "Fine? That's it?"

He didn't feel much like talking anymore. He didn't feel much like discussing his pain, his leg, their work, or the fact that they were going to go out and tell everyone that he needed help.

"I'm pretty tired right now. As we've said, it's really late. I think I should go to sleep."

His father stared at him hard before standing up. "I understand. Yes, let's let you get some rest."

"I'll come check on you before we head to the airport," his mother said, reaching out to brush a strand of hair back from his forehead.

"*Danke*, Mamm."

"Do you need anything before we leave?" Evan asked, looking reluctant to go. "Ice? A fresh glass of water?"

"I don't need a thing."

"Sure? I don't—"

"*Danke*, Evan, but stop worrying. I promise, I'll be fine."

It was only after the door closed behind them that Michael leaned against the headboard, closed his eyes, and whispered everything he'd been aching to say.

It wasn't pretty. It was filled with recriminations and anger and pain and doubts and weakness. It was filled with everything he tried never to think and definitely that no one ever heard. But he couldn't help it. He wasn't a saint, he wasn't even close to that. He was only a man and a flawed one at that.

But after he'd given the Lord the worst of him, Michael went to sleep.

After all, he was the weak one. God was not.

Chapter 6

$\mathcal{B}$y Monday afternoon, Penny had walked into every market and restaurant in Pinecraft and asked to apply for a job. Some let her fill out an application. Others, after learning that she had no actual work experience, showed her directly to the door. Then, just as she was starting to get discouraged, one of the clerks at Yoder's asked if Penny had tried applying at any of the inns or bed-and-breakfasts nearby.

Without delay, she'd headed directly to the Orange Blossom Inn. Though she didn't know the owner, Beverly Overholt, well, the attractive lady with the striking green eyes had always been nice to her. She also had a reputation of being easygoing, which was an attribute Penny knew she would very much appreciate in a boss.

And now, after telling Miss Beverly the reason she was there, the proprietor's eyes brightened like Penny was her long-lost friend.

"You were surely sent here by the angels," she said, wrapping her hand around Penny's elbow. "A set of unusual circumstances has just presented itself, and I've been sitting at my desk praying for some assistance." Her smile broadened. "And now, here you are!"

Penny wasn't sure if she was happier than Miss Beverly or twice as relieved. She'd been starting to wonder how she was going to face her parents if their predictions about her inability to get a job turned out to be right.

The moment after they walked into the kitchen, Beverly deposited Penny in a chair, poured her a tall glass of lemonade, and placed the most delicious-looking slice of strawberry coffee cake in front of her. "Here you go. Job hunting isn't for the faint of heart. I bet you've worked up an appetite today."

"*Danke.*" She smiled hesitantly, briefly wondering if it was ruder to eat while applying for a job or to ignore the plate her potential future employer offered. In the end, her growling stomach made the decision. She was hungry, and the cake looked delicious.

Beverly seemed pleased when she picked up her fork and dug in. "Now, while you eat, I'll tell you the type of job I have in mind for you."

When Penny took a bite, Miss Beverly started talking. "I have been thinking I need to hire some extra help, to assist with cleaning the rooms and such. And with serving afternoon tea." She paused, an almost panicked expression on her face. "Can you work forty hours a week?"

"Yes, I can." Penny took another bite in an attempt to hide the wonder she was feeling. Could she really be landing a full-time job?

Beverly's smile brightened. "You can? Oh, thank goodness. I know we need to talk about what days you will need off, too. Do you mind if we play it by ear? A lot of our schedule will be determined by how busy the inn is."

"I don't mind working different days each week."

"Really? You are indeed an answer to my prayers, Penny."

Penny wanted to say the same thing, that this job was the answer to hers. However, she was afraid to admit it for fear she would sound too eager or that her enthusiasm would reveal her inexperience. Instead, she took another bite of the delicious, moist cake.

"This is wonderful. I've never had strawberry coffee cake before."

"I'm glad you like it. Even though I've been in Florida for a few years now, I take advantage of all the fresh fruits available year round." She shrugged.

"My *mamm* often says the same thing."

Miss Beverly beamed. "Who knows? If everything works out, maybe one day you'll be making this cake for the guests."

"I hope that does happen, Miss Beverly."

Miss Beverly stilled, gazing at her for a long moment before pushing away Penny's offer to rinse her plate. She took it over to the sink herself. "Penny, I forgot to ask, how soon can you start?"

"Oh, I could start today if you needed me." After all, she had no desire to head home. She was certain her news about being hired full-time was not going to be met with smiles from her parents.

"You could really start today?"

Penny nodded, then confided, "I am so happy to have found a job. I really need this."

"*Gut.* And that, well, brings me to something else." Looking wary again, she said, "Penny, I will need you to help with traditional tasks—like cleaning rooms, cooking, serving, and so forth—but . . . well, we have a new development. Please listen to me before you refuse, okay?"

Miss Beverly's sudden disclaimer sounded intriguing, and perhaps a little bit surprising, especially since there was no way Penny was going to refuse this job—but that didn't seem like the right thing to say. "All right."

"We have a guest who will be having surgery soon."

"Yes?"

"It's quite an unusual situation. See, the young man's family travels quite a bit. They are evangelists. Perhaps you've heard of them? The Knoxx Family? They've come to Pinecraft a couple of times over the last few years."

Penny's mouth went dry and a sudden sinking feeling in the pit of her stomach made the strawberry cake she'd just consumed feel like it weighed twenty pounds. "Didn't they speak at Pinecraft Park Friday night?" she asked in an extremely nonchalant way, because, of course, she already knew the answer.

She doubted she would ever forget Michael Knoxx's speech—or how he'd treated her.

"They did." Miss Beverly's eyes shone. "The younger son is going to have surgery on his knee and recuperate here by himself because his family is scheduled to preach abroad."

"That would be awful. I would hate to have to recover by myself in a strange place."

"I would, too. But his family seems to think that the warm Florida air will only help his recovery."

"I see."

"The reason I'm mentioning all this is that part of your job will be to care for Michael."

Penny felt her cheeks heat though there was truly no reason for it. "Michael."

"*Jah*. And perhaps maybe even spend some time with him if you are agreeable to that?"

"Spend time?" She had no idea what that might entail.

Beverly's lips turned up at the corners. "Don't look so worried, dear. I'm simply talking about reading, playing cards, maybe even watching a movie on a portable DVD player I have."

Penny was taken aback. Her parents had been so overprotective that she'd had very few opportunities to spend any time at all with men.

But what choice did she have? This was the job she was being given. Besides, it seemed as if the Lord had been working through the day's events. How else could she have explained the fact that she was looking for a job just when Beverly was in need of help? And that she was going to be helping to nurse Michael, the most famous person in town?

Who just happened to be the same man she'd attempted to help a few nights before.

A verse from Matthew 7 that she'd memorized long ago came to mind: *Ask, and God will give to you. Search, and you will find. Knock, and the door will open for you.*

"What do you say, Penny? Would you like the job? If your answer is yes, it's yours."

With new resolve in her heart, she stood up. "I'm looking forward to this job very much, Miss Beverly. Now, if you'll tell me what you'd like me to do first, I'll get right to work."

As an answer, Miss Beverly pressed a pitcher of water in her hand. "Please go to Michael's room, give him some water, and see if he needs anything. He's in the Lilac room."

"Lilac?" It sounded awfully feminine for a man like Michael Knoxx.

"Jah." Her eyes lit in amusement. "All the rooms—with the exception of the attic room—are named after flowers." Her lips

tilted upward. "Don't worry. You'll see the name to the left of every door."

Penny tried to look competent as she made her way out of the kitchen and through the gathering area. Only when she got up the stairs did she dare allow herself to relax and let her true feelings surface. She clenched her hands and closed her eyes as a terrible combination of embarrassment and something akin to terror churned her insides. This was going to go badly. She had no idea how to care for a grown man, let alone a famous, handsome one.

But then, little by little, she remembered what her alternative was. She could simply stay home and be coddled and protected and have every move watched.

She could not go back to that. She couldn't.

Outside of his room, Penny forced herself to relax, letting her head fall back against the wall and exhaling slowly. She had a job. So what if it was spending time with Michael Knoxx? So what if he was going to be sitting in his bed, in his room?

And did it really matter if it was just the two of them?

Furthermore, the worst that could happen already had. Why, she was fairly sure he believed her to be some kind of awful, crazy stalker. But he was simply going to have to get over that.

As her skin started to prickle with nerves again, she realized she was going to need some help. Luckily, there was someone in her life whom she could always count on for that.

"Lord, you definitely do work in mysterious ways," she whispered. "I'm not entirely sure why You've decided I need to do this particular job, but since You have, maybe You could give me a little bit of help?"

She paused, half expecting to be hit by a bolt of lightning or something.

But when nothing happened, she raised her hand and knocked on Michael's door, then felt goose bumps traipse up and down her arms when no one replied. What to do? Was he asleep? Should she wake him up?

Feeling like the Lord was smiling as He propelled her forward, Penny inhaled, lifted her hand, and knocked again. This time with a good bit of force. Miss Beverly had asked her to bring Michael Knoxx water, so that was what she was going to do.

No matter what was about to happen.

Chapter 7

$\mathcal{M}$ichael barely heard the first knock at his door, he was so tired. But then, when the knock came again, reality returned. He was in Pinecraft. At the Orange Blossom Inn. Alone.

"Come in," he murmured.

When nothing happened, he raised his voice. "Enter!" he called out, though maybe his command was a little harsher than needed. But surely his brusque tone of voice could be excused. He was sore from being poked and prodded, exhausted from his family's announcement, and slightly groggy from the painkillers that had finally kicked in an hour ago. All he wanted was for whoever was on the other side to say what they wanted and leave him in peace. Hopefully, all in three seconds. Unfortunately, it seemed like it was going to take at least three seconds for the person to even open the door all the way.

"Anytime now," he muttered under his breath.

But when a pretty face popped in, he blinked in surprise. First, because he was half expecting the person who had knocked to turn tail and retreat. Second, because he actually recognized the face.

"It's you," he said.

The young woman chewed on her lower lip before meeting his gaze. "*Jah*. It is I." She winced. "I mean *me*. I mean, my name is Penny Troyer. We, um, met Friday night. After the gathering."

"I remember."

She nodded. "*Jah*."

When she added nothing more, he said, "You offered to help me walk."

"Um. Yes, I did." She nodded again for good measure as her gaze darted around the room, at last coming to stop on a point directly above his head.

Realizing she was shy and he was yet again acting like a jerk, he said, "And even though your offer was mighty kind, I brushed it off." He hoped she heard the apology in his tone. "I was rude. I am sorry about that. My knee was paining me something awful."

"I didn't know that. I was simply worried about you." She smiled before immediately letting her expression go blank.

Almost as though she thought she was going to get in trouble if she relaxed around him.

"I should have listened to you," he said. "I barely got here. After Beverly told my family, they took me to the hospital."

Her blue-green eyes flashed back to his, pure concern filling them. "I am sorry about that."

"*Danke*." He eyed her a little more closely, liking the way her blond curls wouldn't quite mind her pins. She looked adorable. Bashful and unsure of herself. "So why, exactly, are you here?"

"Why?" Then her eyes lit on the pitcher she was holding in her hand. "Oh. I . . . well, um, I have brought you some water. Would you like some?"

He pointed to the still-full glass next to his bed. "Thanks, but I have some already."

"Oh." A look of dismay crossed her features as she shifted the pitcher to her opposite hand.

As she continued to shift awkwardly, Michael was suddenly very conscious of the fact that he was sitting in bed wearing a pair of pajama bottoms and an old T-shirt. Wariness coursed through him. "What I meant was, why are you here, at the inn?" And why was she standing in his bedroom? Suddenly, an awful thought hit him hard. "Does Beverly know you came in here?"

"Of course she does! You're my job."

"Say again?" This conversation seemed to be running in crazy circles.

She blinked slowly, obviously irritated with herself. "I guess that didn't come out too well. I meant, I was recently hired here."

His eyes narrowed. "How recently?"

"Today. This afternoon."

He groaned. Maybe his first instinct had been correct. Maybe she really was some kind of celebrity stalker. "You just *happened* to need a job today? And you just *happened* to get one here, where I'm staying?"

"It wasn't like that."

"Uh-huh." He hated to sound like a pompous jerk, but he had a right to be worried. Something like this had happened eight months ago. It wasn't easy to forget that impressionable girl in Lancaster County who had been in need of something and had secretly decided only Michael could give it to her. She'd turned up everywhere they'd been, even finding her way to the hallway outside their hotel rooms. Her infatuation had embarrassed him terribly, caused Evan and Molly no small amount of entertainment at his expense, and had ultimately caused the girl a lot of pain and tears.

Now, the pretty young woman in his room stepped closer. "*Nee*, it wasn't like that at all." Glaring, she continued. "I didn't know you were here."

"Are you sure about that?" That girl in Lancaster County had said much the same thing.

"I'm positive." Her voice turned cool. "This inn was the only place where I could find a job on such short notice."

"I see." It was quite a coincidence. Too much of one. What bad luck! He was stuck here with a girl who was obviously grasping at any reason she could think of to be around him. "Well, *danke* for your help, but I think I'm good now. You may leave."

But instead of accepting his statement and gracefully exiting the room, Penny shook her head. And then stepped closer. "Wait. Miss Beverly said one of my jobs is to see to your needs. Do you need anything?"

"I do not." Feeling exposed, he pulled the quilt up protectively over his chest.

This girl needed to go. Permanently. The moment he saw Beverly again, he was going to tell her that this girl needed to stay away from him at all times.

Penny was starting to look a bit panicked. "I promise, I didn't know you were here. If I'd known, I would have applied at every other inn before coming here."

"If you say so."

"I know so! Why, you have to be one of the rudest men I've ever met. If you cause me to lose my job . . . I don't know what I'll do."

Her words, combined with the outrage on her face, made everything click into place. He had just made a crucial, terrible mistake. Penny Troyer had not been lying about her reasons for being in his room. He really was her job. And if he didn't make use of her efforts, she was going to get fired. And it was going to be all his fault.

He was horrified. Embarrassed. And, well, he could kick himself. When was the last time he had misread a situation so horribly? For that matter, when was the last time someone had only wanted to spend time with him out of obligation?

He couldn't remember.

His ego was truly in need of being taken down a notch or two. "Listen. I'm sorry. Not to sound too full of myself, but sometimes I run into women who, um, want to get to know me better."

Still glaring, she set the pitcher down on top of the dresser. "You can be sure that I am not one of them, Mr. Knoxx."

Obviously she wasn't. Especially not now, since he'd managed to do a pretty good job of hurting her feelings. "I'm sure I'll need something soon, but at the moment I am fine. Thank you for your offer of help, though. I appreciate it."

His gentle tone, coupled with his kinder explanation, visibly relieved Penny. Right before his eyes, that trapped, wary expression that seemed to encompass nearly everything she did eased, and in its place he saw something truly endearing. Her blue eyes brightened and the lines of stress around her lips smoothed away, revealing a small smile.

Suddenly, she was adorable. Innocent and guileless and really, really cute.

Which made him wonder how he'd ever thought she was conniving. Now it was obvious that she was simply a sheltered girl in a small community trying to do the best she could with the job that had been given to her. "Hey, I'm sorry for the way I talked to you the other night."

"It's all right."

"So, you will forgive me?"

"*Jah*. I mean, I probably will. Eventually. I have to, anyway. After all, you are my job."

"*Danke*. I'll try to not be too much trouble."

When he grinned, a blush ignited her skin. "You can be all the trouble you want. I mean, you're going to have surgery. That probably means you'll be a lot of trouble."

"You have a point."

Her smile widened, and a dimple formed in one of her cheeks. Now she wasn't just cute, she was bordering on being really pretty.

Michael couldn't resist teasing her. "I'm sure I will be. My parents have said more than once that trouble should have been my middle name."

To his amusement, she looked tempted to roll her eyes. Good, he thought. He liked that she wasn't going to let him cow her.

"Well . . ." She fiddled with the edges of her apron, obviously at a loss for what to do next.

He guessed she should probably leave, since he'd practically bitten her head off and embarrassed her something awful. But now that he saw there was a bit more to her than he'd first imagined, he wanted to get to know her better.

He'd let his stubborn pride interfere with his family's offer to stay with him during his recovery and he'd let more than pride interfere with the efforts of a nice girl intent on simply doing her job. Now he had nothing to occupy his mind except the knowledge that he was going to have yet another surgery and be forced to sit by himself while the rest of his family went about raising funds to pay for it.

Every time he let himself dwell on that, he felt guilty and

helpless. And, in a way, handicapped. Those thoughts were the ones he'd like to avoid at all costs.

"Since you are supposed to help me and all, would you mind doing me a favor?"

Pure relief settled in her features. "Of course not. What may I do for you?"

"Would you mind sitting with me for a few minutes?"

"That's it?"

"*Jah.* Just for a little while. If you, you know, really have forgiven me for insulting you."

"I've forgiven you."

A new, warm feeling coasted along his skin. Relief? Definitely. But was it mixed in with happiness? Something else? He wasn't sure.

"Yet you still haven't moved." Not even an inch. He smiled again, this time bringing out the grin he used in public. He used it sometimes as a shield. For some reason, he felt like he needed it at the moment. "So, will you chat with me, Penny? It gets pretty boring here by myself, you know."

"I imagine it does." Something new entered her expression, something that piqued his interest even more. But instead of pulling up a chair or even sitting on the corner of his bed, she remained where she was, hovering beside him like a nervous hummingbird.

It was becoming obvious that she was going to need a lot of prodding if they were ever going to have any real communication.

"If you really don't mind then, sit, Penny." He motioned to one of the empty chairs that stood in the corner. As he'd expected, she sat down immediately. But then she did something just as unexpected. She sighed.

"Sorry, am I keeping you from going home?"

"*Nee*. Not at all. I was just thinking that I have no idea what to talk to you about."

He blinked. Pretty much everyone he met had something to say to him. They asked him questions about what his family did. They asked questions about being trapped in the ravine. About how he felt when he'd been rescued. Or, they shared. He learned about diseases and disabilities. Injuries and ailments. Sick relatives and wounds and private pains.

No one ever was at a loss for words.

Therefore, he found himself faltering almost as much as she was. "What made you decide to go out to find a job today?" he asked at last. In his experience, everyone liked talking about what they did, even if they didn't like their jobs.

"I decided it was time. My parents have been sheltering me, you see. Until today, I was never allowed to work."

"I'm surprised by that. You are obviously old enough to be out in the workforce."

"I am, indeed."

Still wary of embarrassing her, he shrugged. "You know, maybe it's not a bad thing that you haven't worked until now. I'm sure your parents really care about you."

"They do. Maybe too much."

Just as he was letting that sink in, Penny surprised him again. Curving her lips, she said, "I guess, Michael Knoxx, I should be thanking you. After all, you are the real reason I have a job today. So even though I am mighty sorry you are ailing, I do owe you a great deal of thanks."

He shook his head in wonderment. "That's really something. Are you glad about this?"

"About having a job? Certainly!"

He laughed. Talk about a girl putting him in his place. Her complete insistence that he was nothing more than an obligation to her should have pinched his ego. Instead, he found it amusing.

"Well, you're welcome, then. I am glad my bad leg is going to bring you some good."

Immediately, embarrassment filled her cheeks. "I'm sorry. I didn't mean that I was glad you are going to have surgery."

"Of course you didn't. Don't mind me. Sometimes I try to make a joke and it falls a little flat. I think that's what happened here."

Looking serious, she leaned forward. "Are you scared about the operation?"

He couldn't lie. "I'm not as much scared as I am dreading it. It's come at a bad time." He didn't know how else to describe his feelings. They were too complex even for him to try to analyze, let alone explain to a stranger.

"There's probably never a good time, I wouldn't think."

She was right, of course.

But he'd been worrying about fulfilling his family's obligations. Determined to keep on their schedule, and do what was expected of him.

Penny was staring at him with such genuine sympathy, it humbled him. "I hope your recovery won't be too terrible. I truly am sorry about you needin' another surgery on your leg."

"Years ago, when I had the first of the operations, the surgeons told me that my surgery was a difficult one. I had secretly wondered if I was going to wake up from it at all. There was even talk of them amputating above my knee. That would have been a far harder adjustment."

Ignoring the way her posture stiffened in the face of his candor, he continued. "So, I think it's safe to say that I've been living on borrowed time for quite a while now. No one has mentioned that they're going to do anything very drastic, but it would be foolish of me to imagine that I could live my life talking about my accident and injury and think that the Lord was never going to give me another hurdle to jump over."

"But still, it must be hard."

He paused, gazing into her blue eyes again, realizing that it had been a mighty long time since anyone had dared to be so honest with him.

It had been an even longer time since he'd been honest with himself about his fears. As the years passed, and he'd become more adept at retelling his story, he'd unintentionally begun to gloss over his feelings, preferring instead to act as if he didn't have any problems. As if he was constantly grateful. Maybe it was Penny's sympathetic look, or maybe it was because, for the first time in a very long time, he was being made to sit still and reflect on the journey he'd had. Whatever the reason, he was feeling inclined to be completely honest.

Taking a deep breath, he nodded. "It is. But at least now I know what is going to happen. The questioning and wondering is over. I won't fear the worst."

"I can understand that. It is a difficult thing, I think, to always be fearing the worst."

Something in her tone compelled him to stare at her more closely. Shadows filled her eyes and a bit of color had drained from her face, making him guess that she was thinking about something far more difficult than his lost leg. He wondered what it was. For a second, he thought about asking her. He knew he was adept at talking to strangers about their problems, offering advice. Counseling them. But he wasn't comfortable doing that now. She obviously had her guard up. Furthermore, they were no doubt going to be in each other's company many hours over the coming weeks.

It was better to simply nod. Let her have her privacy.

Better to keep some distance between them. The last thing he wanted to happen was to form a true friendship with her.

If he did that, then where would that leave them?

Chapter 8

_It_ was almost seven by the time Penny walked up her five porch steps—which her father carefully painted dark forest green every couple of months—and pulled the key out of her pocket to unlock the front door.

The moment she turned the handle, she braced herself. Ever since she'd said good-bye to Miss Beverly and walked the four blocks home, Penny had been preparing how she would describe her first day to her parents. She expected them to be waiting in the entryway, nervously wringing their hands together, ready to pepper her with a thousand questions.

She was going to have to be sure to calm her mother down, first. No doubt Mamm had been driving her father crazy all afternoon, imagining what sort of terrible things had happened to Penny when she'd ventured out into the world.

After reassuring her mother, Penny knew she was going to have to answer a number of her father's questions. No doubt the only way to ease their worries would be to gloss over her insecurities and paint her day as a grand adventure. Then she could set her mother's mind at ease by describing the nature of her job at the Orange Blossom Inn. Though her parents didn't know many people, Penny felt sure they would have heard of Beverly Overholt and approve of her spotless reputation.

There was no need for her parents to hear anything about Michael Knoxx or the fact that Penny was going to be spending a lot of time with him. Besides, Penny was fairly sure she wouldn't be able to describe Michael in a disinterested way. They would probably guess her feelings about him in two seconds.

And then promptly refuse to let her leave the house ever again!

With a shake of her head, Penny returned to the present. She slipped off her flipflops, padded toward the living room, and braced herself for the upcoming conversation. But instead of being greeted by a flurry of questions, she faced an empty room.

Actually, the whole house was quiet. She didn't hear her parents chatting, didn't see them sitting in their chairs on the back porch—their favorite after-dinner pastime. She didn't hear her mother doing dishes, either. She was home alone.

She felt almost as if she'd walked into the wrong house.

Suddenly, all the warnings and cautionary tales she'd been told came to the surface. Maybe something had happened to them. Maybe one of them had been hurt?

She strode into the kitchen. It was spotless and empty. Sniffing the air, Penny couldn't discern what her mother had cooked for supper. Had she even cooked supper?

Just as her worry was starting to transform into something that felt a whole lot like fear, she saw a note on the kitchen counter.

Penny, your father and I decided to go out for pizza.
We will be back later.

Two sentences.

She read it once. Then again. Then set the note back down on the counter. She felt confusion, dismay, and sadness. Followed by a burst of shock. She let the note drift to the floor.

Their family did not go out for pizza. They didn't go out for walks. They didn't visit Pinecraft Park. In a nutshell, they stayed safe.

For the life of her she couldn't imagine her parents going out for pizza on a whim.

Penny had just bent to pick up the fallen note when the front door opened. A moment later, her parents walked in.

"Hi, Penny," her mother said. "It is good to see you home."

"I got back a few minutes ago." Looking from one parent to the other, she held up the note they'd left. "I see you went out for pizza."

Her mother shrugged as she set her purse down on the kitchen counter, then picked up a dishrag and started wiping the already spotless counters. "We did. It sounded like a good idea. We haven't been out to supper in ages."

"I can't remember the last time we went out for pizza," Penny mused. "I wish I would have known you were going."

Her father said nothing, merely glared at her.

That's when Penny knew that they had gone out without her on purpose. And neither of them was holding a pizza box. It seemed they hadn't brought home any leftovers for her, either.

Furthermore, she knew her mother wasn't going to give her a hug and share how worried she'd been. Her father wasn't going to ask about Penny's day. He wasn't going to ask how the job search had gone or if she'd gotten one.

In short, they were going to make certain she knew that they were not happy with her. They were also waiting for her to apologize for going against their wishes. Waiting for her to promise never to stray again. But if she did those things, she'd have to give up the small measure of confidence she'd gained.

Which would be incredibly painful.

As her stomach began to rumble, giving a not-so-subtle reminder that she hadn't eaten anything of substance since breakfast, Penny made another huge decision. Instead of sitting at home, going hungry and begging for their understanding, she turned around and walked back out the front door. She would go over to the Kaufmanns' house to see if Violet was there. And if she was, Penny was going to see if she'd like to join her for supper. It wasn't too late. Most restaurants would still be open.

Once outside, Penny noticed that the sun was just beginning its slow descent toward the horizon and it wouldn't be long before the solar-powered streetlights flickered on, one by one. A tremor coursed through her.

For so long, she'd been ruled by her fears and memories. She'd let herself be guided by her father's warnings and her mother's pain. And though she would never have said that she'd had a comfortable existence, that's what it had been. It was like she'd been stuck in a very plush, very cozy old couch: comforted on all sides, leaving enough room only for a shaft of sunlight and the minimum amount of oxygen.

Now, she was surrounded by air and the evening and possibilities. It was going to be up to her to make friends, acquaintances, and who knew—perhaps even enemies. No doubt, she was setting herself up for extreme happiness and utter fear. But they would be fresh experiences, fresh as the burst of orange blossoms next to Miss Beverly's front door.

It seemed this day was going to be filled with firsts.

Chapter 9

Oh! Pinecraft looked just like the postcards her aunt Beverly had sent her.

As Patricia—Tricia to all who knew her—stared out the window of the Pioneer Trails bus, she was happy that she'd at last taken up Aunt Beverly's long-standing invitation to pay her a visit. She was even happier that she'd decided to come without warning.

Surely unexpected visitors were the best ones.

When the bus driver carefully pulled into the parking lot around what had to be dozens of folks there waiting, she scanned the area, looking for her aunt. Her aunt had written that it was rare for her not to greet the bus from Sugarcreek, even when she wasn't expecting guests. Aunt Beverly said she enjoyed the social atmosphere that surrounded each arrival and departure.

And then, all of a sudden, Tricia recognized her. Even though she hadn't seen Beverly in over three years, she remembered the elegant way she held herself, how her chin lifted just so. And those bright, striking green eyes that everyone had always talked about.

It had to be her. It had to be.

She was standing in the middle of a group of five or six ladies, some of whom were obviously several years older than she, and others perhaps a few years younger. But what was most apparent was that she looked happy. She was smiling and chatting about something. It looked as if one of the ladies had told a joke and they were all enjoying it. Tricia clasped her hands together. She knew it had been the right choice to come for a visit. She knew it.

"Everyone, it's time to go. Make sure you've got all your things. And then double-check again," the driver announced. "This bus will be gone the moment the last suitcase is unloaded."

Tricia looked around and noticed that while all the other passengers were following his directions, it was obvious that no one took his dire warning all that seriously.

"Don'tcha worry about that Tony, dear," the kind woman who'd been sitting across the aisle from her advised. "He's all bark but no bite."

"That's *gut* to know. I don't think I've forgotten anything."

"All you can do is your best, child."

Tricia smiled at her, though she was tempted to point out that she was definitely not a child. She might look like a teenager, but she was twenty-two.

Luckily, there was no time for any of that. People were lining up and eyeing the bus's door like it was the entrance to a grand amusement park. Then, with a snap and a whoosh of air, the driver opened it, stood up, and announced with a bit of fanfare, "Pinecraft, Florida. Everyone out."

The line moved forward. With every step, Tricia found herself being less aware of what was happening on the bus and more interested in the sights, sounds, and smells of her first visit to

Florida. And then, it was her turn to walk down the steps. Instantly, she was surrounded by the warmth of the Florida sun, the bright colors of all the women's dresses, and the scent of flowers blooming in every available bed and terra-cotta pot.

And she was instantly charmed.

Looking to her right, she scanned the area for Aunt Beverly. But now that folks were clustered around greeting friends and family or claiming their suitcases, her aunt and her sea-green dress were nowhere to be found. Tricia was gently nudged forward as the folks behind her descended and filled in the immediate area around the bus.

As she turned to her left, she looked again for Beverly—for any of the women she had seen standing with her aunt—but they were either lost in the crowd or must have already left.

"Excuse me, miss?" a lady called out behind her.

Tricia turned around. *"Jah?"* It was the woman who had visited with her on the bus.

"Did you have some suitcases? Because if you did, you need to head over and claim 'em now. Tony may be all bark and no bite, but he wasn't kidding about his schedule. He won't take it kindly if you keep him waiting on ya."

Tricia nodded her thanks and walked over to the driver who was standing next to a half-dozen bags and holding a clipboard. That's when she realized that she'd been standing there like a lost sheep for far longer than she'd realized. "I'm sorry to have kept you waiting."

The pair of lines creasing his forehead smoothed. "Ain't no problem. But it is time for me to get a move on. Which one is yours?"

She pointed to her spiffy new suitcase. It was covered in bright blue canvas and had not two but four wheels. The card attached to the price tag had said those four wheels were far better than two. "That one," she said with a smile.

He smiled back, grabbed it out of the pile, and deposited it at her feet. "Here you go, doll," he said, tipping the bill of his cap in a rather courtly gesture. "Have a good time in sunny Florida."

Then, before she had a chance to tell him how she had come as a surprise to see her aunt Beverly, Tony turned away and started talking to the person on her right.

Gripping her bag's handle, she pulled it to her. It rolled easily enough, but to be honest, it didn't feel all *that* much better than her suitcase with two wheels.

And as she looked around the now almost empty parking lot, practically bare except for the eight or ten people reading the post office bulletin board, Tricia started thinking that maybe it would have been a better idea to tell Aunt Beverly that she was heading her way.

It seemed that even though Aunt Beverly had written that she met the Pioneer Trails bus every Wednesday, she didn't actually *meet* every bus. And that though she'd written that the Orange Blossom Inn was mighty close to where the buses arrived, it wasn't exactly next door. Maybe she'd let her enthusiasm and ignorance get the best of her.

And now, here she was. Alone in Pinecraft with no earthly idea of how to find the Orange Blossom Inn. Well, she was simply going to surprise Aunt Beverly at her doorstep.

Ignoring the weight of the tote bag on her shoulder and the thought that it would have been a really, really great idea to have taken off her thick boots and slipped on flipflops before stepping out into the warm Florida sun, Tricia gave a sharp tug on the fancy suitcase—and watched as it somehow tripped over a rock, wobbled on two of the four wheels, then landed with a *snap*. Though one wheel had crunched and fallen away—too ruined to reattach—the bag was not too damaged to stop itself from rolling a few feet before coming to rest on its side.

Thus proving that everything was not perfect in Pinecraft, after all. Not by a long shot.

"IT'S ONLY ELEVEN A.M., Beverly," Sadie said as they slowly walked back from their weekly visit to greet the Pioneer Trails bus. "We should go to Yoder's."

Beverly grinned as their other two friends, Wilma and Marta, chuckled.

Her best friend glared at them all. "What did I say now?" It was a long-standing joke that Sadie continually said things that were just a tiny bit nonsensical.

"Nothing. It's only that you suggest we go to Yoder's every single Wednesday. And every single Wednesday you make this suggestion in such a way that it sounds like it's something new." Beverly attempted to say this in a serious way but couldn't refrain from smiling.

Sadie shook her head. "I do not."

"Oh, yes you do," Marta proclaimed. "You add just a touch of surprise and delight to your voice to make it sound like you just thought of it. It's hysterical."

Finally Sadie's lips twitched. "Well, Yoder's *is* always a *gut* idea."

Knowing that her friend's feelings were going to be hurt if they didn't stop the teasing soon, Beverly patted Sadie's shoulder. "You know we're only teasing because you're so much fun to be around, dear. And yes, indeed, going to Yoder's is always a *wonderful-gut* idea."

Wilma pointed to the restaurant. "So, are we going to go? After all, we're right here, and there is no time like the present."

"How long does the line look?" Marta craned her neck to see. "Ugh. It's a long one."

"It would be. The bus just came," Beverly said.

Her girlfriends needed no more of an explanation. Yoder's was one of the most popular restaurants in all of Sarasota and a destination for tourists visiting Pinecraft. Part of the restaurant's charm was its small size as well as the fact that the long lines often became social events—a chance to meet people from all parts of the country.

All four of them had made Pinecraft their home—in Marta's and Wilma's case, for over a dozen years. Sadie had moved to Florida after her husband had passed away seven years ago. Beverly was the newest member of the group, having moved there three years ago.

Still looking hopeful, Sadie tapped her foot. "It is a long line, but we all have two good feet. What does everyone want to do?"

"I'm out," Marta said. "I hate standing in line, especially one that is moving so slowly. Besides, I have food at home. I think I'll eat that and save my time and money."

Sadie harrumphed. "Spoilsport."

Marta just rolled her eyes. "See you all at quilting. Well, except for you, Bev."

Beverly raised a hand. "Yep. See ya."

After a minute, Wilma shrugged. "I have food at home, too, but I have a mind to have a slice of coconut cream pie."

Sadie beamed. "Perfect. So, that's now three of us?"

"I'm going to head on back, too," Beverly said reluctantly.

"Sure? You didn't pick up any guests today."

"I know. But as much as I like Yoder's pie, I'm afraid I have some baking of my own to do. Not to mention I've got my new girl."

"And your celebrity!" Sadie fanned herself. "If I were you, I wouldn't want to ever leave the inn."

"Sadie, he's young enough to be your grandson," Wilma chided.

"I'm not *that* old and he's not *that* young. He could be my son." When they all laughed, she blushed. "And I wasn't even thinking about him that way. It's just that he is so . . ."

"Dreamy," Wilma finished with a smile. "You're right, dear. We're old but we're not dead. That Michael Knoxx is quite the man."

Beverly shook her head in dismay. "You two are ridiculous. As far as I'm concerned, he's simply a guest."

"Uh-huh," Wilma said with a wink. "Well, off you go then. I'm sure you have a lot to do at the inn. See you at tea."

"See you then." Turning in the opposite direction, Beverly headed on her way, feeling better about her decision the farther she walked from Yoder's. She had things to do. Cakes to bake, rooms to clean.

And the new owner, Eric—who was supposed to arrive any day now—to appease.

And since Wilma and Sadie weren't there to tease her, she admitted to herself that they were right. She did, indeed, have her very own celebrity to take care of. Beverly made a mental note to check on him herself when she got back. That sweet Penny had spent quite a bit of time with him the previous afternoon, but Beverly felt responsible for his well-being. Penny had said that Michael hadn't eaten much and didn't seem to have much of an appetite. Since he was going to be staying at her inn for at least a month, Beverly wanted to get things off to a good start.

Even famous men like him needed to feel taken care of.

She'd just begun a mental grocery list when she saw a pretty young lady in a violet dress lugging a broken suitcase with one arm and supporting a very heavy-looking tote bag with the other. Her steps were halting and slow, and when Beverly got a glimpse of her expression, she felt her heart clench.

The poor thing was near tears.

"Excuse me, miss, do you need some help?"

The girl turned to her in relief. "I do. I really do. I need to find the Orange Blossom— Oh, Aunt Beverly!"

Beverly couldn't have been more surprised if the young lady had started tap dancing on the sidewalk. *"Jah?"*

"It's me. Patricia. Tricia! You know, Edward's youngest?"

It had been the question in her statement that had done it. Sweet Tricia, always so hesitant about herself. Immediately, tears sprang to Beverly's eyes. "Tricia? Oh, my goodness, look at you," she exclaimed just before she enfolded the girl into her arms. "The last time I saw you, you were a good five inches shorter. And had chubby cheeks."

Tricia giggled. "I was kind of a late bloomer, but I've made up for it since."

"Indeed you have." Standing back, Beverly eyed her brother's youngest with a happy smile. Edward was her favorite brother, and each one of his five girls had Beverly's heart wrapped around their fingers. But Tricia had always been special to her. From the time she was a tiny thing, she'd had a mischievous way about her. It had often driven Edward to distraction, but Beverly had found her niece's knack for impetuousness to be highly amusing. They'd shared a couple of letters over the years, but nothing recently. Ever since she'd left Ohio she'd found it difficult to remain connected with her friends and family. Even though they'd been nothing but kind when Beverly had been humiliated when her best friend and fiancé fell in love, Beverly couldn't help but be embarrassed about what had happened.

Then another memory filtered through the shock. Beverly recalled a small character flaw—if it could really be called that. Tricia was impulsive—always had been—which spurred a new worry. Edward was nothing if not conscientious. Never would he have allowed Tricia to visit without exchanging four or five phone calls and a half dozen letters with Beverly first.

"What is going on, Tricia?"

"Well, my brand-new suitcase broke. I can't believe it."

"Those things happen." Instead of asking her again what she was up to, Beverly stared at her hard and held on to her patience.

"Aunt Bev, I had to sit at the very back of the bus the whole entire time! And that meant I couldn't get off the bus until everyone else did. So, when I finally did, the crowd around the bus was so thick I couldn't find you. Then I had to get this bag and then the wheel popped off."

"Goodness."

"And I had no idea how to find you," Tricia continued, barreling through her explanation, yet telling her nothing of consequence. "And Tony the bus driver didn't look all that excited to help me, neither. I sure wish he would have."

"Tony is usually ready to get on his way home," Beverly explained.

"So I had to ask everyone I could find where the Orange Blossom Inn was. And the first four people didn't know." She glared at Beverly, as if it were her fault she'd been lost.

"You were heading in the right direction." Hopefully Tricia's explanation was heading there as well. "So, did someone finally give you some help?"

"*Jah.* I ended up asking a pair of boys. They knew right where your inn was." After sighing rather dramatically, she said, "I kind of thought one of them would have offered to help me with my suitcase, seeing how it is broken and all, but they didn't."

"I can help you now, dear," Beverly said soothingly, hoping her dear niece would finally understand that they had so much more to talk about besides luggage and Tony's grumpiness.

Tricia launched herself into Beverly's arms again. "Oh, thank you, Aunt Bev. I knew everything would be okay as soon as I found you. I knew it."

Grasping the handle of the broken suitcase, Beverly positioned it so she could wheel it on just two of the three remaining wheels, and started walking. She realized she was going to have to push a little bit harder for information. "Tricia, dear, I must admit to being mighty surprised to see you. Did you, ah, write me a letter to tell me you were coming?"

"Oh, *nee*! I decided to surprise you."

"You certainly did." Beverly swallowed a retort. There was a time and place for everything and here on the sidewalk wasn't it. "Well, um, you have a fairly big suitcase. How long do you plan to visit?"

"For a while."

Beverly prodded some more. "How long is awhile, dear? One week? Two?"

"To tell you the truth, I was thinking of staying quite a bit longer than that."

Beverly stopped. "Dear, I'm always happy to see you, but now you're starting to confuse me. Why are you being so evasive? I mean, of course you purchased a return ticket?"

Tricia tilted her head down and nudged a pebble with her toes. "Um, actually I didn't do that."

Beverly was at sea. "You didn't do what?"

"Buy a return ticket." After taking a deep breath, Tricia said, "Aunt Bev, I've decided to live in Pinecraft."

"Forever?"

"I had to get out of Sugarcreek and I knew you would take me in," she said in a rush. "After all, if there was anyone who would understand, it would be you." She smiled then. An angelic, lovely, beautiful smile. It was so sweet, so dear, that Beverly felt every retort, question, and comment in her head drift away. Tricia needed her. Tricia had left everything in the hopes that her aunt Beverly would help her.

What was she supposed to do about that?

It was a big question.

A half an hour ago she would have protested that she had no time. Her inn was as busy as ever. She had Eric Wagler, her new landlord, to deal with. She had the famous, attractive, and injured Michael Knoxx to look after. And one very shy, very needy Penny Troyer as her newest employee.

However, it seemed that the Lord had other thoughts about all that.

Beverly was starting to wish she'd said yes to Sadie's invitation to dine at Yoder's. Sometimes the only thing that made something bearable was a slice of coconut cream pie.

And she could surely use one right about now.

Chapter 10

There was a crow outside Michael's window. Or maybe a seagull. Maybe even a pelican. Some kind of large, noisy bird that was enjoying the Florida morning and making it its business to let the world know.

Or, maybe it was in love.

Whatever it was doing, it was doing it noisily. Right outside Michael's window. And it had been doing it since daybreak.

The bird squawked again.

"You . . . You bird." He was somewhat proud of himself for not calling it something else. Or adding a few choice adjectives. But if that creature didn't move along soon, Michael knew his restraint was going to fly out the window, no pun intended. If Michael had been able to easily get out of bed, he would have thrown open the window and shooed it away. Yelled at it. Shoot, he would have happily thrown a rock at it if it would have saved him from the continual squawking.

With a sigh, he shifted and tried to concentrate on how comfortable his bed was instead. If the Lord intended for him to be bound to a bed for the next month, at least He'd given Michael an exceptionally comfortable place to be.

Beverly Overholt's Orange Blossom Inn held everything any weary traveler could want. Fine, soft cotton sheets wrapping a pillow-topped queen-sized bed. Blankets that smelled fresh and clean. Quilts that were soft and pliable, their patches of fabric made of faded colors, evidence of frequent washings and hours spent fluttering in the warm Florida sun.

Beyond the bed was a desk, dresser, and bedside table stained in a pale, white-washed mushroom brown. There was also a comfortable-looking chair and ottoman upholstered in blue, tan, and ivory stripes. The walls were painted the palest blue, the ceiling a bright white. The floor was whitewashed wood. Thick, cream-colored area rugs were soft underfoot.

Since Michael traveled over two hundred days a year and had spent many a night in old guest rooms, dirty hotels, and once, a cabin infested with fleas, he could certainly appreciate his luxurious surroundings.

However, he couldn't recall being plagued by such an incessantly squawking bird.

Picking up his book, he attempted to get lost in the story of a man trying to discover himself in the darkest corners of Alaska, but the descriptions of the snow and ice didn't mean much to him. It all seemed too far removed from where he currently was.

Or maybe it was that bird pecking at his window.

So, he watched the clock's minute hand slowly inch around. And then he watched as it did it again.

The two timid raps at the door just then sounded like choir bells, they were so welcome. "Yes?"

"Michael? It's Penny," she called through the door.

He couldn't resist smiling. "Yes, Penny?"

"Um, may I come in?"

"Jah."

He sat up as the door slowly opened, and Penny stepped in. "*Gut matin*," she said with a sweet smile.

"*Gut matin* to you, too." He couldn't help but smile back. Today she had on a pale blue dress. It highlighted her blue eyes and the golden hair under her perfectly pressed white *kapp*. She looked pretty. Pretty as a picture, as his *daed* would say.

And as she quietly stepped closer, he found himself thinking that she walked with a rolling gait. Going forward but ready to backtrack at a second's notice. The closer she got to him, the brighter pink her cheeks became, finally allowing him to concentrate on something besides one annoying, tapping bird.

"Michael, how are you feeling today?" she asked as she approached. A new, almost clinical look of concern was in her eyes.

At this moment, he felt great. "I am *gut, danke*."

"Are you sure? Your, ah, knee, isn't paining you too much?"

"No worse than usual." He was about to describe his troubles with the squawking bird outside, just to see her grin, when he noticed that her serious expression wasn't actually for him. She seemed to be attempting to cover up her own pain.

And, he thought, doing a fairly poor job of it.

"Penny, I may be doing all right, but I don't think you are."

She blinked those blue eyes, looked tempted to argue, then with a half smile, shook her head. "I'm afraid that is true."

"Want to talk about it?"

"I do not." Looking decidedly determined, she straightened her shoulders. "Miss Beverly sent me up to see what you would like to eat. Would you care for an early lunch?" Still studying him, she frowned. "Or would you prefer a late breakfast?"

Just as he opened his mouth to mention that he didn't care, she continued. "Downstairs, there are banana pancakes, fruit, and coffee cake. Or Miss Beverly could make you eggs. Or grits," she added eagerly. "Would you like some grits?"

"Definitely no grits."

As he'd hoped, she relaxed a bit. "You haven't embraced Southern food yet?"

"Nope."

"It took me some time after I moved here, too."

He zeroed in on that like the bird's inordinate interest in his window. "I want to hear all about when you moved here, and I'll be happy to give you my order, but first I need your help."

"How may I help you?"

He pointed to his crutches across the room. "I forgot to ask Beverly to set those by the bed last night. I need them."

She rushed to get them and didn't blink when he slid to the side and carefully got upright. As he started making his way to the facilities, she merely stood to one side and didn't embarrass him by asking if he needed help. He did not.

She didn't even gape at the way one of his pajama bottoms had been cut and hemmed to just below his knee to account for the prosthesis. He'd long since given up the idea that he had to hang on to that extra fabric to save anyone else's sensibilities.

After he came out of the bathroom, he hid a smile when he saw that she'd straightened his sheets and fluffed his pillows. There was no need to draw attention to her kindness when she'd done so much to save his dignity.

Then he heard that blasted bird squawk again.

"Penny, come here," he ordered as he crutched over to the window.

She rushed to his side. "What's wrong?"

After locating the string, he pulled open the blind and stared at the small gray and white mockingbird that was standing on the windowsill, looking in. "This is what's wrong."

Penny tilted her head to one side. "You don't care for birds?"

The small creature eyed them, pecked at the window, then squawked. "I don't care for *rude* birds. This little guy woke me up the moment the sun appeared on the horizon."

She tilted her head. Then, for the first time, her expression became unguarded, transforming her from a rather charming girl into a particularly lovely woman.

His body jolted in response.

"What do you want to do?" she murmured.

He wasn't sure. Did he want to flirt with her a little? Attempt to make her smile again? Try to figure out why there were shadows dancing behind her eyes except when she spied noisy little birds?

"I can't decide," he answered honestly.

When the bird pecked the window again, she clucked her tongue against her teeth and reached for the latch, which, of course, dislodged the annoying bird. After snapping the window shut, she located a sheet of the inn's letterhead on his desk, then slipped that into the window's wood frame so it was lodged there.

"What does the paper do?"

"Removes the reflection. The morning sun must hit your window in such a way that there's a good reflection on it. Birds are social creatures. When they see their reflections, they will peck and peck until they reach their new friend. This should do the trick."

"That is clever."

She chuckled. "Not so much. I just know birds, I guess." After pulling the blind back down, she continued. "Now, Michael Knoxx, you must tell me what you want for breakfast and do it quickly or Miss Beverly's gonna wonder what I'm doing."

"I'll have the pancakes, juice, and *kaffi*."

"Do you take cream?" Her eyes widened. "Or sugar? Do like sugar in your *kaffi*, too?"

She was too cute. Obviously Miss Beverly had coached her to ask guests how they wanted their coffee.

"Just cream."

She turned toward the door. "I'll be back soon with your plate."

"Wait."

"Yes?"

"Help me with the crutches, would ya?" he asked as he hobbled over to his bedside and lowered himself onto it.

Her hand hovered. "Where do you need me to place them?"

"Against the wall is fine. Usually, I simply lay them on the floor and kind of scoot down to pick them up myself. But my knee is hurting too much for that."

She took the crutches and set them against the wall near the bed's headboard. "How's this? I'll be happy to help you with them if I'm here. But if you have an emergency you can reach them without putting pressure on your knee."

"That is perfect, Penny."

And when she smiled back at him, looking pleased with herself, he couldn't resist teasing her some more. "Penny, you are turning out to be a woman I can't live without," he announced in a dramatic way.

"Is that right?"

"Absolutely! You're able to solve my problems, solve the bird's problems, and make my life easier. All in one very affable way."

"Affable, hmm? You make me sound so special."

He grinned. "You, I think, are more than that."

She rolled her eyes before striding out the door.

But in the quiet of his very comfortable, now very peaceful room, Michael realized that he'd been tempted to say that his words couldn't have been truer. Her presence in his life was serving to lift his mood. A reminder that he wasn't always a speaker or a motivator, or anything special. Really, he was simply a man. Just a man who was kind of, sort of, developing a crush on a girl in the middle of Pinecraft, Florida.

Which, in many ways, was far more discomfiting than a noisy bird outside his window.

By the time Penny finally made her way back to the kitchen, Miss Beverly was waiting for her at the foot of the stairs. Inwardly, she winced, trying to come up with an excuse, but having no idea how to explain herself.

Luckily, Beverly started talking before Penny had a moment to even think. "Penny, at last!" she exclaimed with what looked to be a very relieved sigh. "I've been standing here for the last five minutes, debating about whether to go upstairs and see what was taking you so long or to simply be patient and wait."

The comment was so endearing, Penny took the chance to tease her. "I hate to say it, but you don't look like you've been waiting all *that* patiently."

Beverly smiled, tucking her chin in embarrassment. "You are right about that. I've been more than a little bit concerned."

"I'm sorry. Michael had some things he needed me to do," she said evasively. She didn't want to embarrass him by sharing too much information.

"Like what?"

Well, at least she'd tried to give him a little bit of privacy.

"Michael needed to go to the bathroom. Then, well, then he had some trouble with a bird."

"What kind of trouble?"

"A lonely mockingbird." Penny smiled. "Michael said she'd been pecking and squawking at his window all morning. She woke him up."

"Perhaps he can now count birds among his number of fans," she joked. "I'm surprised he didn't call me to help him shoo it away."

"His crutches were out of his reach. I'm afraid he was stuck in bed." Penny had a feeling that Michael wouldn't have been in a hurry to reveal more weaknesses to Miss Beverly, anyway.

Her expression fell. "Oh, that poor boy. I remember now. I set them next to the door after I checked on him last night. I don't know what I was thinking."

Penny didn't know what to say to that. On one hand, Miss Beverly was exactly right; she hadn't been thinking. Poor Michael had been stuck in bed, which was a difficult thing for any man, let alone a man like him who was no doubt used to his freedom. In fact, he seemed determined to prove his independence at every turn.

On the other, he was definitely not helpless. Which meant that he should have remembered to make sure his crutches were nearby.

"Everything's taken care of now," she murmured, "so there isn't anything to worry about."

"You're right." She clapped her hands lightly together. "Now, what would he like for breakfast?"

"Pancakes, juice, and *kaffi.*"

"Right. Let's go to the kitchen. I'll make his pancakes, you can get him a carafe of *kaffi.*" As she walked, she added, "He's not an easy guest, Penny, but you're doing just fine with him. He said you have a way about you that's warm and pleasing."

"He said that?"

"Oh, *jah*. I must tell you, I'm impressed. I know of too many girls who would be treating him like a celebrity and making him feel self-conscious."

She couldn't help but smile at that. This morning, she hadn't even thought of him as "Michael Knoxx." Instead, he'd been simply Michael. The more they'd gotten to know each other, the less she'd thought about how famous he was. Little by little, she was starting to appreciate his kindness and his humor. "We seem to get along well enough."

"Hiring you was the right decision, Penny. Michael is so used to being independent, I feared he was going to have a hard time recovering from surgery. However, he might let down his guard if you two are friends."

"I'm not sure if we are actually friends. . . ."

"If you two aren't exactly friends yet, you're at least developing a relationship, right?"

Penny supposed so. "Right," she agreed.

"I'm only speaking the truth, dear. Just wanted you to know that I've noticed how well you are doing with such a difficult guest."

Miss Beverly's words were kind, but inside, Penny thought her boss couldn't be more wrong. Michael Knoxx wasn't difficult at all. He was handsome and interesting. Nice.

He was making her think things she had no business thinking about.

Or maybe, instead, he was inspiring her to think things she probably should have thought about years before.

Before it was too late.

PENNY WAS STILL DWELLING on her choices five hours later when she peeked in on Michael before leaving for the day. While she'd spent much of the day in the kitchen helping Beverly or cleaning mixing bowls, baking sheets, and dishes from afternoon tea, Michael had gone to a doctor's appointment. Miss Beverly had told her he was likely sleeping now, but Penny couldn't resist checking on him just to make sure he wasn't in pain after the eventful day.

But when she cracked open his door, she immediately noticed that he wasn't sleeping at all. Instead, he was sitting in the chair she usually sat in and gazing out the window. He turned her way when she stepped inside.

"Time to leave?"

"*Jah.*"

He nodded, his expression tight. "All right then. See you tomorrow."

This was her cue to leave. It's what she should be ready to do, too. Spending the day on her feet in a warm kitchen would make anyone eager to go home and take a cool shower. But his quick, quiet dismissal was so different from how he'd acted that morning, she grew concerned. "Did your appointment go all right?"

He shrugged. "We discussed what would happen during Friday's surgery." After a pause, he added, "Penny, I think I've been fooling myself. I hadn't wanted to really think about the surgery and the extent of the damage. Now I know that it's going to be a tougher recovery than I had imagined."

"Oh, Michael. I really am so sorry. I wish you would have heard better news," she murmured before realizing that it didn't sound very professional.

The corners of his lips curved up. "That pretty much covers it. I knew it was coming, but today it finally sank in."

She stepped a little closer. "Are you worried?"

"About the surgery?" When she nodded, he shook his head. "Not really. The *doktah* says that although they're going to have to do quite a bit of repair work, it won't take all that long. It's not supposed to take over an hour." Looking down at his leg, he grimaced. "I shouldn't even be thinking twice about this. After all, I've been through worse. And I made myself a promise when I was stuck in that ravine never to let myself be disappointed about my leg."

Penny wasn't sure if she could have done that. She knew from experience that sometimes one couldn't help but be human and have human reactions to things that happened. "Then what is bothering you?"

"Truth?"

When she nodded, he said, "It's nothing that I'm very proud of. I was just sitting here, feeling a little bit sorry for myself." He grimaced. "I hate knowing that I'm lying in bed while my whole family is out working hard. I hate that they're all doing their best to pay my medical bills for me. I feel like no matter how hard I try otherwise, I'm still a burden."

"I know that's hard. Once, a lot of people raised money for my family but it was difficult for my parents to accept it." She paused, remembering several men from the church arriving at their house one evening with a large envelope filled with cash they'd collected. But instead of looking relieved, her parents had looked devastated. Realizing she'd been in a daze, she shook her head. "Accepting charity is never easy."

"For what were they raising money?"

It was on the tip of her tongue to tell him about Lissy and how her dear sister's abduction had changed their lives forever. But she had a feeling if she started talking, she wouldn't be able to stop. She'd share how scared and worried she'd been. How lonely she was now. How confused she was about her parents and her future. And before they knew it, the conversation would be all about her, which wasn't right, since he was the one who was going to have surgery soon. "I'll tell you another day."

He narrowed his eyes, looking like he wanted to press her, then nodded. "Hey, I was just looking outside, but no matter how hard I try, I can't see the ocean."

She giggled. "That's because it's not in that direction, silly. It is to our west."

"Too bad for me. I would love to see Siesta Key one day."

"You've never been?"

"Nope. My family has visited here several times, but we've never stayed long enough to visit the gulf."

"Maybe you can visit after you recover," she ventured. "It will give you something to look forward to, and it's not far away at all."

"That's a nice thought, but I think my recovery might be a while. I don't think the doctors are going to be too eager for me to be around a bunch of sand."

"Oh."

He looked at her. Then, right before her eyes, something new flickered in his expression. "Hey, what are you doing tomorrow?"

"Working here. Why?"

"What do you think about going to Siesta Key with me?"

She didn't know what to think about that. "Are you allowed to go to the beach?"

He grinned. "It's my leg that's in a bad way. I'm not being held hostage."

Though she forced herself to smile at his joke, his comment

struck a little too close to home. "If you think you can manage it, then I think you should go. You only live once," she added, hoping she sounded kind of spunky.

His lips twitched. "Does that mean you'll accompany me?"

This was where she could say no. Where she could remind herself that she'd already taken some big steps in her life lately and her parents weren't having an easy time of it. If they discovered that she had agreed to go to Siesta Key with a man? Why, she'd be lucky if they let her out of the house ever again!

But she really did want to go. She'd be a fool to pass up an opportunity like this.

And why wouldn't she want to go? Everyone thought he was a nice man. And he was. Plus, he was beyond handsome.

Plus . . . well, he was Michael Knoxx! What more needed to be said?

"If Miss Beverly says I can, I would love to go."

A mischievous grin suddenly appeared on his face, reminding her that while he was a mighty nice man, he was also a man who was used to getting his way. "She'll let you. I'll make sure of that."

"All right then. Of course I'll go with you." Thinking ahead, she said, "I'll go downstairs and see if she can hire a driver for you. . . ."

"Is that how you usually go? With a car and driver?"

"Well, I've only gone with my parents, but that time we took the SCAT, the Sarasota County Area Transit. And, um, that's how most everyone our age goes." She paused, worried that he would realize that she'd only gone to the beach once and start thinking she was even odder than she felt.

But all he did was nod in agreement. "Then that's how I want to go, too."

"Are you sure you won't get hurt?" What would she do if he got hurt?

"If I get hurt, they can fix the damage on Friday," he said softly, just as if he'd been reading her mind.

Her shoulders relaxed as she realized he was probably right. Besides, there was something in his expression that told her this excursion meant an awful lot to him. He needed to get out of his guest room. He needed to simply be like everyone else.

Trying to do her part to make the day as nice as possible, she hesitantly said, "Would you like me to pack a picnic for us? It wouldn't be any trouble."

His eyes warmed. "Absolutely, Penny."

Absolutely. There was something about him saying that one, special, superlative word that got her every time. "Um, is there anything you don't like to eat? Anything you're allergic to?"

"I promise, anything you make will be fine with me. I'm not picky."

"All right then. I, um, will go talk to Miss Beverly now."

"You do that. Then ask her to please come talk to me, too."

"I will," she promised.

"Then you need to go home because you've been working all day, Penny."

It was becoming impossible to do anything but agree with whatever he said. "All right," she said yet again.

"Michael."

That brought her up short. She turned to look at him again. "I'm sorry?"

"You hardly ever say my name. I was just adding my name to your reply." White teeth flashed. "So you could say, 'All right, Michael.'"

She didn't dare tell him that the reason she rarely said his name was because it felt too personal, too familiar. Admitting that would be letting him in too far. She was starting to realize that she needed as many shields as she could invent to place around her heart so she didn't become too enamored with him.

But even so, she still couldn't resist giving him what he wanted. "All right, Michael," she whispered before turning and darting out the door.

Something was happening between them. She wasn't sure if it was good, but she was certain that it was out of her control.

Completely, utterly, totally out of her control.

Chapter 11

$\mathcal{M}$ichael was mighty glad that New York City and Sarasota, Florida, were both on East Coast time. He was eager to get his promised phone call over with so he could get ready for Penny's arrival and their trip to Siesta Key. If his family were in the mountains or in California, he'd have to wait several more hours to call them.

Every time he thought about sweet Penny Troyer guiding him to Siesta Key, he grinned. She was undoubtedly one of the shyest, most unsure girls he'd ever met—and he'd met a lot of girls through his travels and speaking engagements. Since he was used to most women being the exact opposite around him— practically doing anything to get his attention all while sharing way too much information far too easily—Penny was becoming quite desirable to him. However, he was also discovering that mixed in with her shyness was a quiet strength. He found the mixture fascinating.

And she was pretty, in that girl-next-door way that he found so appealing. He found her easy to look at, easy to be with. And because she was reserved by nature, he was taking his time and learning a lot about her. And he wanted to learn *everything* about her. Why she was the way she was. What secrets she was hiding from the rest of the world. He didn't have any grand expectations that he could help her or anything. But he did hope to be her friend.

She really looked like she could use a friend.

What she didn't know, however, was that he could use a friend, too. He'd traveled so often and for so long, he was beginning to realize just how distant he'd been with most people. Part of the reason was because there simply wasn't enough time for real relationships to take place. Usually, their schedule was so tightly organized that he and his family often arrived just hours before going on stage.

Then, after they spoke, they visited with everyone who came out to see them. And even though those were nice conversations, they usually revolved around either his speech or their experiences. The following day was much of the same, just in a different location. Then, next thing they knew, they were on the bus or plane or train again.

He never complained—Michael didn't believe in complaining or taking the blessings he'd been given for granted—but he did sometimes yearn for some time to himself.

And if he was being honest, he'd like to have a couple of days to be with friends who couldn't care less about amputations and the places he'd been. Who simply wanted to hang out.

Maybe one day he would tell his family that he had had enough, that it was time for God to choose another man or woman to carry on His word.

But before that, he had to get the surgery.

And before *that*, he needed to touch base with his parents.

After taking a fortifying sip of his coffee, he leaned back in

Beverly's office chair in her kitchen and called his brother's cell phone.

Two rings later, he was connected.

"Michael," Evan called out, his voice sounding as bright as ever. "I was hoping this was you. How goes it?"

"About the same."

"Still in a lot of pain?" Evan's voice was laced with concern now, reminding Michael that though hundreds of miles separated them, they were as close as ever.

"Not as much."

"Truth."

"The doctor gave me some prescriptions that help a lot," Michael explained. He hated talking about his weaknesses, hated talking about how needy he was. But taking a deep breath, he made himself share his news. "The surgery is still scheduled for tomorrow."

"Did you learn anything more about what Dr. Barnes expects to do?"

"Some." Frowning, Michael ran a hand through his hair. He didn't like thinking about the damage to his knee, either.

After a beat, Evan prodded. "And?"

"The doctors think it might be a bit more invasive than originally thought."

"Why? Is it bad?" His voice rose. "Have you gotten worse? Are you feverish? Has the infection spread?"

Michael could just imagine how his mother would react to that news! "Settle down, Evan. You're going to worry Mamm and Daed."

"Too late. We're all already worried about you."

"Well, don't be. And reassure Molly and Mamm and Daed that I'll be fine." And he would be. He would make certain of it.

There was no way he was going to let his parents lose sleep over his problems ever again.

Evan lowered his voice. "I'll do my best."

"Danke."

"I don't know how much I'll be able to alleviate *everyone else's* worries, however."

"What are you talking about?"

"You know what I'm referring to. You're all anyone talks about wherever we visit."

"Surely not."

"It's true. Everyone we meet looks for you. And when they realize you aren't with us, a mild bit of panic starts to break out. You've got quite the fan club."

Michael really wished he could see Evan. His brother had such a dry sense of humor that it was sometimes next to impossible to tell if he was teasing or being perfectly serious. "I thought Daed and Mamm were going to preach about the unexpected blessings they've found on the road."

"Oh, they have. And Molly sang last night. She sounded beautiful, too. But after? You were the topic of choice."

"Now you can tell everyone that I'll be just fine."

"I'll tell your admirers that after we hear that you *are* just fine. What time is your surgery?"

"Seven in the morning. I've got to be at the hospital at five thirty."

"Ouch."

"I've been thinking the same thing."

"Is Beverly still going to take you?"

"Yes, Daed," he said sarcastically. Honestly, Evan was asking so many questions, Michael wasn't going to have anything to tell their parents. "Listen, I've got plans for today. Put Mamm or Daed on."

"They're not here."

"No?"

"Nope. They were asked to attend an early-morning prayer breakfast."

"I bet they enjoyed that." While his parents enjoyed prayer meetings, like their sons, they weren't morning people.

"Yep, that about summed up their moods this morning. So, what are you doing today?"

Michael inwardly groaned. He didn't want to lie, but he sure hadn't planned to tell any of his family about his plans for the day. He knew none of them would approve, and probably were much more likely to disapprove. But they loved him. And he loved them back. And that meant that he needed to let them know what he was going to do, on the off chance that he was about to make a very bad decision.

"I'm going to the beach."

After a moment of silence, Evan burst out laughing. "Yeah, right. Of course you are."

Glaring at the blank wall in front of him, Michael struggled to keep the irritation out of his voice. "No, it's true. I'm going to Siesta Key today."

"You're scheduled for surgery tomorrow. It's already going to be difficult. You're already in a lot of pain, so much so that you've been told not to use your prosthesis."

"Thanks for letting me know all that."

Evan ignored his sarcasm. "Michael, why in the world would you put yourself in danger like this?"

"I'm hardly putting myself in danger. And the reason I'm going is pretty obvious. I want to go to the beach. I want to do something besides look out the window and wish I was somewhere else."

"And what does that have to do with anything?" He lowered

his voice. "You know, we can't always do what we want, Michael."

"I believe I've heard that saying once or twice."

"You know what I mean. A man has to come to terms with his responsibilities and duty."

Michael knew all about duty, and thought again that Evan of all people would have been very aware of that fact. "I don't know if you remember, but I've been by your side these last five years of touring. Don't even try to pretend that I don't know a thing or two about making do with what I have."

Evan sighed. "Sorry. I didn't mean that the way it sounded."

"I know. I also know that you know just as much about duty and accepting responsibility as I do. Listen, I don't need another mother, Evan. And we're talking about going to the beach, not hiking in the wilderness."

"I guess I can see your point."

His brother's statement was so grudgingly said, Michael smiled. "Good. Because the fact is that our family has been to Sarasota four times and we've never taken time to go to Siesta Key. I, for one, think that was a mistake. After the surgery, I'm going to be staring at the walls in my room for hours on end. And if I'm going to be doing that, I want some memories to keep me company while I do it."

"Who are you going with?" His voice was quieter now.

"A girl who works here at the hotel."

"Truly?"

Evan sounded both appalled and amused. And that, of course, made Michael frustrated. He was beginning to really regret giving him a call. "Yes, truly."

"Sorry, but I've never known you to make friends with hotel staff." He lowered his voice. "Are you sure she is safe?"

This time, he didn't even try to hide his feelings. He started laughing. "What do you mean by that?"

"Half the girls we meet want to be your wife. They want to tour the world by your side as Mrs. Michael Knoxx."

"Which would be such a treat, because being Michael Knoxx is so exciting," he said sarcastically.

"They think it is. And the other half want to start a rumor about you! Michael, are you sure that this, this maid isn't going to try to take advantage of you?"

"Pretty sure. She's a shy girl." Thinking about Penny, the guarded way she talked about herself, and how she'd never been to Siesta Key except by her parents' side, made him think she might need their excursion even more than he did. "Penny isn't just a maid. She's a sweet girl who's given me a lot of her time. And we're going to the beach, Evan. The beach. Stop making everything into such a big deal. I fear your imagination is starting to get the best of ya."

"I'm going to tell Molly, but I don't know if I'm going to tell Mamm and Daed. Were you going to?"

"I wasn't sure," he said sheepishly. "I wanted to let you all know what I was doing, but didn't want to have this discussion. I'm a grown man, Evan."

"I know."

"And I'm missing the bottom portion of a leg, not my brain."

"I realize that, too." He sighed. "Sorry if I sounded patronizing. It's just that you are you, and, well, Molly and I see how people look at you. They see you as someone larger than life."

"We both know I am nothing out of the ordinary."

"I know that we're all proud of you. I know that you have no idea the impact you have on other people. I'm proud to call you my brother."

Evan's words humbled him. "All I'm doing is going to Siesta Key for the day. That's it."

"Enjoy yourself. And, just for the record, you're right. It is a shame that we haven't taken the time to go to the beach. All this time, we've been preaching to folks about taking what the Lord gives us with an open mind and heart and we haven't even been doing that. I can't remember the last time we took a few hours to tour the beautiful places we've gotten to visit."

"Let's make a vow to change that habit," Michael said. "We owe it to ourselves."

"We absolutely do."

Glancing at the clock on the wall, Michael knew it was time to wrap things up. "Listen, I've got to go. If you want to tell Mamm and Daed about me going to the beach, go ahead, but I won't be here when they decide to give me grief about it."

He laughed. "Gotcha. Have someone call us tomorrow after your surgery."

"Will do."

"Hey, Michael?"

"Yeah?"

"We'll be praying for you tomorrow."

"*Danke.* I appreciate that." He had no doubt that his family's prayers would see him through even the darkest days.

After all, they already had.

TRICIA WAS STILL HAVING a difficult time getting used to the inn's routine. After she'd arrived, her aunt Beverly had encouraged her to spend some time making sure she was at peace with her decision to move to Florida.

But though her aunt imagined Tricia might be having second thoughts, she hadn't had a single one. She wanted a new life. She was ready to give the Lord her burdens and move forward. Of course, she wasn't sure what she wanted her new life to look like.

Therefore, in the meantime, she was determined to be as helpful to her aunt as she possibly could. It was simply too bad that so far Tricia felt she was as out of place in the Florida inn as a grove of blue spruces. Obviously it was going to take some time to adjust. That was the only explanation she could give herself as she rushed into the kitchen and practically ran over one of the guests.

"Hey, now," a man said, holding out a hand to steady her.

Or maybe it was to steady himself? He was holding himself up on crutches . . . and he was missing part of one of his legs! "I'm so sorry," she blurted. "I don't know what—"

He interrupted her. "It's all right." Little by little, his expression eased. "No harm done."

"Thank goodness. I really am sorry." She smiled at him. Then, when he smiled back at her, she got a little flustered. Okay, *a lot* flustered. He was a very handsome man. "Are you a guest?" It was obvious he was, but her mind had suddenly gone blank.

"I am. You?"

"*Nee.* I mean, I'm staying here, but I'm not really a guest. Beverly Overholt is my aunt."

"Ah. Well, nice to meet you." Now that he'd regained his balance, he hopped forward. "Have a good morning," he said as he obviously prepared to leave.

"My name's Tricia," she said quickly.

"I'm Michael."

She felt her cheeks flush as he edged away, almost like he couldn't get away from her fast enough. Gosh, what had she done wrong? But just as he stepped forward, the door swung open again, forcing him to hop backward on his crutches. The moment he did so, he winced.

Now it was obvious that he wasn't okay. Concerned, Tricia reached for his arm. If she could guide him to the kitchen table, she might be able to see how she could help him.

Just then, Penny, Aunt Beverly's shy new employee, rushed to the man's side. "Oh, Michael! Are you all right? I didn't knock into ya, did I? I didn't see you there."

"Don't fret, Penny. I'm learning this doorway is a particularly bad place to take a break."

Without a glance in Tricia's direction, Penny wrapped an arm around Michael's waist and helped him to a chair. The moment he sat, she pulled up a chair next to him and stared at him intently. "Now, please be honest. Are you okay?"

"I'll be fine," he replied.

Tricia raised her eyebrows at that. He'd knocked into a door, not fallen off a cliff. And he was a grown man, not a boy. Why was Penny acting that way?

Still ignoring Tricia, the girl said, "Do you want some ice?"

"I'll be fine," he said again, his voice warm and kind. "What I want to do is get on our way. Were you able to pack a lunch for us?"

"I did." She smiled sweetly as one brow arched. "Were you worried about that? I promised you I would."

"I wasn't worried." Tricia noticed that his eyes warmed for a moment before he adopted a far more friendly expression. With a grunt, he got to his feet. "So, are you ready? If so, let's get out of here."

"Do you mind if I first tell Miss Beverly that I'm going?"

"Of course not."

Tricia was thinking that maybe it was time to say something.

Since, well, it was becoming pretty obvious that both of them had forgotten she was in the room. "Um, I can tell Beverly that you left."

Penny turned to her. "That would be mighty kind of you, Tricia."

"It's no trouble."

Her cheeks flushed. "I'm sorry. I think I walked right by you without even a hello."

"Don't worry about it. You two looked kind of busy." Tricia smiled. "Anyway, I'll be happy to tell my aunt that you two left."

"That would be *wonderful-gut. Danke.* Oh! I didn't even ask if you two have met. Michael, this is Tricia Overholt, Tricia this is Michael—"

He cut her off. "Everything's okay, Penny. We've met."

"Oh, okay."

"Bye, Tricia," Michael said as they walked out.

Tricia raised her hand to tell them a cheery good-bye, but they were already gone. Their behavior was as puzzling as it was cute, she decided, as she poured herself a cup of coffee. She never would have imagined her aunt Beverly would have permitted her employees to be so friendly with the guests. But who was she to judge? Maybe Penny and Michael had known each other for years. Maybe she had a lot to learn about relationships in general.

When her aunt passed through ten minutes later, Tricia was enjoying her second cup.

"Hi, dear," Aunt Beverly said, a dozen neatly folded dish towels in her hands. "How has your morning been?"

"All in all, uneventful." She almost mentioned running into Michael, and then Penny almost running into *him*, and the pained expression he'd worn, but she was afraid Beverly might remind her that the guests' business was definitely not any of hers. Instead, she merely passed on the information she'd been asked to share. "Penny wanted you to know that she took Michael to the beach today."

"I was hoping to touch base with them before they left, but I suppose it's just as well I didn't. Michael needs to have a good day, I think." Tricia held her breath, more than ready to hear the story.

But instead, Beverly merely eyed her carefully. "Now that you've had a good night's sleep, do you feel like you're settling in?"

"Oh, *jah*. I am yearning to simply relax and try to help you as much as I can."

As if she'd finally gotten the opening she needed, Beverly set down the dishcloths and faced her. "I'm so glad you brought that up. I've been wanting to talk to you about why you came to visit me."

She should have known Beverly wasn't going to allow her to stay very long without an explanation about why she'd shown up in the first place. "I told you . . ."

"You told me nothing." After sighing, Beverly stared hard at her. "And because you've told me practically nothing, I called Edward last night."

"You called my *daed*?" A slow, sinking feeling settled in her, mixing with a dark sense of betrayal. "Aunt Bev, there was no need to get my father involved."

"After speaking to him, I'm glad I did." Her mouth settled into a firm, disapproving line. "He was worried about you. Tricia, he said that you came here without his permission."

"I know."

"And then I had to share that I knew nothing of this visit, either." Her glare deepened. "This little escapade was beyond irresponsible. It borders on sheer stupidity."

"Don't say that." She sniffed. All the lightness of her morning had faded and now she felt as troubled as she had before she'd gotten on the bus to Sarasota.

"Why not? Your actions were not smart. At all." Holding out a hand, Beverly started listing off reasons, using her long, slim fingers to illustrate her points. "You went out of state without telling anyone. You got on that bus without even knowing where I was."

"I knew you would be here in Sarasota, Aunt Bev. Everyone knows you are here working."

But instead of reassuring her, Beverly looked even more irritated. Her voice rose. "What if I hadn't been home? What if you had run into trouble on the bus? Did you think of that?"

She hadn't. She'd been too afraid not to count on everything working out. "But you were."

Beverly closed her eyes for a long moment, visibly attempting to maintain her composure. "Tricia, you are a grown woman of twenty-two, not a teenager. It is time to tell me the truth, and it better be the truth, or I will send you back home like the truant child you are being."

Tricia flinched. "You can't do that. Please don't."

"Why? What happened?"

She stared down at her mug. "Things I can't talk about."

"Not telling me isn't an option."

"Aunt Beverly, please, just trust me—"

"*Nee.* You haven't been straight with me. Your father is worried, which means your mother is most likely frantic, and that won't do. I love my brother, but I also love your mother too much to cause her pain. I'm not going to be the cause of her tears. What happened?"

"It's embarrassing."

Obviously out of patience, Beverly waved a hand through the air. "Sweetheart, I was left at the altar by my fiancé and best friend. *That* is embarrassing. I doubt you have experienced anything close to the like."

"It was bad."

"*What* was bad?" When Tricia didn't immediately reply, Beverly's eyes flashed. "Spit it out, Tricia. Your parents are waiting to hear—and I've got too much to do to wait for you to think of the perfect way to tell me."

"I was being bullied."

Her aunt stilled. "What? By whom?"

"By some girls who didn't like me." Though she tried to stop them, tears formed in her eyes as all of the terrible pain and embarrassment and, well, total humiliation came back. "I liked a man. One day, during a particularly long sermon, I wrote some stupid notes about him. Then I did something even more stupid. I was in a rush so one of my girlfriends said she would throw out my notes on her way home. Except, she didn't throw them out."

"That is too bad, but things pass, child. Next week, it will all be forgotten."

"No, Beverly, it wasn't forgotten in a week. It's been months. And things have snowballed."

"Oh, Tricia. I am sorry. What happened after she took the notes home?"

"She showed them to Ian."

"Really? She wasn't much of a friend, was she?"

Tricia shook her head. "It gets worse. After the man—Ian— saw what I'd written, he was shocked. And then my girlfriend decided to tell tales about me." Closing her eyes, she gathered her courage and shared some more. "They told everyone I was sneaking out at night. Spying on him." Actually, they'd made up far worse things, but Tricia wasn't in any hurry to share that with her aunt.

"Were you spying on Ian?"

"*Nee!* But it didn't matter. One of the girls? One of the girls has a lot of freedom. Her parents don't check on too many things she does. She lied and said she was with me."

"Therefore everyone believed her."

Tricia nodded. "She made up awful things. I don't even know why people would think they were true," she added, "but they did."

"What did your parents say? I can't imagine Edward putting up with that for a minute."

"I never told them," she whispered.

"No? Why on earth not?"

"I was afraid they'd believe those rumors, too." She'd been afraid to find out if they believed the worst of her because she had started to believe the worst of herself.

"They wouldn't have. But they could have helped you."

"They might have had doubts. I already had so many people thinking I was terrible, I couldn't risk them thinking that way about me, too."

"But you made things worse by keeping them in the dark."

"Aunt Beverly, by the time I boarded the bus, it wasn't simply my word against three or four girls. It was me against almost everyone I knew. People didn't want to be associated with me."

Beverly reached out and clasped her hand. "Oh, Tricia. I am so sorry."

Tears filled Tricia's eyes. This was why she'd come to Pinecraft. Not simply to run away but to be accepted. "I had to come here, Beverly. I couldn't wait. I couldn't risk you refusing me. I couldn't stay there another second."

"How did you get the money for your ticket?"

"I had most of it saved."

"And the rest?"

"I took it from the envelope in the kitchen," she admitted, hating how that made her sound. "It was my mother's grocery money."

Beverly shook her head. "Oh, Tricia. That was bad of you."

"I know. I'm really sorry. I promise, I really am. But you don't know what it's like. If it had just been those stupid letters, I could have dealt with it. If it had been just a week or two? I would have stayed. But it's been months and months of dodging questions and comments about things I didn't even understand. I didn't know what else to do."

Wrapping an arm around Tricia, Beverly squeezed her tight. "While I don't agree with your actions, I feel for you. What you've been going through was very, very hard."

"Terrible."

"Terrible, indeed."

"What should I do now?"

"First, you need to call your parents." When Tricia started to shake her head, Beverly said, "Tricia, it is time to start acting like the person you want everyone to see. That means you need to put your parents' minds at ease. "Call them and tell them everything."

"And then?"

"And then you may help me with the inn today. Since Penny is away for the day, I've got a lot of cooking and cleaning to do."

Tricia braced herself. She knew this phone call was going to be one of the hardest things she'd ever done. But Beverly was right. It was time to start doing the right thing, not simply running from everything that was so very wrong.

Chapter 12

*Y*ou know, if you keep looking at me the way you are, everyone is going to start to stare," Michael chided as they walked down Bahia Vista's sidewalk toward the SCAT stop.

Penny started. Was her attraction to him that obvious? "How am I looking at you?"

"Like you think I'm about to fall down any second."

Relief made her smile. "Sorry. I'm afraid I can't help it. See, I *am* kind of afraid that you are going to fall down any second." Unable to help herself, she examined him again.

He didn't look especially hurt or offended, which was good news. Instead, he wore a weary expression, as if he was reluctantly resigned to being coddled.

"I can't seem to catch a break," he said after she'd looked her fill. "Pretty much everyone I talk to only wants to make sure I'm not making things worse." As he stared off into the distance, he added, "When I called my brother this morning, he made sure to tell me I was being an idiot. My quick check-in turned into an exhausting conversation where I had to defend myself the whole time. Within five minutes, I felt like I was his pesky little brother again."

She couldn't help but grin at that. Though she was thinking of him more and more as just plain old Michael, there were still times when he said things that made her shake her head—like the idea of someone treating him as a "pesky" anything. To her, he was still a bit larger than life. It would be hard to deny him anything—which was part of the reason why she'd agreed to go with him to Siesta Key.

"I'm sorry about your conversation with your brother," she said as they continued walking, passing English tourists, their pale legs peeking out from under cotton shorts, and sunglasses framing their faces.

He shrugged. "It's irritating, but it's no big deal. He cares about me, you see. That's a blessing."

"Indeed."

"Do you have siblings?"

As it always did, the question cut through her. "I used to have a sister," she finally admitted. "But she died."

His expression grew serious. "I'm sorry to hear that. What happened?"

"I'd rather we didn't talk about that right now." There was no way she could even attempt to explain Lissy's abduction and her own loss in a few succinct sentences. It would also mar the joy and excitement she'd been feeling about the day.

She simply wasn't ready to lose that feeling of happiness yet.

"Are you sure you don't want to talk about it? I'm a mighty *gut* listener."

"I'm positive."

"Why?" His gaze turned searching.

"Because we're here, you see." Pointing to the SCAT stop crowded with people, she added, "We'll need to take the shuttle, then transfer to the bus going to Siesta Key. Are you sure this won't be too hard on you?"

"If things get too bad, I'll tell you. Okay?"

"Okay," she said as they came to a stop at the edge of the crowd, the faint scent of sunscreen infusing the air around them.

"*Gut.*" He smiled. Then, as if he'd just realized that most of the Amish men and women at the stop were staring at him, he lifted his hand. "Hi."

"Hi," one teenaged girl in a bright pink dress replied, then promptly giggled.

No one else responded, but Penny guessed that while they were watching him silently, more than a couple were probably wondering if he was *the* Michael Knoxx or if he just happened to look a lot like the headliner for the famous evangelists.

Over the next hour, Penny noticed him receiving similarly appraising looks when they transferred buses, and again as they walked through the parking lot on the way to the beach. He didn't look fazed by it in the slightest, however. He simply smiled at whoever was staring at him, then looked away before they got up the nerve to ask him any personal questions.

When she saw him politely ignore a middle-aged couple who looked intent on making his acquaintance, she said, "This happens a lot, doesn't it?"

"Walking to Siesta Key with a pretty girl? Never."

She laughed. Not because she knew he'd never been to this beach before, but because she knew she wasn't anything all that special to look at. "I mean, people approach you a lot, don't they? Even when you're not speaking in a crowd?"

He shrugged. "It doesn't happen as much as you'd think. Usually, the only time people stop me to ask questions is at a speaking engagement. And that's to be expected." He frowned. "I promise, usually I am a lot more receptive to folks. I'm glad for their interest and grateful for their support. But that said, I need a break this week."

"I don't blame you for that."

"You sure?"

His hazel eyes searched hers as they reached the edge of the parking lot. It was almost as if her opinion really mattered to him, which was ludicrous. But perhaps this was exactly why he was so well known. He had a way of looking at a person as if he or she mattered. It was a mesmerizing thing to experience when he was speaking to a crowd, but in person? Well, half the time his intense gaze left her tongue-tied.

"Penny?"

"Oh. *Jah*. I am sure. You're only human."

"You're right about that," he quipped, his expression easing. "So, are we finally going to go to the beach now?"

She pointed ahead. "It's right there. All we have to do is go down those steps and you'll be walking on the softest, silkiest sand in the world."

Stepping forward, he grinned at her. "How could a guy refuse an offer like that?"

She chuckled. "Put that way, I have no idea." When they started down the cement stairs, she noticed some added strain in his expression. "Michael, will you be all right, walking on the beach?"

"I'll let you know if I'm not."

His reply didn't alleviate her worries one iota. "I don't intend to be mean, but I feel I should point out that you're much bigger than me."

She felt his gaze travel the length of her body. "*Jah*," he said with a nod. "I've noticed that as well."

She felt her skin flush. "Um, what I'm saying is that if something were to happen . . ." Her voice drifted off, because, truly, how could she say what she was trying to say without ruining his day?

"I know you can't carry me, Penny," he said softly. "Don't worry. I would never let things get that bad."

"Michael—"

"This pain is new, but my disability is not. I'm used to dealing with it."

"If you're sure."

His eyes brightened with an amusement he didn't attempt to conceal. "I am sure. *Danke*, Penny. Thank you for worrying about me."

Feeling as if her whole body was lighter, she took the canvas bag filled with their lunch and towels off his arm. "In that case, Michael Knoxx, please enjoy Siesta Key."

He took three steps onto the sand. Looking right he focused on a group of kids playing volleyball. Glancing left, she watched him eye the bright blue lifeguard tower with interest. Then, at last, he stared straight out over the water. As the waves rolled forward, he breathed deep. Then sighed.

"It's beautiful," he murmured. "Penny, it's exactly like you said. And absolutely worth coming out here for."

Something new and warm and wonderful filled her. It felt a lot like happiness, but stronger. Something inside her whispered that it felt like love, but of course that couldn't be. Maybe it was more along the lines of intense satisfaction.

Because she knew for a fact that the man by her side wasn't the only person stretching his limits today. She had taken some giant steps of her own. And the day had only just begun.

PENNY WAS A WONDER. After scanning the area, she'd found a secluded cove that was a relatively short distance from the water. Then, she'd held his hand when he'd walked down to the surf, somehow making it look like she was the one holding on to him instead of the other way around.

Though Michael never felt self-conscious about missing part of a leg, for the first time in years, he found himself wishing he had two good legs. Maybe it was because the sand felt like heaven under his bare left foot. Or maybe it was because he feared he looked like quite a sight, walking on crutches toward the waves with one pant leg rolled up to his midcalf, the other pant leg brushing his tennis shoe.

Or perhaps it was because Penny looked more light of heart than he'd seen her all week. Her feet were bare and she'd knotted the sides of her skirt so they kind of billowed around her calves. Her cheeks were glowing from the sun, and her smile was so broad and bright it was infectious. And her laugh! She giggled and chuckled at crabs and jellyfish. She laughed outright at a child who was attempting to bury his older brother's legs in the sand. She beamed at the teenagers playing volleyball and the elderly couple enjoying a bucket of Kentucky Fried Chicken.

In fact, she had so much joy on her face, Michael was starting to wonder if he'd ever been so happy. He honestly couldn't remember.

After his daring toe-touch in the ocean, they walked back to their spot and she helped him sit down. Then she carefully spread out another beach towel and handed him a thick roll filled with roast beef, Swiss cheese, lettuce, tomato, and brown mustard. Another container of sliced strawberries was set to one side. Then she handed him a bag of potato chips and a plastic cup filled to the brim with sweet tea.

"This looks amazing, Penny."

She looked so pleased, he knew that she'd been the one to prepare the meal instead of Beverly. He took a bite of the sandwich and it tasted just as good as it looked. "The sandwich is delicious."

"I'm glad you like it." She took a bite of her own.

After a few more bites, something occurred to him. "I was in the kitchen when you arrived for work, no?"

"You were."

"Well, then when did you have time to make everything?"

"I made it all at my house this morning." Looking guilty, as if he'd caught her in a fib, she added, "I made the turtle brownies last night, though." She pointed to a covered container that he hadn't even noticed yet.

"So, this is your food? Not the inn's?"

"Well, *jah*." She looked at their sandwiches with some concern. "Is that okay?"

"Of course it is." He lifted up the remains of his own sandwich. Barely a fourth was left. "I, um, was simply worried about the expense. I hate the idea of you using your own money to pay my way." Thinking of her working late into the night, he added, "And time. I didn't think about you having to spend your evening baking."

"Brownies don't take long. And as for our meal? It is only sandwiches."

He knew she wanted him to leave it alone, but there was something about what she'd done that gave him pause. "Why didn't you use the kitchen's food?"

A line appeared above her brows. "I didn't do that because, um, after I asked Beverly for the day off, I didn't know how to ask about your lunch, too. Besides, I enjoyed making the brownies and sandwiches."

"Now things are starting to make more sense. When I told Beverly last night that I was going to the beach with you today, she seemed surprised. You're not getting paid for today, are you?"

"Of course not. I'm at the beach, Michael."

"But that doesn't seem fair, you carting me to the beach on your own time."

"I told you I wanted to go." Irritation was seeping into her words now.

But the more he learned, the guiltier he felt about taking up her whole day off. "Did you have to cancel some other plans?"

"Not at all."

"Why not?"

"I don't think that's any of your business."

"I think it is." He didn't want to call her a liar, but he was pretty certain that she'd canceled all kinds of things in order to babysit him for the day. He simply wanted her to admit it so they could have it out in the open.

She pursed her lips together. For a moment there, he was genuinely worried that he'd made her so upset she wasn't going to answer. Then she sighed. "I didn't have to cancel anything because I don't really have any friends and my parents are mad at me."

He was stunned. He put the last of his sandwich back on the sheet of waxed paper and gave her his complete attention. "Why?" he asked. "Why don't you have any friends? And why are your parents upset with you?"

"Michael, honestly, this doesn't concern you. Can't we leave it at that?"

Even though he heard the stress in her voice, he shook his head. "*Nee*, I don't think so." When she practically rolled her eyes, he pushed a little more. "Come on, Penny. You know all about me. You're going to have to help take care of me for the next few days. Don't make me feel like we're completely on uneven ground."

"We are, though."

"Please? I'm not just asking because I'm being nosy. I'm asking because I care."

"It's kind of a long story."

He leaned back on his elbows. "I've got time." But more than that, he was eager to learn more about her. When she wrapped up her half of the sandwich and set it to one side with a resigned expression, he knew he'd won. "What happened to you, Penny?"

She closed her eyes, as if mentally preparing herself for what was to come, then began. "It all started when my sister, Lissy, was kidnapped walking home from school one day."

It took every bit of experience he had to not betray how shocked he was. Instinctively, he knew if he reacted too intensely, she would shut down. "So, what happened to her, then?"

"About everything one might wish to never happen, Michael. After, she was found in a field."

He blinked. He'd seen enough of the world to have a very good idea of what had happened to her sister. But for some odd reason, he wished she'd said the words anyway. Almost as if he was hoping that his darkest imaginings were completely off base.

But he would never ask her to speak of such things.

"So that's how she died," he murmured to himself. He swallowed hard, hoping she didn't notice how much her story was affecting him. She needed him to be her support now.

"*Jah.*" She leaned forward, ran her finger in the sand. "Lissy was . . . She was dead when the police found her."

"I'm so sorry, Penny." He was such an idiot. Here he had been pushing and prodding her to tell him private information about herself, thinking he could use his wealth of experience to ease her pain in some way. But now it was so very obvious that she had much to teach him.

"*Danke*, but it's okay." Visibly steeling herself, she added,

"They did find the man who murdered her. He was arrested and later sent to prison."

"Ah."

"He, uh, died there. Someone murdered him." She took a deep breath. "As you might imagine, it has been a difficult thing living with what happened to my sister. I've often wondered why that man didn't kidnap me." She met his eyes. "I've wondered why the Lord took Lissy so young. Why did He have to make her suffer so?" Lowering her voice, she added, "And why did He decide that nothing should happen to me?"

As she paused for breath, Michael struggled to find the right words to comfort her. But what could he ever offer that would comfort Penny?

She continued. "Lissy's death, um, drew a lot of attention to our community. In the news."

"I can only imagine."

She looked down at her feet, as if it was too hard to face him. "Some reporters acted as if what happened to Lissy was doubly bad because she was Plain." She shrugged. "I don't think that matters though, you know? I mean, it was all bad."

Practically unable to speak, he nodded.

"Anyway, after a time, my parents decided to move here, to Florida. They wanted a fresh start. And, well, Lissy died in the middle of winter. There was something about the cold, gray skies that my *mamm*, especially, couldn't deal with."

"How old were you when that happened?"

"Twelve."

"Twelve," he repeated. Twelve was far too young to experience such a tragedy.

She nodded. "I, ah, was almost fourteen when we moved here." A few minutes passed as she shifted, fussed with the makeshift knot in the hem of her dress. "Anyway, we moved here, but time hasn't really helped my parents all that much. They are angry and bitter and so very sad."

"I imagine lots of people would be that way still."

She nodded. "The way they dealt with their loss was to keep me close. They don't want to lose another daughter, you see."

Now he was beginning to understand her lack of friends. "Even though you might've been perfectly safe, they didn't want you to be out of their sight."

"Not at all." She pressed her lips together before continuing. "At first I felt the same way. Then, when it began to chafe, I tried to understand and give them time. But then something snapped, I guess. I couldn't do what they wanted anymore."

She turned to look at him directly. As if she needed him to understand. "Michael, I knew if I stayed one more day in that house I was *never* going to leave. My sister may be dead, but I felt like *I* was dying inside. I told my parents that I was going to go see your family speak in Pinecraft Park. I do know some folks from church and one gal, Violet, had said that she was going to go. So I went."

And that very night, when she'd offered to help him, he'd acted like a jerk. What was wrong with him? "I'm sorry I was so rude to you."

"You weren't rude. You were in pain. And there's no reason for you to apologize."

"Still, I could have been nicer."

"Michael, you were yourself. Believe me, I'm glad you acted like yourself. I'm glad you weren't perfect."

"I was far from that. I *am* far from that."

She shook her head, chuckling softly. "Don't be so hard on yourself. If you had been perfect, I think I would have been even more nervous the first time we met." She rolled her eyes. "It would have been even more awkward than it was."

"So, you really did just start working at the inn?"

"*Jah*. On Monday."

"Monday. Miss Beverly needed an extra pair of hands, and here we are. Sitting on the beach." He forced himself to smile, even though so many emotions were running through him, his insides felt raw.

"*Jah*."

"So I take it your parents aren't happy with you working?"

"*Nee*. They're punishing me by ignoring me. I was mighty happy I had something to do today."

He gazed at her. Saw her dimples, her freckles. Her dark blond hair, blue eyes. Her general awkwardness. And knew he'd never before felt so unworthy of someone's friendship.

Here he'd gotten into an accident, lost half a limb, and turned that experience into a way to travel the world with his family. And though he believed in the power of the Almighty, he would be lying if he didn't admit to feeling self-righteous at times.

Now he cringed as he recalled some of his speeches, especially some of his first ones, when the pain and fear of being stuck in that ravine was so fresh. He had probably come across as thinking that he was the only person on earth who had ever been in a bad accident. Or who had been alone and frightened while waiting for help to arrive.

Or who had lost part of a limb.

But here was Penny. Losing a sibling was undoubtedly traumatic, but to lose her sister like that? Michael couldn't imagine.

And she'd spent years reliving that experience. Trying to help her parents heal by allowing them to force their will on her. She'd been hurting but she'd kept everything to herself. Never making a big deal about her own issues. In fact, she probably wouldn't have told him anything if he hadn't pressed.

But instead of dwelling on everything that had happened, she'd still opened herself to him and given him so much. Her strength and modesty were awe-inspiring. Yet, she didn't seem to even realize it.

Michael glanced at her, noticing that she was holding herself still and steady. She was alert. Wary.

She was worried about what he might think.

"Penny?"

"Jah?"

"Have you ever talked to anyone about everything? You know, sought help?"

"Like a counselor?"

"Jah. Or a preacher. Or even some close friends?"

She nodded. "I have. Michael, losing my sister was a terrible thing. But I know she's up in heaven. And I know I'll understand why that happened to her when I get there. I've made peace with it. What I haven't been able to do is dare to live my own life. I've been afraid of what might happen. Afraid to cause my parents more worry."

"But you're doing that now."

"Jah. But they aren't happy with me. They don't understand. And I'm old enough now to realize that they may not ever understand."

"But you are going to keep moving forward?"

She nodded. "Well, I'm going to try."

"Penny, I think you are pretty incredible."

She blinked. Then, to his relief, she slowly smiled. "Thanks."

He liked that. He liked that she didn't try to brush off what had happened to her or make it seem like something less than it was. He was glad that not even her shyness and worry would make her discount what had happened.

"You're welcome," he said simply.

She didn't say another word. Instead, her smile became brighter, as if he'd just given her a beautiful gift. Seeing that smile, Michael knew there had never been a better moment in the midst of a better day.

Chapter 13

What a day! Beverly was still reeling from Tricia's announcement this morning about being bullied. And her ears were still stinging from Edward's scathing words. He'd been hurt and angry that Tricia had come to her instead of confiding in her family there.

Not surprisingly, the conversation between Edward and Tricia hadn't gone any more smoothly. Edward felt she should have shared everything that she'd been going through weeks ago. Tricia's belated honesty also hadn't made up for the fact that she'd left Sugarcreek and her family with nothing more than a note. Tears were streaming down Tricia's face when she finally hung up the phone.

"Well, that was awful," Tricia said, wiping her eyes with the side of her hand.

"Indeed it was," Beverly agreed.

"Do you think Daed will ever forgive me?"

"Of course."

"Anytime soon?"

Thinking back to the anger in her brother's tone, Beverly

shrugged. "I can't answer that question. He's not happy with me at the moment, either."

Tricia glared at the telephone. "Oh, I wish I could have recorded that conversation! Daed should have heard himself. Then he would have understood exactly why I didn't tell him anything. He doesn't listen." Wiping at her tears again, she whispered, "Mamm never intervenes."

"I'm sorry about that, but most wives don't."

"When I'm a wife, I'm gonna intervene when I don't like what my husband has to say."

"I'll look forward to seeing that," Beverly said with a smile.

What she didn't bother adding was that she didn't think Edward and his wife's relationship was all that unusual. In many Amish households, the husband was always right. Beverly herself had grown up imagining that her future husband would make most of the major household decisions.

But then, Marvin had also made the decision to fall in love with her best friend while they were engaged.

Now Beverly wasn't sure if she would ever be okay with always following her husband's lead. Somehow she didn't think so. But who was she to say what was right and what was wrong for others? After all, Edward and Kathleen had enjoyed a successful marriage for almost thirty years. Beverly, on the other hand, hadn't even been able to keep her fiancé from straying.

Tricia coughed, bringing Beverly back to the problem at hand. "Daed kept saying it was rude of me to come here uninvited. Was it? Are you mad?"

Tricia was trying to hide it, but Beverly noticed she was trembling. She was anxious and worried. Preparing herself to be rejected again. But in her eyes was a slim ray of hope. A hope of acceptance. To be loved, no matter what she'd done.

Beverly couldn't have ignored that silent plea for help even if she had wanted to. "I'm not mad. Of course I'm not."

"Promise?"

"I'm not mad at all." She curved a hand around Tricia's shoulder and pulled her into a hug. "There was a time when my aunt Patty gave me comfort here. I'm glad that I can do the same for my sweet niece." She was just about to add something more when the doorbell rang.

"I'll be back," she said before hurrying to the front door. When she saw that it was Eric Wagler, the man who owned her inn, Beverly barely stopped herself from taking a step back in alarm.

Unfortunately, she didn't do nearly as good a job holding her tongue once she opened the door. "What are you doing here?"

He raised his eyebrows. "I told you I'd be coming back."

"I had assumed you would have given me a little bit of warning," she hedged, because what she really had wanted was more time to pretend her life wasn't about to drastically change.

"I told you I'd be back sometime this summer. And it is April." He tilted his head to one side. "Is this a problem?"

Actually, it was. He was tall. And had beautiful brown eyes. He was handsome. But most of all, he made her feel things that she'd nearly forgotten about after her fiancé had broken her heart. In short, Eric Wagler was the very last person she wanted to see . . . and the only person in the world able to make her blush and stammer like a schoolgirl.

Since she still hadn't invited him in, he folded his arms across his chest and smirked. Smirked! "Bev, I had hoped you'd be happier to see me than you were last time, but it doesn't look like that's the case."

"I'm happy to see you," she lied. "Come on in. As a matter of fact, you are the highlight of my day."

Concern drifted over his features. "You okay?"

"*Jah*. It's simply been a day of surprises. Want to set your bag down and come into the kitchen? I've got a niece for you to meet."

He tossed his duffel on the ground, then gestured toward the back hallway. "You lead and I'll follow, Beverly."

That was a strange thing for him to say. What was even stranger was her reaction to it.

Her palms had become a little damp and she felt, well, giddy. Almost.

AFTER THEY'D FINISHED THE sandwiches and brownies, Michael had simply wanted to sit and watch the surf. Penny had been okay with that. Actually, she'd been fine with anything he wanted to do. She simply enjoyed being by his side.

"I can't believe this is my fourth time in Sarasota, but my first time here at Siesta Key," Michael groused. "I hate that."

"If you'd been here before, today probably wouldn't seem as special," she replied easily. Personally, she was glad Michael hadn't been to Siesta Key before. It gave her hope that he would always remember their day together, too.

"Today would still seem special, Pen."

She turned his way, but his eyes were closed. Just in case they weren't completely closed, she faced forward again. No way did she want to be caught staring at him.

"I'm going to rest my eyes for a couple. 'Kay?"

" 'Kay," she replied, liking how he shortened words and phrases when he was comfortable.

When his breathing turned steady, she pulled her dress up to her knees and let her calves and feet get some sun. Wiggled her toes in the warm sand. Then, as the clouds cast a shadow over them, and Michael's breathing became deeper, she glanced his way again and looked her fill.

It turned out that Michael Knoxx was just as handsome asleep as he was awake. She'd secretly hoped that it was just his bright personality that made him so attractive to her, but that hope fell by the wayside now. The fact was, the Lord had certainly given him more than his share of attractive attributes. He was tall, broad-shouldered with dark blond hair and hazel eyes. He even had straight, white teeth! The only flaw—well, what should've been a flaw—was his right leg.

But it seemed to only enhance his appearance.

Glad she'd brought a watch, Penny saw that almost an hour had passed since he'd closed his eyes. The next bus came at four o'clock, and they were going to have to be on it. And since they were going to have to gather their things and be at the stop in plenty of time, she was going to have to wake him up soon.

She scanned his sleeping form once more as a group of ladies walked by. Then, when they were relatively alone again, she reached out and gently shook his shoulder. "Michael? Michael, it's time to wake up."

His eyes opened instantly. "Hey. Did I fall asleep?"

"You did."

"I'm sorry." He smiled sheepishly. "That was pretty rude."

"Not at all. I was sorry to have to wake you."

He stretched, then sat up. "Is it time to go?"

"Pretty soon. We have to walk to the stop." With his leg paining him like it was, she feared it might take him a bit longer than usual.

He nodded. "Do we have a minute? Or do you want to go right now?"

"I think we have a good five minutes or so," she replied, enjoying the novelty of being in charge of the schedule.

"We have just enough time, then."

"Time for what?" She really, really hoped he didn't want to go swimming because they didn't actually have time for that and she didn't want to have to tell him no.

"I have a proposal for you."

"A proposal?" Penny didn't even attempt to hide her confusion. "What kind of proposal is on your mind?" she teased. The only proposals she'd ever heard of happened when men proposed marriage.

He turned to face her directly. Then, to her shock, he reached for her hand and held it between his hands. "I've been thinking about this all day and have been trying to summon the courage to ask you."

"Ask me what?"

"Penny, after my surgery, when I'm doing better and can get around good . . . will you bring me back here?"

"Of course." She smiled at him. "I'll be happy to."

"No, I mean, let's make a plan, Penny. How about we start learning to embrace each hour. Each day. How about we promise to cherish each moment?"

"Cherish?"

He nodded. "That's going to make us stronger. Better."

"I can do that."

"*Gut.* Then you can make some new friends, too."

"And you're going to heal."

He shook his head as he gently caressed her knuckles. "I'm going to do that, but I think I need to follow your lead, as well. I, too, need to become more aware of what I want and need."

"But, Michael, you're already—"

"*Nee.* I am not. But you've given me hope. So, will you accept my proposal?"

She stared at him a long moment, then nodded. "I do. I will accept your proposal, Michael. In one month's time, I promise to know a lot more about myself. We'll come back here and have sandwiches and celebrate."

"Nothing would make me happier, Penny. *Danke.*" A new light shone in his eyes. A heady mixture of promise and satisfaction.

Spurring thoughts about a future she shouldn't even be imagining.

Without a word, she slipped her hand from his. Before she got too used to it being there.

Chapter 14

*B*everly figured she'd put off the conversation she needed to have with Eric long enough.

After she'd introduced him to Tricia, he'd moved his things into one of the two empty rooms. Then, as if they'd been living together for weeks, he'd found her and politely informed her that he had some errands in Sarasota to run, and that he'd be back later.

That had been hours ago.

In the meantime, she'd fretted about all the possible reasons for his return. She'd served tea. She'd chatted briefly with Penny after she'd brought Michael home. She'd helped Michael make his way back up the stairs and made sure that he'd gotten in and out of the shower without any problems.

After that, she'd said good night to Tricia, who had announced that she was heading upstairs to read and write letters.

But now that he'd returned from his errands, it was time to find out what he wanted to do with the inn. Just as she needed to finally come to terms with the fact that although her aunt Patty had indicated that she'd wanted Beverly to continue running the inn after her death, she'd never actually owned it in the first place. In fact, up until a few months ago, it had been owned by Patty's husband—who'd willed it to Eric.

Yes, it would be better to know Eric's intentions about the Orange Blossom Inn. Did he want to take things over right away? Did he want her to move out immediately?

She had no earthly idea, but it was beyond time to find out.

Eric must have thought the same thing, too, because when Beverly returned to the kitchen she saw that he'd poured himself a cup of decaf coffee, sat down at her kitchen table like he owned it—which he *didn't*, well, at least not yet—and proceeded to watch her put out the dishes for the morning breakfast rush.

While she checked the sugar bowls, refilled the pretty glass containers with homemade granola, and measured out coffee, he asked questions here and there. None of his questions were all that taxing. None were intrusive. He mainly seemed to be making conversation and whiling away the time until she was ready to sit with him.

Only when there was absolutely nothing else to distract her, did she finally pour herself a cup and sit down across from him.

"What have you decided to do?"

"I'm going to move to Sarasota," he said.

"I see." Well, now she knew.

But honestly, that was all she appreciated. Even though she'd spent many nights imagining this conversation, coaching herself about what to say and how to say it, his news hit her hard. Surely if he was moving to Sarasota, that meant that she would need to move out of the inn. She was really disappointed. So much so, she couldn't think of a single thing to say.

He stood up and poured the remainder of his coffee down the sink. "Did the lawyers call you?"

"Oh, they called," she said. "And they told me that you were correct, that the Orange Blossom Inn was yours."

He grimaced in a funny way as he sat down again. "Listen, this is awkward for both of us. I bet you feel like I'm taking over your life."

"No. I know you didn't ask for this surprising inheritance. And I don't blame you for wanting the inn." After all, she'd been thrilled when she'd thought her aunt Patty had given it to her.

"I'm glad you feel that way," he said slowly. "But still, I wish this conversation could be easier."

"It is what it is, *jah*?"

"*Jah*." He smiled, letting her know that he wasn't being snarky. Instead, he was clearly feeling as awkward about things as she was.

She smiled, hoping to soften her next words. "So, when do you plan to move here permanently?"

"Not for a bit. I'm going to stay here for a couple of weeks, then go to PA and put my place on the market. I'll return after my home sells."

"Ah." He'd already put a lot of thought into this. She'd known he would. Why hadn't she made plans, too? "So you'd like me out as soon as possible."

His eyes widened. "No," he said quickly. "No, not at all." He looked at her chidingly. "Beverly, I'm not going to kick you out. I can't believe you thought I would."

"It's not kicking me out if it's your inn and not mine."

"You know what I mean."

"Actually, um, I don't. It doesn't take two of us to run an inn, Eric." Before he gave her another glare, she continued. "And please don't think that I'm upset with you. Because I'm not. Anymore." Oh, why was she telling him everything on her mind? It was as if she'd just swallowed a pint of truth serum. Eric did *not* need to know everything she was thinking.

He rubbed a hand across his mouth, as if he was attempting to hide a smile, which didn't make sense. Then, at last, he spoke. "Beverly, I'm really glad you're not mad at me. Anymore. But, uh, what I've been trying to say is that I'm going to get an apartment or a condo or something in Sarasota." He shrugged. "I might rent or lease a place. There are a lot of vacation properties available."

"You aren't going to move in here?"

"No. At the moment, I don't intend to move in here."

"Why?"

He shrugged. "I'm not ready. And honestly, after the excitement of inheriting a place in sunny Sarasota wore off, I started thinking about how running an inn would change my life. I don't know if I'm ready to put myself at everyone's mercy twenty-four-seven."

"It's not like that. Most people are not much trouble," she blurted, then wondered yet again why she couldn't just keep her mouth shut.

"It's close to that," Eric said. "Listen, I should have called you. I should have told you what I found out from the lawyers as soon as I knew. And I should have told you my decision as soon as I made up my mind. I'm sorry. It was unfair of me to leave you hanging like this."

She agreed. He should have done those things. But at the moment, she was glad he was telling her face-to-face. She didn't think she would be feeling the same way if she'd been sitting alone and merely listening to his voice over the telephone. "What's done is done."

"Is it? Is it, really?"

He was speaking cryptically again. "Eric, I just want to know where I stand and what you want me to do."

"I want you to keep your same job. But in addition, I want to help you as much as I can when I'm here."

"With what?" She couldn't really see him making beds or blueberry muffins.

"First, I want to make sure our work relationship is taken care of. I've asked the lawyer to visit with us in a day or two so we can draw up a contract."

"Contract?"

"Salary, days off. Benefits. She is also going to take care of all the accounting."

"So I'll only have to worry about the guests."

"Yes. Then, after we get that settled, I want to talk to you about improvements. This is a pretty inn, but it looks like some of the rooms and such could use a little TLC. I thought I could handle that part."

Beverly's hands started shaking. Her financial worries would be eased, but she'd still be able to do her job. She wasn't even going to have to move. As far as most people would be concerned, nothing would change. She was going to be okay.

It was so incredible, so much better than her worst fears, her eyes watered.

"Are you crying?" He got to his feet, true panic in his voice. "Please don't start crying on me, Bev. I'm no good at tears."

Now, there was a story. He sounded so adorable, she grinned at him through her tears. "Seeing a woman cry distresses you that much?"

"Absolutely. I hate when Amy cries."

Amy? "Who's Amy?"

"My girlfriend."

"Ah." Her throat felt tight as she fought to hold back an unwelcome wave of jealousy. He had every right to a girlfriend. For that matter, how in the world had she imagined that he wouldn't have someone special? He was handsome, self-assured, and rather kind.

And funny, too.

Who wouldn't want a man like him?

Hoping she didn't sound too fake, she said brightly, "I, um, didn't know you had a girlfriend."

"We've been off and on for a couple of years." Looking satisfied, he said, "Currently, we are back on."

"That's good." Frustrated with herself, she shook her head. "I mean, that's great, Eric. I'm happy for you."

Now she felt like crying for a whole different set of reasons, reasons that didn't bear thinking about. Turning away from him, she walked across the room and pulled a tissue from the box and dabbed her eyes. Took a deep breath. When she faced him again, she had almost completely regained her composure.

"Everything sounds good, Eric. You know what? The inn is fairly quiet right now. Why don't you simply walk around a bit and inspect some things? Then later I can answer any questions."

A line formed between his brows. "Did I upset you again?"

"Not at all. Knowing I'll get to stay here made me happy. Actually, I might be the happiest woman in Pinecraft."

As his gaze drifted over her face, his expression grew thoughtful. For a moment, it looked like he was going to say something, but instead, he smiled. "Good. That's real good. Great."

Before she could comment on that, he turned away.

PENNY TOOK THE LONG way home from the Orange Blossom Inn. She didn't know why, exactly. She was in no hurry to face her parents, but other than them, she had no one else to see.

But what a day it had been! All day she'd felt deliciously decadent, going off to the beach with Michael Knoxx. Of course, her adventure had brought forth a myriad of feelings, too. She'd had moments of giddiness and depression. She'd been hopeful and scared to death. Worried and sleepy and so blissfully content, she wasn't even sure there was a way to describe it.

Now, her nose was surely sunburned, her dress was full of sand, her feet were sore, and she was tired. But also so happy.

It had been a *wonderful-gut* day. The best.

Still, she knew that the moment she walked into her house it was all going to take a turn for the worse. Her parents were going to be angry and worried. Sullen and obstinate. They were going to want answers and she was afraid that she wouldn't have any for them.

She was so lost in her thoughts, she hardly heard Violet Kaufmann call out to her. When she turned, she saw Violet, her brother, Zack, and his fiancée, Leona, all sitting on the front steps of the Kaufmann house.

"Hi," she said awkwardly. "I'm sorry, I wasn't paying any attention."

"That's okay," Violet said with a smile. "We were just wondering if you'd gone to the beach today."

"I did." Glad for a reason to delay the inevitable, she walked closer. "It was *wunderbaar.*"

Leona smiled. "I bet. Zack and I might go sometime this weekend."

"Who did you go with?" Violet asked.

"Um, one of the guests at the inn."

Violet's eyebrows rose. "Really? You went with a stranger?"

"Not really. He's staying there for a month, and one of my duties is to look out for him."

Violet frowned. "That sounds awkward. Is he old?"

"*Nee*. He's um, about my age. One year older."

Zack grinned. "So it was like a date."

Though she tried hard to hide it, Zack's playful words made her feel even more awkward than she usually did. She was starting to wish she hadn't taken the long way home. "Not that at all. I mean, a man like him wouldn't date me."

"Why not?" Leona asked. "Is he English?"

"Mennonite."

"I'm dating a Mennonite man," Violet said, as if she had all the answers to Penny's problems. "My parents weren't exactly thrilled about me seeing him, but they came around."

"It's not that."

"Then what is it?" Violet asked.

"You don't have to tell us if you'd rather not," Leona said quickly. "Or is it that he's not nice?"

This game of twenty questions was making Penny's head spin. Realizing that someone might have seen them together anyway, she said, "I was with Michael Knoxx."

All three of them looked stunned. "You mean *the* Michael Knoxx?" Violet practically whispered. "Of the Knoxx Family?"

"*Jah*. He's staying at the inn. We've become friends."

"Why's he staying here in Pinecraft?"

"I'm afraid I can't say. That's his story, not mine." She braced herself, ready for them to argue, but instead of pushing her, Leona and Violet merely nodded.

Zack, on the other hand, just looked at her as if she'd said something amusing. "Why would you think he wouldn't be interested in courting you, Penny?"

She blinked at him. Was he teasing her? "You know."

He shook his head. "You're pretty. And though no one really knows you well, it's obvious you're kind."

"Zack's right," Leona said. "Why, I'm sure any man would thank his lucky stars to spend time with you."

"Um, I had better go. My parents are surely upset with me for being gone all day." Taking a chance, she confided, "Putting it off isn't going to make it any easier."

Violet got to her feet. "Penny, didn't they get mad at you and not let you eat supper on Monday?"

"Kind of. I mean, they, um, decided to go out for pizza and didn't bring me anything to eat. That's when I stopped by your house." As soon as she said the words, she wished she could take them back. Not because they weren't true, but because they revealed too much about how things had been. "I'll be all right tonight."

"How about I go with you?" Violet offered.

She felt like she'd already shared too much about how uncomfortable her home life had become. The last thing she needed was for Violet to actually witness her parents giving her the silent treatment. "*Danke*, but—"

"Penny, I'm starting to realize that you don't like to ask for help. Why don't I go with you so if your parents are upset with you, you can come stay at my house?"

"I couldn't."

"Sure you could. My parents love to have company," Zack said. He got to his feet, too, then pulled Leona up by the hand. "Hey, why don't the three of us go with you?"

Ack, but this was getting awkward! "I think having Violet with me is enough. Thank you for the offer, though."

Violet picked up Penny's tote bag and started walking down

the sidewalk. She was smiling, but other than that, she didn't let on a thing.

Which made Penny realize that Violet couldn't have planned this better if she'd orchestrated it herself. Now, instead of facing her parents alone, she had Violet by her side. Which was exactly what Violet had suggested in the first place.

$\mathscr{B}$y the time Penny and Violet reached her house, the sun was beginning to set. Its rays sent out a spectacular glow, casting the usual blue sky into shades of pink and rose. The cooler temperature had brought out many of her neighbors. Snippets of conversation and laughter lit the air.

The lovely sunset, the chirping of birds, and even the faint perfume of blooming rosebushes created a wonderful atmosphere. Penny would have remarked on the beauty of it all—if she hadn't been worried about what would happen when she arrived home.

It turned out that her suspicions were correct.

Her parents were not happy. As a matter of fact, they were so eager to discuss their disappointment in her—their words, not hers—that they looked completely flummoxed seeing Violet walk through the door by her side.

"What are you doing here?" her mother asked her the moment they walked in the front door.

Penny grimaced. Her mother was practically glaring at Violet! "Mamm, I invited her here."

Instead of looking intimidated, Violet merely stood by Penny's side and smiled politely. "My brother Zack and I started talking to Penny when she walked by. When she told me that she wasn't sure what she was going to do for supper, I decided to accompany her on the off-chance that you both had already eaten." She smiled again in a winsome way, practically daring Penny's parents to argue with her reasoning.

Of course, what Violet had alluded to was the fact that the kitchen was completely neat and tidy. No meal was waiting for Penny.

Her father rested his closed fists on his hips. "If you will excuse us, we need to speak with Penny in private."

But instead of apologizing and scurrying off—which was absolutely what Penny knew her parents wanted Violet to do—Violet looked her father directly in the eye. "Before she eats or after?"

"She missed supper."

"How about I wait for you in your room?" Violet asked Penny. "Then when you're done, we'll go get something to eat."

"It's late," her mother said. "Too late for Penny to leave the house for supper."

Violet nodded as if that made perfect sense, which, of course, it did not. "Penny, would you like to come to our *haus* for supper and then spend the night?"

"You wouldn't mind?" she asked. "I need to be at work in the morning."

"You can simply leave from our *haus*." Her lips curved up in a half smile that seemed to convey everything she was thinking but didn't deem appropriate to share. "Which way is your room, Penny?"

"It's down the hall. The door on the right."

Once Violet stepped inside her bedroom and closed the door behind her, Penny faced her parents. "What did you want to speak to me about?"

"You know. You *must* know," her father said around a glare.

"I'm sorry, but I'm not sure what, exactly, you are upset with me about."

"We don't like that you've been gone so much, Penny," her mother murmured.

She knew they worried about her. She knew Lissy's kidnapping and death had everything to do with their worry. But she also knew that her independence was a long time coming. Still, any retreat she made now would be closely guarded.

Therefore, she kept her answer short but respectful. "I do know that."

After a moment's silence, her mother's patience erupted. "That's it? You don't have anything else to say?"

"Mamm, what more can I say? I've taken a job. It has kept me busy."

"Not that busy." Pointing at the grains of sand still stuck to her toes, her mother said, "You went to the beach today."

"I did. I took one of the guests at the inn." As she said the words, she practically willed her body not to flush. She knew she was not telling the whole truth. However, she didn't feel as if she had any choice.

"I think we all know that you chose to go. I think we all know that you wanted to go."

"You're right. I did choose to go to the beach." Mentally she shook her head in wonder. When, exactly, had her parents decided that everything needed to be twisted and turned? They were speaking of Siesta Key like it was a den of iniquity! "Mamm, spending the day at the beach was fun. I'm glad I went! The sand was soft and silky, the water was beautiful, and everything smelled fresh and clean. I saw lots of people there who were at least six or eight years younger than me."

Her father harrumphed. "I don't know what that has to do with anything."

"It has everything to do with everything." When he merely looked at her myopically, she attempted to explain. "It has everything to do with how I'm feeling. With how I've *been* feeling. For years."

He blanched. "Years?"

At last he was listening to her. "Daed, I was sad when Lissy died. I was scared, too."

"Don't talk about your sister," Mamm blurted.

"I'm not," she retorted impatiently. "I'm talking about *me*." She stressed the last word, hoping against hope that something about what she was saying, something about her words this time would sink in. And that her dear father would notice her as a person instead of as a reminder of all they'd lost. "I was glad when we moved here. Glad when you and Mamm kept me close. But that was years ago. Time has moved on."

Her father folded his hands behind the back of his neatly tucked-in white cotton shirt. "The years passed, but the dangers didn't change."

"But I have. I'm not a scared twelve-year-old little girl anymore."

"So what? You're going to ignore everything we taught you?" he asked. "You're going to ignore everything we've done for your welfare?"

Penny pulled herself inward. He wasn't hearing her. Yet again, nothing was going to change. But still, she decided to say her piece, if for no other reason than to know that she, at least, was making strides. "Father, I saw a lot of teenagers at Siesta Key."

"Well, sure—"

"Listen. Those teenagers weren't at the beach with their parents, they were with their friends. They were having a *gut* time, simply enjoying a sunny day. And it was obvious that this wasn't the first time, either. Daed, they were doing things that I should have been doing for years now. All I'm doing is catching up."

After looking awkwardly at her father, Mamm picked up a dishrag. "You never said you missed those things."

"That is because I knew you would be upset if I said anything. And I knew there was no way when I was sixteen or seventeen or even twenty that you would have let me go to Siesta Key alone."

Instead of commenting on that, he waved a hand toward Penny's bedroom. "We're not just talking about your sudden need to act like a teenager, Penny. You keep doing all sorts of strange things."

"Like what?"

"Like bringing Violet Kaufmann to our house."

Penny felt her cheeks heat with embarrassment. She certainly hoped Violet hadn't overheard that. "There's not a thing wrong with Violet, and there isn't a thing wrong with me inviting guests over. What *is* wrong is the fact that you are denying me meals if I don't come home early enough."

"You have been receiving the consequences of your actions."

"Consequences of your choosing."

"*Nee*, daughter. You have been making the choices. Things don't have to be this way."

"I'm starting to feel that the only way things will change is if

I move out. Unfortunately, because I've hardly had any freedom, I have nowhere to go."

Her mother looked stricken. "Unfortunately?"

"Mamm, you must see how unfairly you're treating me. I'm too old for this."

"Watch yourself, daughter."

Never before had she dared to verbalize her thoughts. But now, realizing that if she didn't speak up in this moment nothing was *ever* going to change, Penny knew she had no choice. Suddenly, she felt so angry at herself for having lived in a fearful fog, so disappointed that her father wasn't even trying to see her side of things, so betrayed that her mother simply glossed over everything that had been happening to her, that she lost her temper. At last. "Watch myself? Father, that is *all* I have been doing! Things need to change. *I* did not die. I am going to live my life and make friends and go to work and one day, with God's help, find the right man and get married. Those are normal, right things that I should be doing."

"We never said you couldn't marry," her mother interjected timidly.

"Mamm, all three of us know that even if I met the perfect man on Sunday at church it would not be all right. What you have to decide is whether you want me here at all. If you don't, I'll start looking around for a new place to live."

"You wouldn't do that. You wouldn't actually leave us, would you? After everything we've been through? Penny, I can't lose another daughter."

And that was the problem, Penny realized. Her mother couldn't differentiate between Penny growing up and moving forward and Lissy being kidnapped and killed when she was twelve.

In her mother's mind, both girls were still leaving her.

And her mother was doing everything she could to bend Penny to her will. Even using manipulation and guilt.

"I never thought I would leave, but I'm afraid I will now. It's time you both accepted me and accepted my future." Before they could answer, she turned and walked down the hall to her room.

Her hands were shaking and she knew her cheeks were flushed, too, but when she opened her door and saw Violet standing with tears in her eyes, Penny knew she'd made the right decision.

Sometimes, the hardest path to take was the only path worth walking on.

Chapter 16

The next morning, Penny found herself sitting between Beverly and Tricia at the hospital. On the other side of Beverly sat Eric Wagler, who, as best as she could figure out, was kind of Penny's boss, too. Neither he nor Miss Beverly seemed in any great hurry to actually explain their relationship, but it sure seemed to be a rocky one. From what Penny could discern, Eric owned the inn but Beverly ran it. Mr. Eric seemed all right with this. In fact, he seemed to take it in stride.

Miss Beverly, on the other hand, seemed far less comfortable with their relationship. Penny wasn't sure if it was because they didn't like each other much or if they simply didn't know each other well.

Penny found the tension floating between them a bit odd.

But perhaps not any stranger than how the four of them had come to accompany Michael Knoxx to the hospital. Beverly had needed to go, of course, since she had been the one to whom Michael's parents had entrusted his care.

Eric came because he was English and had a rental car.

Tricia came because even though she didn't know Michael,

she was Beverly's niece and had said she felt strange staying back at the inn without her. But if Penny were being completely honest, it didn't seem as if Tricia knew her aunt all that well, either.

Yet when Tricia, Beverly, and Eric had begun shuttling Michael out the door, Michael had stared at Penny in confusion.

"I need you to come as well."

"Michael, there's no need," Beverly said gently. "Besides, I need her to stay for the rest of the guests."

"I think differently."

As Penny had looked on, embarrassed by the situation and torn between listening to Michael's request and following Miss Beverly's wishes, Michael, for the very first time, had displayed his star power. "I'd like Penny to be there. And since I believe she was hired in part to help me, it makes perfect sense that I should get my way on this." Then, after launching that zinger, he raised one brow. "You don't mind, do you, Pen?"

Penny didn't think she minded. But then, she was discovering that when he called her Pen, she agreed to just about anything he asked of her. "I don't mind," she said at last.

"Great." He'd smiled. "Now I'm ready."

Beverly sighed. "Let me go ask Sadie to come over for a few hours."

When they'd arrived at the hospital, Michael had signed himself in before being whisked away by a pair of nurses. An hour later, they were told he had been taken into surgery.

And two hours later, they were still waiting.

Penny was starting to get worried. Though she'd tried to find something of interest to do in the waiting room, the flashy magazines about English celebrities didn't mean much to her. The same could be said for the shows on the television.

She got to her feet and started walking around, looking down the hall every couple of minutes and waiting for the doctor to come out and talk to them.

A moment later, Tricia joined her. "Do you mind if I wander around with you? I can't sit in that chair for another minute."

"I don't mind at all." Penny smiled softly at her, glad for the company but a little confused as to why Tricia had sought her out. Though they were about the same age, they seemed very different. She wasn't sure what they could talk about.

However, it didn't seem Tricia was of the same mind. "Are you Michael's girlfriend?"

Penny was so flustered by the question, she blurted the first words on the tip of her tongue. "Definitely not!"

Tricia blinked. "Sorry. I, um, just thought you two seemed pretty close."

"We're not." Still, it was tempting to imagine that she and Michael were close, that she meant something special to him. "As a matter of fact, I hardly know him." Though, that wasn't really true. Not anymore.

Tricia didn't seem put off by Penny's outraged tone. Not at all. Actually, it seemed to only spur her curiosity. "But didn't you go to the beach together yesterday?"

"We did." Penny rubbed the knot of tension that was forming at the base of her neck. She ached to share with Tricia that she was feeling close to Michael. That he was becoming important to her. Really important to her. But that would only be setting herself up for embarrassment. A month from now, Michael would be gone and she'd have to face everyone knowing that she'd made a fool of herself over him.

"At first I thought you took him because Aunt Beverly asked you to. But then she told me it was your day off."

"Going to the beach wasn't any big deal."

"It seemed like a big deal to him." With a smile, she added, "I went to his room with Aunt Beverly last night. He kept saying that it was the nicest day he'd had in some time."

Penny kept her eyes averted. "He really wanted to go to the beach. And I did go with him, but that was mainly because he needed someone to go with and he doesn't know anyone else. I've been helping to take care of him, you see." Yes, that should be the spin on her obvious affection for him. She was spending time with Michael because she was so dedicated to her job.

"I get that, but I don't know, Penny. He sure seems taken with you." She smiled again, showing Penny that she was being completely sincere. For some reason Tricia didn't see that there was anything strange about *the* Michael Knoxx liking Penny Troyer in a special way.

"Well, he isn't. He's simply nice."

Tricia looked tempted to say more, but she simply shrugged. "You're right. He is nice."

Yes, that was how she should think of him. A nice man. Because when he was healed and feeling better, he would leave and be off traveling again. Being everything everyone needed him to be.

Thinking about him on stage and about how, well, *compelling* he'd been, she realized that was exactly how she could make Tricia understand. "Have you ever seen him speak?"

"*Nee.* To be honest, I had only heard of the Knoxx Family and the message they preach in the most general terms. They visited Berlin a year or two ago, but no one in my family went to hear them speak."

"I heard them here. Michael was . . ." Her voice drifted as she struggled to find the right way to describe his charisma, and the way his talk had made her feel.

"He was mesmerizing," she finished.

Tricia grinned. "I bet. He does seem to have a way with words. And, well, he is terribly handsome."

He was the most handsome man Penny had ever seen. But reducing him to only his looks felt like a travesty. "*Nee*, it was more than that. He was speaking to over a hundred people, but the way he looked at the audience made each person feel as if he was having a private conversation with only them. It was meaningful and real."

"He talked about being trapped in the ravine, didn't he? And about how he's coped with losing a leg."

"He did. But it was more than that," she said. "He . . . He made me believe in miracles."

Tricia's eyes widened. "Wow. I wish I had seen him. I would like to believe in miracles again."

"Do you not? Sorry. Forget I asked that."

"I don't mind answering," Tricia said softly. "If you want to hear."

"I do. Of course I do."

Tricia looked pleased. Or maybe it was more like grateful? "Back at home, I had trouble with some girls. One made up a story about me and everyone wanted to believe it. I had to get away, so I came down here to see Aunt Beverly without an invitation." Looking away, she added, "Actually, she didn't even know I was coming. But I had complete faith that I'd find her and she'd take me in. And she did. So maybe I do believe in them after all. Do you?"

"I haven't for a long time. But lately, it feels as if everything is coming together for me." Not comfortable with sharing her past or discussing her feelings about Michael, she said, "Some things have happened to make me and my family wary about most things. But the evening Michael and his family spoke, something made me decide to make a change. And once I did that, it set a lot of other things in motion."

Tricia looked at her in wonder. "Do you think that's all it takes? That each of us needs to have the presence of mind to make that first step, even when we aren't sure where it leads us?"

"I don't know. I'll let you know a year from now when I can look back on how things turned out."

Tricia grinned. "Let's make a promise, then. In one year, we'll write each other and say if we thought it was *gut* that we went down that path. Or if it had been a bad mistake."

"That's a deal." She was about to add something more, but Beverly stood up just then and motioned them closer.

"Girls, the *doktah* is coming."

Penny rushed to Beverly's side just as the doctor was introducing himself.

"How is he?" Penny blurted, unable to wait another moment.

"Michael is in recovery, so he's a bit groggy," he said around a smile. "But when he's more himself, I'm going to tell him the same thing I am telling all of you. The surgery went well."

"Oh, praise God," Beverly said.

Penny sighed in relief as the surgeon continued. "We repaired the scar tissue that had gotten a bit aggravated during the last month and found the source of that infection. We cleaned that area well, too. He's going to be just fine."

"This is such *wonderful-gut* news," Beverly said. "Michael is such a nice man. I've been hoping and praying that you wouldn't find anything unexpected." Looking at the four of them, she grimaced. "I'm embarrassed to say that at times I was afraid that you would have worse news for us."

The surgeon's expression turned serious. "The worst of it was seeing the damage done to his limb. He made a bad decision ignoring his pain for so long. If he'd simply told his family and made an appointment, everything could have probably been taken care of in an office visit."

Beverly nodded. "I'll be sure and share that with his family."

The doctor grinned. "I'll be telling him my feelings about that, too. I know he likes to think he is invincible, but none of us are. The Lord expects us to take care of ourselves to the best of our ability."

"Those are words to take to heart," Eric murmured.

"Is there anything else, Doctor?"

"Just be sure and let Michael's family know that they can call me if they have questions, though I doubt they'll need to. Michael asked me quite a few questions before we put him under anesthesia. He might not always take care of his leg, but he knows its limitations well."

"What happens now?" Eric asked.

"As I said, he's in recovery. When he's feeling a little less woozy, we'll put him in a room and keep him overnight. Unless something unexpected happens, he'll be able to leave around noon tomorrow."

Penny smiled at Tricia. "That's *wonderbaar*. I thought he might be here for days and days."

The surgeon shook his head. "These days, we send folks home as soon as we can. People like being in their own beds. Now, who is Penny?"

She was so surprised, she held up a hand. "I am."

"Would you mind coming with me? Michael has been asking for you." He smiled to himself. "He's asked for you so many times, the nurses decided it would be a good idea for you to keep him company for a spell."

"Are you sure he asked to see me?"

Behind her Tricia giggled. "He's sure, Penny."

And the surgeon nodded. "I'm very sure. Come along now."

She took a step forward but looked over her shoulder as she did. "Do you think this is all right, Miss Beverly?"

She was wearing the same amused expression as Tricia. "I think it's more than all right, Penny. If he's asking to see you, I think that's a mighty *gut* sign. You go on ahead. I need to call Michael's parents, anyway."

"All right then." Steeling her shoulders, she followed the doctor through the big set of automatic doors and realized that her conversation with Tricia had been perfectly true. One never did know what the future had in store.

Or what miracles were about to take place in their midst.

Chapter 17

$\mathcal{F}$eeling awkward, Penny followed the doctor down a wide hallway filled with all sorts of metal carts and empty gurneys, as well as several orderlies and nurses who were standing next to complicated-looking equipment. More than one nurse looked up as they passed, greeting the surgeon and sending an encouraging smile Penny's way.

After turning a corner, the doctor pulled back a white curtain. "Here we are, Penny. Why don't you take a seat. Michael looks like he's drifted back to sleep, but he should be waking up again in a few minutes."

Before she could ask any questions, Penny was alone with Michael. She was secretly pleased he wasn't staring at her at the moment because she needed some time to settle down. The patients, the carts, the smells, the tubes, and machines and noise . . . it had all been a little frightening. Furthermore, she was still trying to figure out why Michael had asked for her. Had he, too, sensed that something important was happening between the two of them?

Or was he simply asking for her because he had no one else to turn to?

These questions spun in her head as she crossed the room to his side, each step feeling like a huge distance instead of mere inches. When she got to the side of his bed, he opened his eyes.

"Hi," she said, wishing she had some interesting comment or amusing quip to utter. But seeing him in the hospital bed, surrounded by machines and attached to wires and cords, that one word was the best she could come up with.

His eyes warmed. Seconds later, his lips turned up in a smile.

That small response was all she needed to pull over one of the hard plastic chairs that lined the wall. And when he reached for her hand, she held his.

Then it became a matter of simply following directions: When the nurses asked her to step back into the waiting room so he could leave recovery and get settled into a regular room, she returned to Beverly's side.

An hour later, a nurse came to get her again.

As she stood up, Beverly told her that she and Eric were going back to the inn and to call when she needed to be picked up.

Penny nodded, though she was already thinking about Michael. This time, she accompanied a nurse into the elevator, down a long hallway on the third floor, and at last to a doorway on the right. When she peeked inside, Michael looked much better. He was sitting up and sipping on juice, and he stared at the door as it opened.

"Here you are. I was wondering if someone had forgotten to bring you." His lips twitched, as if he were thinking about a secret joke. "Or that maybe you had left."

"I wouldn't have left without telling you," she said in a rush.

Then she realized he'd been teasing. "You shouldn't tease me, you know. I've been worried about you. I'm glad the surgery went okay."

"Sorry," he said quickly as much of the humor lighting his eyes fled. "You were worried about me?"

"Of course I was." Unable to help herself, she leaned close. "Michael, how are you? Are you in much pain?"

He held up a hand, which was decorated with tape and gauze and an intravenous tube. "These tubes are taking care of the worst of it."

"I'm glad about that. The doctors said you did *gut*."

"They told me the same thing." He looked down at his right leg. "They seem to think I'll heal quickly. I hope so."

She looked around the room. "Where is your prosthesis?" She stumbled on the word, it was so unfamiliar, but she was glad she'd said the proper term.

"It's with a technician. They're going to adjust it or simply order me a new one."

"So, you'll be without it for a time."

A new, guarded look entered his eyes. "Will that make you uncomfortable?"

"Why would you think that?" She really had no idea what he was talking about.

"Some people can't handle looking at my leg like this." When she frowned, he said, "It, um, makes my disability seem more real, I think."

"But it's you," she protested. Furthermore, she didn't consider him disabled in the slightest.

Looking down at his lower thigh and knee, covered in bandages, he frowned. "It's imperfect."

"We are all imperfect, Michael." Gazing down at the part of the hospital bed where the lower portion of his leg would've been if he hadn't lost it, a variety of emotions filtered through her. But none of them had anything to do with feeling uncomfortable about him not having a right foot. "I don't understand how people would feel that way."

"It's unsettling. And weak, I suppose. Men like to feel as if they can handle anything. A man with only a leg and a half? Well, it shows that I am not invincible."

"I'm not either." Because she was a woman, because she supposed most men would laugh at her bravado, she lifted her chin, practically daring him to make fun of her.

"You are strong, though."

"Not as strong as I'd like to be, but I'm getting stronger every day."

"Penny, I thought a lot about your sister last night when I was trying to go to sleep. I thought about her this morning when I was waiting for surgery, too."

"I appreciate that, but you should have been thinking about yourself."

"I hope you know that I am sorry for your loss," he said, basically ignoring her protest.

"*Danke.* But, if you don't mind, can we talk of something else? I mean, we've already spoken of Lissy."

"That we did. Well, since you're stuck here with me, want to play cards?"

That was definitely not what she'd expected to hear. "You feel that well?"

"I think so. If I'm not, I guess we'll find that out," he said. "Do you know any card games?"

"A couple."

"Are you any good at them?"

Enjoying their lighthearted banter, she teased, "It depends what game you want to play."

"Uno?"

"I doubt there are any Uno cards around." She glanced at the deck of cards on his nightstand. "Gin rummy?"

"You know how to play that?"

"I do." She hoped she looked more humble than she felt. She was actually very good at cards.

He waved a hand. "Uh-oh. You picked the wrong game, Penny."

"Is that right?"

"Absolutely. Because it just so happens that I'm the gin rummy champion of my family." He waggled his eyebrows.

She had a hard time not laughing. "That's just as I suspected. You have not an ounce of modesty."

"It's not bragging if it's the truth."

"You're not being modest if you are bringing your accolades up in conversation."

He smiled, making little fans form at the corners of his eyes. "I knew asking you to be here was a good idea, Penny. I've hardly felt any pain the last couple of minutes."

"Glad I could help." Meeting his gaze, she smiled back at him. Part of her wanted to tell him that his company was just as beneficial to her.

It was ironic, but when she was with him, she felt more like herself. The more they got to know each other, the more she relaxed. So much so, she was beginning to feel as if she'd only discovered who she was once she was in his company.

Leaning over, she grabbed the deck of cards and started shuffling them. "Because you are slightly out of it, I'm going to give you a break."

"How so?"

"I'm shuffling, dealing, and keeping score."

An eyebrow rose. "That's it?"

"You're weak, you know. So, do you trust me?"

"Absolutely, Pen."

She paused, swallowing, and realized that for all their banter, neither had been more serious. He trusted her to keep score and help him ignore his pain.

As for her, she trusted him with, well, everything.

"WANT TO GO OUT for ice cream?" Eric asked Beverly, as if their going out for dessert was a common occurrence.

They'd just returned to the inn. The moment they'd arrived, Tricia had announced that she was going to go upstairs and take a shower and read her book.

Beverly had been about to tell Eric that she'd see him later, sure he was ready to take a break after spending most of the day at the hospital. She knew she was going to be running around the inn for the next couple of hours since they'd been gone for most of the day.

"Um. Well, I don't know."

"You don't know? What's not to know?"

She shrugged. "I kind of feel like I should stay around here."

"Why?"

"You know why. And if you don't, you should."

"Enlighten me."

"Well, when you run an inn, there's always work to do, you see. I'm sure I've got dishes to do and lists to write. Then I need to check the reservations. And probably make sure Tricia is actually all right."

He folded his arms over his chest. "Those are all good reasons to stay here. But why don't you ignore them and come get ice cream anyway?"

"Eric . . ." She was desperately attempting to keep their relationship professional.

Eric, on the other hand, seemed just as determined to turn them into friends. "Come on, Bev. I know you're thinking about it."

"The last thing I need is to be eating ice cream."

He reached out and grabbed her hand. "We both need this. You know it."

"Oh, all right."

He smiled. "I was hoping you would give in gracefully. Come on," he added before she could think of a good, scathing retort.

Dutifully, she followed. "Want to go to Olaf's?"

"That's the only place around, right?" he asked as he held the front door open for her and then started walking down the steps.

"It's not the only place, but it's the best place."

"I'll remember to use that description with future guests."

The thought of them working together, maybe even eventually greeting guests together, sent a little shiver through her.

When they reached the bottom of the porch steps, Eric turned to her. "So, do we go left now?"

"Right."

An eyebrow quirked. "Right, we go left?"

"Right, we go right," she said around a giggle.

He returned her smile as they turned right and started down the sidewalk. It was after six o'clock, suppertime for most people. Consequently, the area was far emptier than usual. It allowed her to pay more attention to the man beside her.

It was becoming obvious that they were never going to be able to maintain only a professional relationship. Maybe that was for the best, after all. They would be able to get along better in the long term if there was more between them than just the fact that he was her new boss.

"How are you liking Pinecraft now?" she asked, attempting

to steer their conversation back toward something safer for her heart, back to the proper tone between employee and employer. "Is it feeling more familiar?"

"In some ways it does. But then today, when we were at the hospital, it felt like we could be anywhere in America."

"What's wrong with that?"

"It confuses me, I guess. I keep feeling like everything should be all Amish, all the time."

"The hospital was in Sarasota. Pinecraft is just a part of the city. The Amish enjoy good medical care as much as anyone else, you know."

"That makes sense." He nodded. "But then, when we walk down these streets, it seems like almost everyone is wearing a *kapp* or a hat. And the pace is slower." He shrugged. "I like it, though."

"I'm glad." To her surprise, she realized that she meant what she said. She'd noticed his interest in the brightly painted bicycles so many Amish rode, the abundant flowers on nearly every corner, and even the almost daily gathering to meet the Pioneer Trails buses. She was glad he was happy to be here. "We should probably talk about what happens next, Eric."

"We should. But not now."

The ice cream store loomed in the distance. As usual, there was a crowd of people standing around its entrance. Teenaged girls, some in traditional dresses and *kapps*, some in short shorts and tank tops, were standing in groups of two and three. Boys were doing the same thing.

Sitting on the neighboring benches were younger children and older folks. All were eating ice cream cones with obvious enjoyment.

"Actually, I can't think of a better time. I'm not busy with guests and you're not preparing to meet with lawyers. No one else is around to interrupt. It's perfect."

"It's a perfect time to relax, Bev. And it's important, too. We're spending time together."

His comment took her aback, mainly because she'd just been thinking that very same thing. So why was she attempting to direct things back to business? "We are, but—"

He cut her off. "No buts," he said, softening his words with a smile. "Beverly, we're getting to know each other. That's important, too, I think. I want to get to know you."

When was the last time a man had said such things to her? Had it been Marvin? Had it really been that long? Was that why another small shiver just rushed through her at his words?

It made her uncomfortable. And embarrassed! The last thing they needed was for her to imagine that there was something of a romantic nature brewing between them. "How is your girlfriend?"

He blinked. "What?"

"What was her name? Annie?"

"It's Amy. And she's fine. Thank you for asking."

Was it her imagination or had he really just retreated into himself? "Is she going to move down here to Sarasota?"

"I hope so." He didn't smile though. Instead, he looked a little irritated. "What kind of ice cream is the best?"

"What?"

He waved at the line of people practically snaking around them. "We're here. What kind do you usually get?"

Strawberry was her favorite. Usually she could wax poetic about Olaf's ice cream and exactly why she enjoyed strawberry so much, but she'd ruined his mood. It was obvious the enjoyment he'd felt about their short excursion had come and gone.

"Anything is good here," she said as they got in line.

"That's it? You come here all the time, you say it's the best around, but you have no preference for a flavor?"

"It's ice cream, not anything that really matters."

"It's your opinion," he said as they moved forward. After another couple of minutes, he continued. "Your opinion matters, don't you think?"

"I think it doesn't matter all that much."

After giving her a long look, Eric shook his head.

Making her feel worse than she already did. Eric had been nothing but kind today, and now he was even attempting to get to know her better. She needed to stop feeling jealous of a woman she'd never met dating a man she hardly knew. "I'm sorry," she said. "I know I sounded kind of snippy."

"What did I do?"

"Nothing." Well, nothing that she was ever going to admit out loud! Then, because she hated how she was acting—and they likely had another five minutes or so of standing in line— she changed the topic. "I don't know if you knew this, but Big Olaf's has been around since 1982. It's quite famous."

His eyes lit with amusement. "I actually did not know that."

"Oh, *jah*. They have all kinds of flavors. And you can even ship their pints of ice cream all over the country. Can you imagine that?"

"I like the idea of being able to get a little something from Pinecraft up in Pennsylvania. I'll have to keep that in mind."

As they stepped forward, Beverly chattered on, telling Eric all about the other location out on Siesta Key. When she finally paused to take a breath, they were at last at the front of the line.

"I'll take a scoop of mint chocolate chip. What would you like, Bev?"

"Strawberry," she said with a smile.

"And a strawberry cone, too," he told the server.

After they got their cones, they headed home. Beverly told herself that the reason they weren't talking was because they were busy with their ice cream.

However, she was fairly sure that both of them had a whole lot more on their minds than that.

Chapter 18

"So how bad do you feel, really?" Evan asked over the phone two days after the surgery.

Michael grinned as he stared out the window in his bedroom. Yesterday Eric had driven him back from the hospital. Though the journey had been a bit painful, the result was worth it. Now he was propped up against a trio of down-filled pillows in a snug bed instead of constantly shifting positions in an attempt to get comfortable in the middle of a drafty, smelly hospital room.

"If you were here instead of in the middle of a tour, you would know that I'm doing better than any of us expected."

"So am I allowed to call you ten times a fool for not getting this surgery done a year ago?"

"Nope. Nothing was wrong a year ago." Well, not too much had been wrong.

"I wish I could say I believed you. But I don't."

"Why don't you concentrate on the good things instead? I got through the surgery and I'll be joining you in a couple of weeks."

"That will be great. It's not the same here without you."

"I bet. I am the star of our show, you know."

"I was going to say that it was *quieter*. Everyone's more easygoing. Things are running like clockwork without your fans following us around."

"That's so funny. Not."

Evan gave a bark of laughter. "If you were here, you could watch Mamm about to jump out of her chair and grab the phone from me right now."

Michael smiled at that. It was impressive that she had allowed Evan to be the one to talk to him. "She said to be sure to let you know that we have our own fans chasing us."

This time Michael was the one laughing. "Tell her I'm real sorry to be missing that."

"I don't think I will. She never cared for your sarcasm, you know."

"I know." Michael's smile widened. He missed his brother. They knew each other well—so well, that a dozen thoughts could be conveyed in just one or two words. "It's really good to hear from you. I'm glad you called."

"Of course I'm going to call. So, are you bored and restless already?"

"Not yet."

"That's *gut*. I'm surprised, but happy to hear that. Actually, I was afraid that you were going to have a really hard time when we left you. You don't always do that well when you're alone."

"I haven't been alone."

"Who have you been spending time with?"

"With Penny."

"The girl who's been looking after you?"

"*Jah*, she works here," he said, "but she's become a friend, too.

We went to the beach together the day before the surgery. Then she sat with me at the hospital until visiting hours were over."

"Why?"

"Why what?"

"Why is she spending so much time with you, and why are you putting up with that?"

"It's not a hardship." It was the opposite of that, of course. Seeing Penny was quickly becoming the highlight of his day.

"Really."

Michael knew the meaning of that "really." Evan had perfected it when he was about eight years old, and it was the ideal combination of sarcasm and polite response. He'd pull it out at different times, in all kinds of situations, much to the irritation of Michael and Molly.

And that was why, now, he sighed in exasperation. "What is that supposed to mean?"

"Nothing."

"Uh-huh."

"Okay, fine. I'm just wondering how much you know about this lady."

"She's twenty-four. Her sister died in a violent crime twelve years ago, and it pretty much messed up her whole family. She was hired at the Orange Blossom Inn for the express purpose of helping me. She's a nice girl."

"Are you sure she didn't get the job to get close to you?"

He winced, hating how that sounded. Hating even more that he'd thought the same thing at first. "I'm sure. *She's a nice girl*," he repeated, thinking there was no better way to describe her. "She's shy."

"Oh. So she's only in your company because she's getting paid. You're her job," Evan said matter-of-factly.

Michael scowled. He didn't like the idea of anyone trying to classify his relationship with Penny. He knew for a fact that there was more between them than his neediness and her paycheck.

At least, he hoped so.

But how could he convey that without giving too much away? "Yes. But we're becoming friends, too."

Now, why had he said that?

"Didn't know you needed a new friend in Pinecraft." Again, Evan's tone was careful and controlled. It was obvious that he was feeling his way around the conversation. But what Evan didn't know was that he was walking a thin line between sounding careful and condescending.

"I can always use a new friend. Don't worry about it, Evan." Evan sighed. "Michael—"

"Listen, I've got to go. Penny's about to bring me supper."

"What does that have to do with anything? She can wait, right? After all, she's getting paid to bring you food."

It was time to change the direction of the conversation before he said something he regretted. "When do you all hit the road again?"

"In four days. Molly or Daed or I will give you a call in a day or two."

"Great. I'll talk to you then."

"Michael. Listen, I'm sorry if I sounded like a jerk, but we both know that nothing can happen between you and that girl."

"I know. Because we have to continue the tour."

"It's what we do, brother," Evan stated, his voice sounding as firm as their father's.

And though Michael did completely understand what his

brother meant, he resented it. "Evan, don't you ever wish it *wasn't* what we did?"

"*Nee*. Never."

"Really?" He found that hard to believe.

"It's given us the opportunity to travel all over the country. We've spread the Lord's message. We've given money to charities, too." After a pause, Evan added, "Michael, our work is a blessing to so many."

"I didn't say it wasn't . . ."

"You are a gifted speaker," Evan continued, his voice sounding a bit harsher. "It's what you were meant to do."

Michael wondered if Evan even heard himself. Did he realize that he was touching upon everything they'd gotten to do but not much about how their schedule had affected them?

Michael knew in his heart that the five of them were a team. He might be the face of their group but only teamwork made the Knoxx Family the success that it was. And that was terrific. Great. It always had been. Except now he'd started wondering what life might be like if he left the group. If he dared to walk away, would he ruin his parents' and his siblings' lives?

Was he willing to do that?

Michael realized then that the whole time he'd been talking with Evan, he'd had the strange sensation of being on the outside looking in. And he'd been happy with that. Though he'd missed his family, to be sure, he didn't miss what they were doing. He hadn't even been all that interested in their itinerary or how things were going. Had he really moved on? If that was the case, how was he going to tell his family?

And what was he going to do then?

A soft knock interrupted his thoughts. Thankfully. "Evan, listen, I've got to go. We'll talk again soon."

"Hold on. When—"

"Sorry, I've got to go. Bye!" he said as the knock came again. "Come in," he said with relief.

A turn of the knob brought in pretty Penny. Her arms were laden with a tray filled with supper, a tall glass of iced tea, and what looked like two pieces of pie.

This afternoon she had on a pretty coral-colored dress, which did amazing things to her blond curls, her lightly tanned skin, and her mesmerizing eyes. But beyond her looks, it was her sweet, almost demure temperament that had trapped his heart. He liked how shy she was. He liked that she seemed to see him for who he was, not for what he was.

"Penny! You are my favorite person in the world," he declared, intentionally making his voice sound effusive so she'd do the next thing he absolutely loved to see. As he'd hoped, she blushed prettily, and two seconds later, that darling dimple made an appearance.

Adorable.

"I have a feeling you say that to all the girls who bring you pie," she teased.

He pressed a hand to his chest in mock distress. "No I don't."

"*Nee?*"

"Lately, I only say that to girls who bring me pie *and* supper. And Beverly's iced tea."

She closed the door behind her with one hand before crossing the room to him. A faint smile played on her lips. "Then I must remember to thank the Lord tonight when I say my prayers. Because it seems I am blessed enough to be that girl today."

He winked. "Amen to that."

But instead of another dimple appearance, her eyes widened. Obviously, he'd gone too far with his wink.

"Hey," he said as she approached awkwardly. "I'm sorry. I didn't mean to be so forward."

"It's all right. I suppose you can't help yourself."

"What does that mean?"

She set his tray down on the bedside table, then expertly shook out a linen napkin and handed it to him. After he took it from her, she continued. "Nothing. It's just that I'm fairly sure you're used to women bringing you supper."

"No." When she tilted her head to one side, he patted the side of his bed. "Have a seat, wouldja?"

Instead of sitting where he'd gestured, she pulled over the chair. "What is wrong?"

"Penny, I want you to understand something. This isn't my life. I don't sit in bed and ask to be waited on. That's not who I am."

"Michael, what you do is none of my business."

"We're friends now, right?" With obvious reluctance, she nodded. "Then it is your business. When I'm on tour with my family, we are usually traveling to our new stop, preparing to speak, or sleeping. I'm not complaining or saying it's a terrible way of life. It's not. Not at all. But I don't sit around and hope someone will wait on me."

"I see."

"I hope so." Then, before he lost his nerve, he added, "And furthermore, I hope it's not going to be my life forever."

"What do you mean by that?"

"I want to stop touring. I want to simply be Michael Knoxx, the guy who lives down the road."

She stared at him hard. Then, to his surprise, her lips twitched. Right before she burst into giggles.

"What?"

"What? You!" Still giggling, she leaned close and grabbed his hand. The one that was still raised in the air, ready to make a grand point.

Almost against his will, his fingers immediately linked through hers. His lips seemed to take on a life of their own, too, because he started smiling, though he wasn't even sure what he was smiling about. "Talk to me."

"Michael, you will never simply be that guy down the street. It's not going to happen."

"Sure it can. When I stop touring, everyone will forget about me being some kind of celebrity."

She shook her head. "No one is going to forget. You shine so brightly, it would be impossible for anyone to forget you." Looking down at their linked fingers, she gave his hand a little squeeze. "For now and forever, you are Michael Knoxx. That is all there is to it."

He liked the way their hands were joined. He liked the feel of her slim fingers threaded through his own. He liked how soft the fragile skin over the top of her knuckles was. But most of all, he loved that she'd reached for him. And how she seemed to enjoy the feel of her hand in his as much as he did.

Just then, the door opened. "Excuse me, Michael. Is Penny in—" Beverly paused as she took in how they were sitting. The way Penny was leaning toward him.

And most of all, how they were holding hands.

As far as compromising situations went, theirs was hardly noteworthy, Michael knew that. But as far as the two of them—especially with Penny not only working for Beverly but being Amish—this was not good. He knew it, Beverly knew it, and by the way Penny dropped his hand, jumped to her feet, and nearly toppled his tray, it was very obvious that she knew it, too.

"I should go," she whispered.

Beverly's expression was as angry as he'd ever seen it. "Yes, Penny, you should. Go down to the kitchen, if you would. We need to have a talk."

Penny nodded and rushed out of the room.

"Beverly, don't be upset with her. What happened is my fault."

"That's big of you to say. And you might even be correct," she replied. "But it doesn't change what I saw."

"All you saw was two people sitting together. Holding hands. It wasn't like we were in some passionate embrace. She wasn't even sitting on my bed," he added for good measure, pushing away the knowledge that he'd tried to get her to sit there in the first place.

"She was hired to bring you meals. To get things you need. To help you hop over to the bathroom. She was *not* hired to flirt with you at your bedside."

"She wasn't flirting. She wasn't being inappropriate."

"I've been an innkeeper for over three years now, Michael. I think I have a better idea of how my employees should conduct themselves than you do."

"It wasn't like that," he said again.

"I'm not blaming you. Though I must say if you are used to picking up women in hotels, you've definitely come to the wrong place."

"Don't," he bit out. "Don't make this into something like that."

"I don't need to make it into anything," she replied, her voice turning frigid. "I know what I saw."

"It was nothing like that." He couldn't help it, but his voice rose.

He never lost his temper. Sometime around the twelfth hour of sitting in that ravine, he'd decided to stop sweating the small stuff. He'd also decided that "small stuff" included everything that wasn't being trapped in a ravine, pain shooting through his leg, and feeling like he'd give up a hand, too, if he could simply have one tall glass of water.

But now—for reasons he wasn't a hundred percent sure he was ready to investigate—his temper returned with a vengeance.

"Beverly, first of all, don't make me into something I am not. I don't flirt with hotel workers. I don't take advantage of women. Ever."

She blinked. Maybe it was his tone or maybe she'd finally realized how ludicrous she was being, because when she stared at him again, there was a new softness in her green eyes. "I realize, of course, that you are pretty much held captive here. I know your surgery has made you helpless. I know you couldn't have moved away from her even if you had wanted to."

Captive? Helpless? "I am not helpless."

She flinched. "*Nee*. No, of course not."

"And I was not being held captive in my bed, at the mercy of Penny Troyer." He ran a hand through his hair, grabbing a chunk and pulling hard. "Where are you coming up with this stuff?"

She flinched again. "Perhaps I misspoke."

"You did more than that," he retorted, still hating, *hating* the way she'd portrayed Penny. "This is sweet Penny Troyer we're talking about. You know what she's like. I mean, I thought you did."

Beverly stiffened her spine. "I'm not saying that she isn't sweet. But she did, however, overstep her boundaries."

"No she didn't. Penny isn't like that."

"Forgive me, but you don't really know her all that well."

"I know her far better than you do. Beverly, what you walked in on was nothing more than two people talking."

"I'm not blind and I'm not a fool."

He tried again. More softly, he added, "Penny and I are becoming close. What is happening between Penny and me is special. That is what you walked in on."

"She works here."

"She has to work somewhere, Beverly."

Now she looked like the one who wanted to pull out her hair. "You're right. She needed this job. And that is precisely why she should have been more professional." With a sigh, she continued before he could respond to that. "And as far as what you two have being special? Michael, forgive my bluntness, but how could that be? She is a small-town girl who lives in Pinecraft. In a couple of weeks, you'll be back to being who you are."

"And who am I?"

"Don't start playing games. We both know who you are and what you do. It's a fact. It canna be changed. And if you think it can, then you need to consider how it could. One day very soon you will be back on your way and she'll still be here. Pining for you." Her eyes flashed. "Or something worse."

"Worse?"

"Yes, worse. You'll leave behind a vulnerable girl who's a little shy and a little awkward. You'll move on to another city, maybe even another country. A year from now you'll probably have forgotten her name. But Penny won't have forgotten a minute of your time together. She'll have a head and heart filled with regrets. Long after you've forgotten her, she'll be bearing the consequences," she said softly. Then she turned away and walked out his door.

Leaving him staring at the empty chair by his bedside and his empty right hand.

He was so aggravated, he was tempted to raise his hand and shove that whole tray off the table. He was also alone. Unable to go after Penny. Unable to make her any promises.

As much as it pained him to admit it, he knew that some of what Beverly had said was true. He would be moving on, and she would stay here. He was a little more worldly. Okay, he was about a thousand times more worldly than her, but that didn't mean she wasn't perfect the way she was.

Yet, knowing that didn't really matter.

He picked up one of the pillows beside him, closed his right hand in a fist, and punched it hard. It wasn't even close to what he yearned to do, but sometimes a man had to know his limits.

And sometimes a man had to make do with what he had. And at the moment, he was willing to only harm a down pillow in his frustration.

Still, it was better than nothing.

Chapter 19

*F*uming and feeling like every step was yet another obstacle, Beverly stormed down the stairs.

She was mad. Mad about what had happened between Penny and Michael.

Mad at the way she'd handled it.

But more than both of those things, she was mad that her little speech had served to remind her of her own pain. It was becoming obvious that she hadn't yet dealt with everything that had happened between her and Marvin.

It was becoming obvious? Even that seemed like an understatement! And what a shame that was.

She was a grown, independent woman in her thirties who operated a successful business. Yet, it seemed she only needed a fresh reminder of how emotions could get the best of a person and then all that awful hurt and betrayal—feelings she'd thought she held firmly at bay—rushed forth as if from a faucet.

When was she going to stop being a jilted bride? When was she going to realize, in her heart, that being betrayed by Marvin and Regina before their marriage had been for the best?

She would not be the same person if she were living back in Sugarcreek as Marvin's wife. Perhaps she wouldn't even be very happy. Looking back on it, it was hard to ignore his selfish ways. When she'd been engaged to him, she'd thought she admired a man who looked out for himself. But then, he really only *ever* looked out for himself.

Never her.

Beverly stopped at the foot of the stairs, closed her eyes, and asked the Lord for yet more help. More opportunities to grow and strengthen. And, yes, to help her find the right words to apologize to both Penny and Michael. As she stood quietly, praying for help and guidance, she felt the tension ease in her shoulders as a newfound sense of peace surrounded her. She needed to remember to ask for help more often. Nothing good happened when she attempted to fix everything on her own.

Her temper and emotions were much more firmly in check by the time she got to the kitchen. After first wondering where Penny was—after all, she was pretty sure she'd told Penny to wait for her there—Beverly decided to give herself a couple more minutes to cool off and brew a cup of chamomile tea. She knew the soothing properties of the tea, mixed with a couple of her favorite almond shortbread cookies, would settle her spirit and give her just the boost she needed to go back upstairs, apologize to Michael, and then go talk things over with Penny.

"Feeling better?" Eric said.

Beverly jumped a good two inches off the floor. "Eric!" she called out, at last locating him lounging against the counter next to the refrigerator. "You startled me."

He smiled tightly, though his gaze was devoid of any humor. "Looks like it. Sorry, I thought you saw me."

"Obviously, I did not." After catching her breath, she said,

"I'm, uh, going to make a cup of tea. Would you like one?" She really hoped he'd say no. He was staring at her with a bit of distaste, almost as if she had a stain across the front of her dress.

"No, thanks."

"All right," she said, growing a little uncomfortable with the way he was still staring at her. "Well . . ."

"The last thing I want right now is a cup of"—he paused to read the label of the tea bag she'd just pulled out of a drawer—"soothing chamomile." His voice was laced with sarcasm.

Beverly really didn't know how to respond. What she wanted—no, needed—was to keep a tight rein on her emotions so she didn't burst into tears in front of her new boss. "Okay."

But unfortunately, her easy acquiescence didn't seem to appease him. His eyes narrowed. "See, I've just spent the last ten minutes attempting to calm Penny down."

Valiantly pretending her cheeks weren't turning beet red, she kept her eye on the kettle. "Oh? Why?"

"You know why, Beverly. Actually, she was so upset I sent her home."

Beverly flinched. She hated that she'd made Penny so upset, but she didn't appreciate that Eric was acting like he had every right to chastise her for behaving badly.

How she ran the inn and talked to her employees wasn't any of his business. Not yet. Right now he was simply a guest at the inn. Happy to watch and observe. He had no desire to help manage things. He'd said so several times. Besides, this was a personal problem, one between her and Penny and Michael. Eric butting in wouldn't help anything.

But when he continued to stare at her, she knew she was going to have to talk to him about Penny whether she wanted to or not. "You're right. I know why Penny was upset."

"What are you going to do about it?"

"Ask you to let me handle it," she replied pertly, still looking at that teakettle. Surely it would start whistling soon. "I made a mistake. I also might have overreacted a bit. I'll talk to her in the morning."

"I doubt that is gonna happen."

His words were so laced with derision, his tone so matter-of-fact, that she lifted her chin and turned to him. "Why is that?"

"Because I'm fairly sure that you embarrassed Penny so much, she isn't going to come back to work," he replied as he folded his arms over his chest. The pale blue T-shirt he was wearing stretched across his shoulders, hinting at the muscles underneath.

She really, really wished she hadn't just noticed that.

"She can't just quit, Eric," Beverly retorted.

His expression turned thunderous. "Sure she can. And once more, I wouldn't blame her." He paused. "You know, it took me forever, but I finally got the gist of what happened from her. Did you really accuse that sweet girl of making a move on one of your guests?"

"It wasn't *one of my guests*, it was Michael Knoxx."

"So?"

"Eric, you wouldn't understand this, but he is a very handsome young man. Charming, too. It's no wonder that she let down her guard. But she can't do that. She's here to do a job, not flirt with the guests."

"Beverly."

"When I walked in, they were holding hands."

"So this handsome and charming Michael is so helpless that he can't pull his hand away from the *conniving* and *brazen* Penny?"

The kettle started whistling. Grabbing a towel, she pulled it from the burner, then filled her mug. Hopefully Eric didn't notice that her hand was shaking. "I don't know what, exactly, is going on between them, but Michael has already given me an earful. I don't need to hear it from you, too."

"I think you do." He shifted, dropping his hands to rest on the counter. She glanced at him again, noticing that his faded jeans were almost the same color as his T-shirt. And that he was barefoot.

"Eric, stay out of this."

"You're going to have to go to her house in the morning and apologize."

"I'm sure Penny will have realized I let my temper get the best of me by tomorrow morning," she replied, trying to remain businesslike but likely failing. She hated what had happened. Hated feeling so guilty. And hated that Eric was now pointing out how badly she'd behaved. "Plus, I know she needs this job. She'll be here."

His expression solemn, Eric shook his head. "I really don't think so." More softly, he added, "I saw how she was with him at the hospital. I heard the doctors and nurses say that he asked for her. Clearly, there's a bit of a romance brewing. What's wrong with that?"

"Everything. Penny works here. Michael is a guest."

"So? People meet everywhere. It's obviously mutual, too. It's not as if she's been entering his room uninvited." When she took a breath to speak, he raised a palm. "And don't start telling me how scandalous hand-holding is. I'm not an idiot, and you're not that sheltered. You run an inn. I'm sure you've seen and heard your fair share of amorous situations."

Beverly couldn't help but smile at that. Yes, the thin walls had sometimes given her a surprise or two.

After taking a fortifying sip of tea, she grabbed a jar of shortbread cookies and sat down at the table. Since this conversation wasn't likely to end anytime soon, she needed cookies. Lots of cookies.

Still eyeing her, Eric shook his head again. "Their hand-holding isn't what's bothering you. What is it?"

"I don't know." Then, knowing she was a liar, she corrected herself. "I mean, I do know. Michael is going to leave when he's healed, Eric."

"And?"

"And he'll likely move on."

"You don't know that. Men don't always do that."

"I know," she said quietly. With a sigh, she said, "The truth is that when I saw them together, Penny so trusting and Michael's future so different from hers, something inside of me snapped. I felt like the jilted bride again. All I could feel was how hurt I'd been when my fiancé cheated on me."

Surprise lit his eyes. "That's what happened to you?"

Was it more embarrassing to admit being jilted or to admit it to Eric? "Yes."

He came over and sat across from her. "Not all men are like that," he said quietly.

She scanned his face, noticing the concern in his eyes, the faint stubble on his cheeks. She pretended she *didn't* notice how handsome he was. "I know."

"And what happened wasn't your fault."

His voice was so suddenly gentle, so surprisingly, well, *kind*, it enabled her to lift her chin and meet his gaze. "You don't know everything that happened, Eric."

"I know you. I know myself. And I've been around enough to know people. Who knows why this guy decided to cheat on you?" He shrugged. "He was most likely just a jerk."

"He fell in love with my best friend."

To her bemusement, he shrugged again. "All right. Who knows why this guy decided to cheat on you with your best friend? All I do know is that most men don't become engaged and then start looking for additional relationships. Excuse me, but this guy was a . . . a piece of work."

Almost against her will, she smiled. "A piece of work?"

He smiled softly as he dipped into her jar and pulled out a cookie. "Obviously, I'm watching my mouth around you. He was worse than that."

"He was." It felt good to be so open and honest. It felt good to not take the high road, to finally admit that she'd held herself at least partially responsible for Marvin straying. Reaching for a cookie of her own, she said, "I'll go speak to Penny tomorrow morning."

"Want me to come with you?"

It was on the tip of her tongue to refuse, but he'd shown a lot of insight, and if Penny had told him what happened, that meant she trusted him. And there was a mighty good chance that Penny didn't exactly trust Beverly at the moment. "*Jah*," she said. "I'd really appreciate it if you would come with me tomorrow."

His gaze warmed, letting her know that he was glad about that. "What time?"

"We better go early. Seven?"

"I'll be ready," he said. "Now, pour me a cup of that soothing tea and grab me a plate for the cookies."

Getting up from her chair, she did as he asked, feeling a little bit disappointed that he didn't want to enjoy his snack in her company. "So, are you going to have them in your room?"

"No way. These aren't for me."

"Who are they for?"

"Michael Knoxx." He grinned. "I thought I'd take them up to his room for you."

"Wait a minute. That's not necessary—"

He cut her off neatly. "Let me, Bev. He's probably ready for a break from all the women around here. And I could use a bit of his company, too."

She knew what he meant, but she didn't entirely appreciate the way it made her sound. "Eric, this afternoon's little rant aside, I usually do well with all my guests, both men and women. It's not like I go around causing scenes all day."

"I know. That's why I think a little break from the world might do you a bit of good, too. You have a lot on your plate."

"I'm all right," she said, because admitting that she wasn't would be a very bad thing.

Pressing a light hand to her shoulder, he murmured, "Relax for a bit, Bev. I've got this."

And because she believed him, she decided to take his advice. She added more hot water to her mug, grabbed a couple more cookies, and did just that.

Chapter 20

Penny had already gotten dressed, cleaned her room, and made her bed before she remembered that she didn't have a job to go to anymore. Suddenly, she was alone all over again. Feeling darker than she could remember feeling in a very long time, she sat down on the side of her double bed and wondered how she was ever going to be brave enough to leave her bedroom today.

When she'd arrived home earlier than normal yesterday evening, a jumble of emotions had crossed her parents' features when they'd stood up to greet her: surprise, followed by curiosity, and then concern.

"Why, Penny, you have been crying!" her mother had exclaimed.

Her father had gotten to his feet. "What on earth has happened? Did you run into trouble on the way home?"

As upset as she'd been she knew his worry about her being attacked was very real. "*Nee*, Daed. Nothing like that."

"Are you hurt?" her mother had added.

Their questions and the caring looks they'd treated her to were such a welcome change, it had only made the tears fall again. She'd missed her parents.

But how could she tell them what she'd done? She'd practically thrown herself at Michael. And though he'd defended her, it hadn't really made a difference. He was the guest, she was the employee. Worse, she'd somehow taken advantage of both him and Beverly.

"I had a tough day at work," she'd finally said.

"What happened?"

"We had a mis . . . a misunderstanding." When her bottom lip started to tremble, she'd decided to get her terrible news over with. "I'm pretty sure I was fired today."

Inhaling, she'd steeled herself against the expected barrage of *I told you so*s and recriminations. But instead of looking pleased by the event, her father had looked thunderous.

"They fired you for a misunderstanding?"

"Um, it was just Beverly got upset with me. But . . . *jah*."

"What did she say happened?"

There was no way she was going to share her shameful behavior with them. "I don't want to talk about it." But she'd braced herself for more questions.

Then, instead of nagging her or ignoring her pain, her mother had placed her arm around her shoulders. "Have you eaten lunch or supper?"

"*Nee*."

"Then come sit down in the kitchen and we'll talk. I'll make you a sandwich."

"Mamm, I don't want to tell you what happened."

"Why ever not?"

She'd glanced at her *mamm* who was dressed neat as a pin. As usual. Her light-blue dress had looked as crisp and clean as it had that morning. Her blond hair was still carefully smoothed under her white *kapp*. For Penny's whole life, her mother had been the picture of modesty and grace.

How could Penny reveal what she'd done?

"You're going to think less of me."

To her surprise, it was her father who'd answered. "No matter what happened, we're not going to think less of you."

"Daed—"

"I promise," he'd said, emotion thick in his voice. "Please, trust us."

She hadn't wanted to.

But she had been more afraid of being alone with her thoughts than telling her parents everything. And so she had. She'd told them about the inn and her responsibilities and the friendship that had been growing between her and Michael. Through it all, she'd also waited to be chastised for her actions. But instead of looking angry, her father had merely looked thoughtful. And her mother had looked bemused.

"Hand-holding, hmm?" she'd murmured pulling out two slices of bread.

Penny had been sure every inch of her skin was now beet red. Too embarrassed to even glance at her father, she'd answered her mother directly. "I promise, Mamm. That was all it was."

"I'm sure of that, dear," Mamm had replied.

Penny had gaped. "You're not disappointed in me?"

"Penny, I might not have liked you working and being out on your own, but I surely don't think you've turned into the girl of loose morals Beverly Overholt is making you out to be." She'd fanned her heated cheeks. "Goodness!"

"Your mother is right, Penny," her father had said, his deep voice clear and precise. "I know you, and I know how we've raised you. You have done nothing to be ashamed about."

Her parents' support had felt so good. It was if they were finally mending their broken past and building something new. "I don't know what to do now."

Her mother had stopped slicing roast beef for her sandwich and gave her another long look. "It seems to me that you're simply going to have to be patient. It's out of your hands."

"You mean it's in the Lord's?" For some reason, Penny had been disappointed. She knew everything was ultimately in the Lord's hands, but at the moment that had felt like a bit of an excuse.

"Of course everything is in Got's capable hands, but that wasn't what I meant." She'd gone back to fixing Penny's sandwich. "It seems to me that either your boss will come to her senses on her own or she'll get some prodding from Mr. Michael Knoxx."

Penny had been bowled over. "You think he'll say something?"

"From what you told me? I do."

"We know you, daughter, and we know that you would never be such *gut* friends with anyone who didn't deserve your friendship," her father said. Looking mildly uncomfortable, he'd added, "Besides, once you told me about Michael and the Knoxx Family, I did a little bit of asking around." Looking her in the eye, he'd said, "I couldn't find a single person who didn't think this man was a good one. I'm sure he was anxious to defend your honor. And his."

PENNY HAD KEPT THAT conversation and advice close to her heart all night long, hugging it to her as she'd fallen into a restless slumber.

But now, in the bright light of day, all of her optimism felt misplaced. It was a lot to ask Michael to stand up for her, and even sillier to imagine that Beverly would change her mind about Penny's behavior. All she had to do was let it be known that she needed another worker and any number of girls would probably be at her doorstep in minutes.

But what could she do now? She had no other job offers, and

if she applied at another bed-and-breakfast, they'd soon find out that she was fired from the Orange Blossom Inn.

She was stuck.

It was going to be a hard adjustment to go back to spending her days helping her mother around the house. But the hardest adjustment would be making peace with the fact that this was her future.

A knock on the front door interrupted her thoughts. She stilled, half listening for voices, trying to recall who might be stopping by this early in the morning. Unfortunately, the guest's voice was muted.

Moments later, her father rapped his knuckles on her bedroom door. "Penny?"

"*Jah*, Daed?"

"*Maydel*, Daughter, there are some people here to see ya."

He sounded hesitant and perhaps careful, as if he wasn't sure how to deliver the news.

Crossing the room, she opened her door. "Who is it?"

"It's, ah, Beverly Overholt and a man."

"Really?" Never, ever would she have thought that Miss Beverly would come to her house looking for her.

"Really." Everything in her father's manner and tone indicated that he wasn't particularly thrilled about this news, either. "Do you want me to ask them to leave? I will, you know. I'd be happy to do that."

After last night's conversation, his heavy-handed ways didn't upset her. Instead, she counted it a blessing that her father cared enough to want to shield her from further unpleasantness.

"*Nee*, Daed. I'm certain that Miss Beverly has only come over to officially fire me. Since I got the job on my own, I think I should get fired on my own, too."

Eyeing her steadily, he rubbed his beard. "I'm not so sure about her wanting to fire you, child. Beverly looks a bit shame-faced, if you want to know the truth."

"Really?"

"Come out and see for yourself," he said in a gentle way.

She nodded. "I suppose I had better."

After giving her another encouraging smile, her father turned and walked to the living room, where Beverly and Eric were sitting uncomfortably side by side on the couch. Her mother was standing in front of them, her arms crossed over her chest, her dark coral dress practically matching the flush in her cheeks. Obviously, her mother was still upset. She hadn't even offered them coffee or some of her banana bread.

When Beverly caught sight of Penny, she smiled in relief. "Hi, Penny. I'm so glad you are home. I wasn't sure if you would be here or not."

Penny couldn't imagine where Beverly thought she might be instead. But rather than sharing those thoughts, she simply nodded. "*Gut matin*, Miss Beverly, Mr. Eric."

Eric's smile looked far more genuine and relaxed as he leaned back on her parents' couch. Today he had on a white short-sleeved cotton shirt with buttons down the front, jeans, and some black flipflops. He looked as if he were ready to settle there for the next hour. "*Gut matin* to you, too, Penny."

Penny couldn't help herself from grinning at his awful pronunciation of Pennsylvania Dutch.

As if reading her mind, he chuckled. "I'm hopeless, aren't I?"

"Not quite hopeless . . ."

"But definitely not good." He wrinkled his nose. "No matter how hard I try, I can't seem to get my tongue around these German-sounding words."

She couldn't deny the truth in his words. "I'm sorry to say you might be right about that. It's *gut* you weren't born Amish," she teased.

"Penny," her mother interrupted, "Eric and Beverly said that they came over to speak with you about an important matter."

"Of course." Right then and there, she felt the seriousness of the moment hit her full-force. "I'm sorry. Miss Beverly, how may I help you?"

"Penny, if you don't mind, I wanted to talk to you about yesterday."

A lump formed in her throat. Glancing at her parents, she bit her lip. "I thought that was probably the reason."

Her mother waved her over. "Come sit down, Penny."

Feeling like she was back in school, she did as her mother asked.

As soon as she sat, her father clasped his hands behind his back and glared at Beverly. "I'm mighty interested in hearing what you seem to think happened."

Penny couldn't have been more shocked if her father had announced that he wanted to take her to Disney World. He really was on her side! However, she'd meant what she'd said earlier. She needed to have this conversation on her own, if for no other reason than to prove to herself that she really had grown up and was becoming more independent. "Daed, Mamm, may I speak to Beverly and Eric on my own?"

"Are you sure that is what you want to do?" her father asked.

She wasn't. But she knew it was the right thing, and that was what counted. "*Jah*. I think it would be best."

Her father nodded, but her mother acquiesced with far greater reluctance. However, to her credit, her *mamm* merely gave her a quiet, searching look, then followed her father out to the back patio.

When it was just the three of them, Beverly looked more relaxed. Eric looked bemused. And Penny? She felt even more unsure about what to do or say. She really hoped Beverly would say her piece and then leave. Then Penny could spend the rest of the day moping around the house and planning the rest of her life.

Miss Beverly cleared her throat. "Penny, there's no easy way to say this."

"Yes?" She inhaled, preparing herself for the worst.

"I made a terrible mistake yesterday."

All the air in her lungs flew out in a rush. Penny knew she was gaping, but she couldn't help herself. "I'm sorry?"

"When I walked into Michael's room, I completely misunderstood what was happening." Twin spots of color appeared on her cheeks. "Furthermore, I completely overreacted. I knew that you and Michael had become friends, that there was nothing untoward happening between the two of you." She bit her bottom lip. "I'm ashamed to say that I let some things in my past color what I saw. I hope you will forgive me."

Penny glanced at Eric. When he met her gaze, he nodded in an encouraging way, letting her know that he was on her side. Perhaps another day she would wonder why and how she came to trust him so easily. But at that moment, she was simply grateful for his support.

"You are not here to fire me?"

Beverly's green eyes darkened with obvious remorse. "*Nee*, Penny. I am here to ask your forgiveness."

"Of course I forgive you," she blurted. How could Miss Beverly even imagine that Penny wouldn't?

But instead of looking eased, Miss Beverly still seemed hesitant. "If I promise to not accuse you of such things again . . . Will . . . will you come back to work?"

"*Jah*, if that is what you would like me to do."

"That is what I would love for you to do." She smiled brightly. "While you haven't been working at the inn very long, you've already shown a lot of initiative and promise. You're dependable, have a great disposition, and a calm way about you."

"*Danke.*"

"You're welcome. Though it's not so much a compliment as it is the truth. I'm grateful for you." She smiled again.

Penny couldn't help but smile back. "Do you still want me to come in today?"

"I do. I've come to depend on you, you see."

"And there's also a certain young man who would likely create quite a stir if you don't come back," Eric added with a ghost of a smile.

"Michael?"

Eric nodded. "I sat with him for a while last night. Almost the whole time, he was fretting about you."

"Truly?"

This time it was Beverly who answered. "Yes. See, after you left, he told me what he thought of my treatment of you but he wasn't exactly thrilled with how my words reflected on his character, either. He was right, of course. I really messed up yesterday."

Penny knew it would take her quite some time to process everything that Beverly and Eric had told her. However, two things were already shining through. The first was that she'd done a good job at the inn; she was mighty pleased about that. The second bit of news, however, left her fairly breathless.

Michael Knoxx had come to her defense.

She had no idea what was going to happen next. All she knew was that she wasn't about to go backward.

That was enough for now. "I'll be there as soon as I can."

Eric looked at his watch. "Why don't you take your time? I'm sure this has been a difficult morning and you probably want to visit with your parents."

"Or would you rather I speak to them for you?" Beverly asked. "I'll be glad to let them know that what happened was my fault and my fault alone."

Penny wasn't entirely sure that was the case. Beverly had rushed to some conclusions, but Penny *had* let herself get too attached to Michael. She couldn't deny that. She should have remained a bit more distant with him. It wasn't like they would ever have a future together. "There's no need to talk to them. I will."

"All right then," Eric said. "How about we see you in an hour or two? Just come back whenever you are ready."

"I can do that. I'll talk with my parents, have some breakfast, then head over. Thank you again."

"You're very welcome," Eric said before he and Beverly walked out.

As Penny closed the door after them, she knew she needed to talk to her parents. No doubt they'd be on pins and needles, wondering what she, Mr. Eric, and Miss Beverly had all been saying to one another.

But instead of being mad at Penny, her parents had been concerned. And that, she realized, was something that had made it all worthwhile. She and her parents were making progress. After living in limbo for twelve years, they were all moving forward. At last.

Chapter 21

*W*hen Tricia walked into the inn's small upstairs sitting area the next morning, she was brought up short. There, on one of the couches, just as if he hung out there all the time, was none other than Michael Knoxx.

Though she knew he was in the house, of course, she hadn't seen him since he'd returned from the hospital on Saturday. She'd kept track of her aunt's reports about his surgery and recovery, though. After all, he was pretty much the main topic of conversation around the inn. Eric seemed to enjoy his company but Aunt Beverly continually fretted that she wasn't doing enough for him. And Penny, of course, seemed completely smitten with him.

But then, there had been all the commotion she'd heard last night. Tricia hadn't been brave enough to ask her aunt what had happened between Michael and Penny, but she figured it must've been something pretty awful to send the whole place into a state of turmoil.

"What are you doing in here?" she asked. The last Tricia had heard, Michael was still basically bedridden.

His eyebrows rose. "Hello to you, too."

She rolled her eyes. "Dwell on good manners if you must, but you and I both know that you aren't supposed to be out of bed."

"Tricia, don't be a worrywart," he said in a breezy way, which was strangely appealing. "I'm feeling much better. And since you're neither my nurse nor my mother, I have no concerns about where you think I am supposed to be."

"You know, it's no wonder you speak on stage," she said sarcastically. "You certainly like to make your point."

He grinned. "Loud and clear."

She walked closer. "Michael, your recuperation has the whole household tied up in knots. My aunt has been worried sick."

For the first time in their acquaintance, she thought he looked a bit unsure. "I'm sorry to hear that. I've been trying to not be too difficult a patient."

"She didn't say you were and I'm not telling you this to worry you. I'm telling you this so you will understand why you shouldn't be out of bed."

He ran a hand through his hair. "I couldn't stay in that room another minute."

"What's wrong with it?" Maybe she needed to freshen his sheets or something?

"You know why. Sitting in one room for days is tedious. I was bored." He scowled. "Not that it is any of your business."

He sounded so irritated and saddened, Tricia felt guilty. "Sorry I lectured you."

His eyes lit up. "Don't be. It's kind of fun sparring with another person for a change. You remind me of my sister."

"I'll take that as a compliment."

"You should. Molly is great. She keeps me in line. I never thought I needed that, but maybe I do. Penny is far too patient and kind. Sometimes I really have to watch myself or I'll mow her over."

"Penny *is* patient and kind." She was also adorable in that girl-next-door way, shy, and had that lovely, curly hair. She was everything Tricia had hoped to be. However, the Lord had given her a gregarious nature, a temper, and a rather tomboyish figure. No matter how hard she'd attempt to mind her manners and watch her tongue, she'd never be able to adopt Penny Troyer's purely feminine demeanor.

He smiled. "She is."

"I haven't seen Penny yet today. I guess she has a day off."

As if she'd flipped a switch, the light left his eyes. "I hope that is the case."

Knowing he was referring to the big fight, she didn't respond. "Since I'm here and Penny is not, may I get you anything? *Kaffi?* Iced tea?"

"Maybe in a minute. Why did you come up here anyway?"

She pointed to a book on the table. "I left my library book here." She'd had to stop in the middle of a really good section and was eager to read the next couple of chapters.

"What are you reading?"

"Oh, it's, um, just a romance." When he smirked at the Amish woman on the cover, she felt her insides bristle. "It's a good one, though."

Still staring at the book, he asked, "Aren't all romances good?"

"Are you speaking of books or real life?"

Lifting his gaze, he met her eyes. "Both."

Again, she was struck by how his personality seemed to fill the room—even a small sitting room like this. "I'm not sure about that," she said slowly. "I've never been in love."

"No?"

"*Nee.*"

He leaned back against the cushions and shifted. "Tricia, come sit down. My neck is starting to get an awful crick in it."

The light in his eyes told her he wasn't above using sympathy to get his way. "I doubt that." But still, she took a seat.

Once she was sitting primly next to him, wondering if the bright pink fabric of her dress might be a bit too bright, he asked, "So what's your story?"

It was a bit disconcerting to receive his complete, undivided attention. "I don't have one," she sputtered.

"Sure you do," he said impatiently. "Where are you from? Why are you here?"

"I'm from Sugarcreek, Ohio, and I'm here to visit my aunt."

He looked at her so intently, she could swear he was trying to read her mind. Then he shook his head. "No, that's not it."

"That is exactly it," she lied.

"That is the bare bones of the story. Come on, Tricia, give a guy something to think about besides missing part of a leg."

She gaped at him. "I can't believe you said that!"

He didn't look the least bit shamefaced. "Tricia, it's not a secret."

"But still . . ."

He chuckled. "See, this is why you need to talk to me. If we leave the subjects up to me, we'll venture into all sorts of awkward areas."

"Obviously."

"So. Why are you here, really?"

Maybe it was the way he listened so carefully. Maybe it was because she was more afraid to talk about his injury than her past. Or maybe, just maybe, she needed to tell someone who could be objective. Whatever the reason, finally, Tricia said, "Something happened back in Sugarcreek that I thought was important."

"You don't think it is important anymore?"

"I'm not sure," she said honestly. "Now that I have some distance and some time has gone by, I'm starting to wonder if everything that I thought was so important was minor after all."

"If it matters to you, it's important."

His comment, so sure and simply stated, startled a laugh from her. "You don't even know what I'm referring to!"

"Maybe I don't need to know."

"You are beyond frustrating. If you didn't need to know, why did you even ask?"

"I asked before I realized your reason was such a closely guarded secret."

"I had some trouble with my friends," she blurted. "A rumor had been started about me, and I was getting teased." Almost against her will, she felt her gaze drift toward his injured leg. Pretty much everyone knew his story. He'd survived a terrible accident. Even now, he was recovering from injuries sustained in it. Her problems seemed minuscule in comparison.

Embarrassed, she stood up. "You know what, I have to go."

"I'm sorry," he said. "I'm sorry you were being teased. I know that's hard."

She was about to brush off his apology when his words—and his tone—hit her hard. "You know about being teased?"

"Of course I do."

He was famous. He was handsome. She assumed most people wanted to be his friend. That, at least to her mind, left only one area where people could target him. "Do people tease you about your leg?"

To her surprise, he looked amused by the idea. "About how I had to have part of it amputated? *Nee*. Not so much. Comments like that kind of cross the boundaries of good taste, don't you think?"

"Then what?" she asked. Realizing she was about to cross those boundaries of good taste herself, she flushed. "Sorry, it's none of my business."

"Of course it's your business. I'm the one who wanted to talk. Ain't so?" After she shrugged, he said, "Tricia, when you have a job like mine, being out in public, speaking on stage? It kind of opens a person up to a lot of criticism."

"I suppose it does. I never thought about that."

"Some of that criticism hurts." His expression clouded. "Sometimes people see me on stage, hear me speak for ten minutes, learn something about my life, and then think they know everything about me. They don't, of course."

"How do you deal with it?"

"I'm lucky. I rarely do much without my family. We support each other." He grinned. "We're also honest enough to give criticism if it's deserved. Do you have that support?"

"I do. But the things they were being mean about? They weren't things that I wanted my parents to know."

"So who did you tell?"

"My aunt Beverly."

"I'm glad you told someone. That's *gut*."

She nodded. "Aunt Bev is super kind, and I'm glad she understands, but it doesn't really change anything." She shrugged. "But I'm getting through it."

"All you can do is take things one day at a time, *jah*?"

His eyes were gentle, gentle enough that she wished she were a whole lot more like Penny Troyer and a whole lot less like his sister. But perhaps instead of having a crush on him she could foster a friendship? That was something that would be more meaningful and longer lasting.

"*Danke*," she whispered. "Talking to you helped."

He looked pleased. "I'm glad."

She liked that. She liked how he didn't brush off her thanks, or make light of her words. She was just about to tell him so when his warm gaze lifted from hers and settled on someone behind her. Curious, she turned and saw Penny Troyer staring at the two of them, confusion written all over her face.

Hoping Penny hadn't mistakenly misread the situation, Tricia smiled brightly, in what she hoped was a welcoming way. "Hi, Penny."

"Hello. I'm sorry. I didn't mean to interrupt. I was just looking for Michael."

"You didn't interrupt a thing," Tricia said in a rush. "We were just talking. About nothing important." She glanced back at Michael, but either he didn't hear her or he didn't feel the need to respond. Because he was still staring at Penny.

"I'm glad you found me," he said. "I was just telling Tricia here that I needed a break from my bedroom's walls." He lifted a hand. "Come here and talk with me. I want to know how you are. I've been worried sick about you."

"You have?"

"Absolutely."

As Penny stepped forward, Tricia edged out of the room. It was painfully obvious that there was only one girl Michael had eyes for.

And it certainly wasn't her.

Chapter 22

The moment they were completely alone, Michael spoke. "Penny, you seem a little worried. Are you upset about last night?"

Her blue eyes widened before closing briefly. When she met his gaze again, it was obvious that she'd placed a firm hold on her emotions. "*Nee*. Believe it or not, I talked to my parents about what happened between us and neither of them thought we'd done anything wrong."

"That's because we didn't."

"And then, this morning, both Miss Beverly and Mr. Eric came to my *haus*."

Michael was surprised to hear it, but he was pleased, too. "That's *gut*. What did they say?"

"Miss Beverly apologized." Penny shook her head in wonder. "Oh, Michael, I had thought I was fired, for sure."

"I'm glad you weren't." Then, instead of rehashing all the events from last evening, he attempted to lighten things up. "We should probably have a bowl of ice cream or something this afternoon. A celebration is in order, I think."

"Because?"

"Because I'm out of my room." When she slowly smiled, he added, "I couldn't sit there another hour. I was too restless."

"You're right. We need to have some ice cream and celebrate. If you're out here, it means you're feeling better."

"Will you get some for us when you take your break after lunch?"

"Of course I will." Eyes sparkling, she added, "I might even buy some hot fudge sauce, too."

"I can't wait." Glancing at her, Michael was once again struck by how pretty she was. He loved her curly blond hair, and how strands were constantly springing out from under her white *kapp*. Her eyes were mesmerizing, and he was certain he'd do just about anything to see that dimple of hers.

But he could still tell that she wasn't completely herself yet. She seemed far more tentative around him. Almost shy. "Maybe we should talk about yesterday after all," he said quietly. "Are you really all right?"

"I'm not quite sure. Yesterday really confused me."

"Because Beverly got mad at you?"

"*Jah*. And other things." Straightening her shoulders, she looked directly at him. "She was right. I shouldn't have been sitting so close to you, holding your hand."

"I was glad you were holding my hand. Everything that has happened to me since I arrived in Pinecraft—the pain, the surgery, my family leaving, the recovery—it's all been difficult to deal with, though I actually didn't think much could faze me anymore." Taking a breath, his expression lightened. "I mean to say, everything's been mighty hard to deal with . . . except for you."

"You have been a good friend to me, too."

Two steps forward, one step back. "Do you remember what I proposed on Siesta Key?"

"Of course I do."

"Tell me," he coaxed. Honestly, it was taking everything he had not to reach for her hand right now and link their fingers together.

"We vowed to cherish each moment," Penny recalled, a winsome smile on her lips. "To embrace each hour. Live each day."

"And we have."

"We've certainly tried." She paused. "Maybe too hard."

Her comment made him smile. "Make fun of our pact if you want, but I took it to heart."

"I took it to heart, too. And I think I have moved forward." Leaning closer, so close he could smell the faint lemon scent of her hair, she said, "I still can't believe that my parents were on my side."

"Well, of course they were. You did not do anything wrong."

"You don't understand. They've been mad at me for going against their wishes. They've refused to see me as a grown woman, as an adult. But when I told them about holding your hand, my mother started chuckling."

"She laughed? Why?"

"She said that it seemed like a lot of nothing for Beverly to get excited about."

He smiled at her, genuinely pleased. "My *mamm* would have said the same thing. I'm so glad for you, Penny."

"I am, too. It's been hard. My parents have been all I've had for a long time."

"But that isn't the case any longer. Now you have your job, and you're making more friends."

"This is true. Every day, my circle seems to be getting bigger."

"Plus, now we have our friendship."

"*Jah*. Our friendship is special to me."

It was special to him, too. "Though the reason I've gotten to know you has been hard, I'm mighty glad my family encouraged me to stay here longer."

"Me, too. I only wish time hasn't gone by so fast. You've already been here for more than a week."

"Just three weeks to go."

"Do you know what date you're going to leave?"

"*Nee*. I should probably call my brother and talk things through with him."

"I bet you can't wait."

Though his first instinct was to agree, he was discovering that with Penny he couldn't do anything but be completely honest. With that in mind, he said, "Actually, I'm not in any hurry to call him. See, the last time we spoke, things were fairly strained between us."

He glanced at her, half expecting her to begin peppering him with questions. But Penny was simply sitting quietly. She wasn't grilling him with questions or expecting him to entertain her or to spout encouraging or insightful stories. She never did. Instead, she looked content to follow his lead, to allow him to take the time he needed.

It was a wonderful thing.

Penny Troyer calmed him. She cleared his head.

She made him feel like he didn't have to try so hard. And having been around many, many people, in many, many parts of the country and even in different parts of the world, he knew what a gift that was.

How in the world was he going to give a woman like her up? Why would he want to?

Feeling her support, he said, "Penny, remember yesterday, how I told you I wanted to stop touring and speaking?"

"Of course I do."

"Well, I feel even more certain about my decision this morning. I need to stop soon. Very soon."

"I can't help but fear that might be a mistake, Michael. I know I only saw you once on stage, but you seemed to really enjoy speaking to everyone. Actually, you seemed kind of larger than life. Why would you want to give that up?"

There she went again. Asking him simple questions, questions that made him think and consider . . . but didn't press him for more than he was willing or able to give. And because she was so considerate of how he was feeling, it made him want to share even more.

"See, the thing is, I'm not larger than life."

"Of course you aren't. I only meant that you were mesmerizing."

When he smiled at that, her cheeks turned bright red. "I'm sorry, I don't want to embarrass you." She looked a little sheepish. "Or maybe I don't want to mortify myself any further."

"Don't be embarrassed. I like your honesty. I admire it." Taking a fortifying breath, he said, "Truthfully, I'm tired of the pace."

"Maybe you could slow down? That sounds like a *gut* compromise, *jah*?"

He was finding it hard to verbalize everything he had kept to himself for so long. But her blue eyes, so clear and kind, made him want to be as frank as ever. "I'm tired of always living out of a suitcase. Of never being home. I'm tired of staying in other people's homes and feeling like I need to be something I'm not so they're not disappointed."

Finally looking at her again, he said, "But most of all, I can hardly stand the idea that there is no end in sight. I need an end."

"Oh, Michael," she whispered. "I had no idea."

"I'm not going to say it's been a sacrifice, because it hasn't. I've been blessed to have had so many adventures and opportunities. But of late, my life hasn't felt full of blessings. It's felt full of burdens."

She pursed her lips, then said, "Do you mind if I share something?"

"Of course not."

"Michael, after what happened to Lissy, with the trial and the reporters and the anger and the pain . . . Well, my parents and I felt like we were living each day only half-alive. The other half we spent looking over our shoulders. That was one of the reasons we moved here to Sarasota." She breathed in deeply. "We wanted to be normal. We *yearned* for normalcy."

"You do understand."

She nodded. "I think I do. The lure of having a home and stability and to simply live? Those things are as valuable as diamonds and gold to some people."

"For people like you and me, their worth can never be overstated."

She smiled. "Exactly."

"Penny, what am I going to do without you?" he whispered around a breath. Only after did he realize he'd mistakenly uttered that question loud enough for her to hear.

"Maybe you'll miss me," she said simply. Then, as if she'd just realized what she said, her eyes widened and her cheeks bloomed brightly. "I mean, maybe you'll miss our friendship."

He knew he was going to miss a lot of things. "I *know* I'll miss you, Penny."

"I'm going to miss you, too."

But when he met her eyes, it occurred to him that they both knew something else, something they hadn't said aloud. They might want the same things, they might even yearn for things to be different. But that didn't mean they would be able to get what they wanted. Sometimes that was an impossibility, better left to the dreamers and romantics.

Not to people like them.

Chapter 23

$\mathcal{B}$y Thursday evening, Beverly had a full house. While she was glad about that, she couldn't resist thinking that she would've appreciated one or two empty rooms. As it was, she found herself running back and forth between the kitchen and the gathering rooms, the bedrooms and the office, doing her best to keep all of her guests happy and satisfied. She'd learned long ago that it only took one bad experience for a guest to elect to never return and tell their friends about it, too.

She couldn't have that.

To his credit, Eric was helping quite a bit. He had volunteered to take over the reservations and billings, and it was amazing how much her mind eased knowing that part of her business was in his capable hands.

But at the moment, with Eric wrist-deep in dough, she was beginning to fear for her bread's safety.

"Now what, Bev? Should I knead it some more?"

Eyeing the dough critically, she frowned. It looked a little too shiny, a little too smooth. Actually, it bordered on being kneaded into something resembling old gum. "*Nee!*" she called out, perhaps with a bit too much force.

When he flinched, she smiled apologetically. "Sorry. I mean, um, it's been kneaded enough. More than enough."

Immediately, he raised his hands in surrender. "Uh-oh. Did I use too much pressure?"

She grinned. "I don't know if that's the right descriptor. It's more like you've been declared the winner in your fight with the dough." Looking at the sad lump he'd just placed in the bowl, she teased, "It didn't stand a chance."

He frowned. "Did I ruin it?"

"I don't think so." Grabbing a clean white dishtowel, she flicked it open and covered the bowl, then pointed to the sink. "It should be okay. But now you should probably wash your hands. I'm afraid my kitchen won't be the same if we don't get you cleaned up." As it was, almost every inch of the counters and floor were covered with a fine coating of flour.

Walking to the sink, he smiled at her. "Thanks for letting me in your domain today. It's been a lot of fun."

"Eric, you don't have to thank me. It's your kitchen, too."

"I might own the building, but we both know which of us belongs at the Orange Blossom Inn."

His words were so sweet, she looked at him gratefully. "Thanks for saying that."

"It's the truth."

Their eyes met again, and suddenly something soft and sweet and dear passed through them. Maybe they were going to become friends, after all. Amazing how the Lord always seemed to make everything turn out all right.

"You know," she began, "it sure seems as though—"

"Excuse me, Aunt Beverly," Tricia said as she peeked through the opening of the swinging kitchen door. "But there's someone here for Eric. Have you seen him?"

Eric turned off the sink. "I'm right here, Tricia."

"Oh! Well, yes you are. You have a visitor."

Grabbing a handful of paper towels, he asked, "Is it John from the bank?"

"*Nee.*" Looking right pleased with herself, she said, "It's Amy from Pennsylvania."

"Amy?" Grabbing another paper towel, he rubbed it vigorously between his hands before tossing it on the counter. "Where is she?"

"I put her in the gathering room. Is that all right?"

"Perfect," he said before flying out the door . . . and reminding Beverly that although they might be forming a friendship, there certainly wasn't going to be room for anything more.

Not that she'd been hoping for that, of course.

Unable to help herself, Beverly left the kitchen and peeked into the gathering room, making sure to keep out of sight. The last thing she wanted was for Eric to see her spying on him. Though she wasn't *spying*, exactly. She was simply interested in who this mysterious Amy was. Yes, it was simply curiosity. That was all. But the moment she caught sight of them, Beverly realized she could have strode into the center of the room and danced in circles.

She would have bet money that they wouldn't have noticed a thing.

Eric had a very pretty, very petite, brown-haired woman in his arms. The woman's arms were looped around his neck. Probably holding on for dear life, Beverly mused, because Eric was currently kissing that woman like he was a starving man and Amy's lips were all he needed for sustenance.

Beverly's cheeks flushed. She knew she should look away. They obviously thought they were alone. And though she was slightly shocked, there was nothing wrong with what they were doing, either. Eric had told her he had a girlfriend. And, well, they'd been apart for weeks now.

So there was no real reason for her to feel the things she was feeling.

Turning on her heel, she rushed to a back hallway, wishing with every step that she had never peeked into that room in the first place.

Because now, that vision of Eric and Amy locked in a passionate embrace had firmly embedded itself in her brain. And for the life of her, she couldn't seem to stop replaying it.

Beverly knew why, of course.

Seeing Eric and Amy had spurred visions of her and Marvin together, back when they were mere months away from marrying. Though, never had Marvin kissed her like *that*. His kisses had been sedate. Quiet. Controlled.

She'd assumed that had been how everyone kissed, but now she realized that some key components had been missing: Passion. Desire. Yearning. It had all been missing and she hadn't even realized it.

Suddenly she understood why he had turned to Regina.

Oh, of course what they'd done was bad. They should have told her about their feelings for each other long before they did, but now, at last, Beverly could at least understand what Marvin had been searching for.

Tears pricked her eyes. This awful realization—that not only had she never experienced such passion, but she'd never imagined it could exist—was as painful a lesson as any she'd ever learned. It was also, she believed, a fairly terrible thing to come to terms with at thirty-four years of age.

As she returned to the kitchen in a daze, Tricia looked up from the casserole dish she was drying and frowned. "Aunt Bev, you okay? You look kind of like you've seen a ghost."

Beverly forced herself to laugh. "Of course I'm fine, dear. I've never been better."

Lying about herself, unfortunately, was something she *did* have experience with. In spades.

MICHAEL HAD JUST SETTLED into one of the comfortable chairs by the kitchen when Tricia handed him a portable phone. "It's for you, Michael," she said before returning to the kitchen, the smell of freshly baked bread wafting through the swinging door in her wake.

"Hello?" Michael asked, wondering which member of the family had decided to call this time.

"Hi! How are you feeling?" Evan asked.

"Better."

"How much better?" he pressed.

"I'm out of bed today."

"Really? That's *wunderbaar.*"

"I think so, too. I'm sitting in a chair just outside the kitchen. Beverly's been baking bread. It smells like heaven."

"It sounds like heaven. I'm standing outside of tonight's amphitheater. We've got a record crowd, though half of them are rapidly turning churlish because they've already heard you aren't here in upstate New York. It's also pouring down rain."

Glad Evan couldn't see him, Michael grinned. "The rain is a real shame, especially since you all are touring the area."

"Yeah. I hate wearing wet clothes."

"Don't blame you for that." He hated it, too. "Hope Mamm and Daed are keeping warm and dry."

"They're fine," Evan muttered in a distracted way as he shuffled his cell phone against his cheek. "Listen, I can't talk too long, but we do need to get something settled."

"What's that?" Though, of course, it was practically a rhetorical question, because he knew what Evan was going to ask.

"Do you have your calendar in front of you?"

Unfortunately, he'd had Tricia help him with his book and his calendar when he decided to go downstairs. So his planner *was* standing open right in front of him. As he stared at the expanse of beautiful empty squares, he swallowed back a lump of regret. "*Jah*," he said at last. "I've got it open to May."

"How does being in Texas in June sound?"

Too soon. Hedging a bit, he asked, "When in June?"

"June first." Impatience settled in Evan's voice. "When do you think?"

"Hey, I'm just asking."

"Well, I'm just asking, too. I'm getting mighty tired of disappointing your fans."

Evan sounded beyond tired and cranky. He sounded exhausted. Guilt bit at Michael, making him realize that he'd been fooling himself to actually think he could give everything up and start a new life in Sarasota. "I'll have to double-check with the doctors but I'll let you know as soon as I can."

"When?"

"I don't know. By the end of the week?"

"Michael, I know your stump has got to heal and all, but the rest of the world is moving forward. I've got to tell those folks in Brownsville yay or nay. They're waiting on you. We're waiting on you."

"You all can go to Brownsville without me."

"*Nee*, we actually can't." Evan's voice was flat. "This group only wants to book us if you are going to be there."

"Why don't we wait on it, then? Maybe push it back a few months?"

"Because they've promised they can bring in a big crowd if

you are there then. As much as it pains me to remind you of this, you are the main draw. The rest of us are simply filler."

"You know that's not true."

"No, you know that *is* true. Michael, I'm not giving you false compliments, merely saying how it is."

"It's not exactly that way."

"It is. What's happening in Brownsville ain't a surprise and we both know it. Everywhere we go, you are the star, not the rest of us."

"I didn't ask for that."

"I know, but just because you didn't ask for it doesn't mean it didn't happen. God gave you a gift, and it's being able to tell a crowd your story. There's no shame in acknowledging that."

Staring at the blank slate of his calendar, Michael knew what he had to do. There were some things far more important than mere wants or feelings. "Tell Mamm and Daed that I'll meet everyone in Brownsville."

"You sure?"

There was such hope in Evan's voice, Michael knew he'd be there even if his stump was not completely healed. "I'm sure."

"Thank the Lord. Okay, then. I'll let them know. And now I'll be letting you go. See you in a couple of weeks."

That much time had already passed? *"Jah."*

"Let me know if you want me to fly to Sarasota and help you travel. I'll be happy to."

Michael knew that to be true. Evan would fly all night, would do whatever it took to be there for him. He'd always been there for him. "I think I'll be all right, but I'll let you know."

"Great. See you then."

When Michael hung up, he grimaced. As much as he might talk or act like he was ready for a change, he wasn't ready to let his family down. He owed them too much. He loved them too much.

And that meant, of course, that he was going to have to find a way to tell Penny that he was leaving for good about a week earlier than planned. For all his big talk about proposals and living life to the fullest, it seemed dreams weren't always meant to come true.

At least, not yet.

Chapter 24

$\mathscr{M}$r. Eric's Amy was a nice lady. Since arriving on Thursday, she'd not only made her bed but also left Penny a small tip every morning.

Penny was coming to understand that these types of thoughtful gestures were typical of Amy, who had gone out of her way to be nice to everyone she came in contact with during her long weekend at the inn.

Amy was also a talker. Hardly a minute could be spent in her company without hearing how *beautiful* Florida was, or how *adorably quaint* she found Pinecraft. She also loved the *gorgeous, fragrant flowers*, and couldn't wait to stroll on the *incredible, so-sandy beach* again, or have just one more slice of the *almost-irresistible, perfect pie* at Yoder's. Amy, it seemed, enjoyed incorporating both adjectives and alliteration into her vocabulary.

The flowery, effusive compliments amused Michael, enamored Mr. Eric, and annoyed Miss Beverly to no end. One could almost see Beverly gritting her teeth when Amy started discussing how cute and charming the Amish were when playing shuffleboard at Pinecraft Park.

Though Penny wasn't really exactly sure how the older men could be thought of as cute, she didn't mind Amy's description. It wasn't mean-spirited. Rather, it seemed to be indicative of the way she went through life: constantly commenting on everything.

There were worse ways to be, Penny figured.

Since Amy's room was the last to clean for the day, once she was done she put away her supplies in the hall closet, then joined Michael on the back patio.

Now that over a week had passed since his surgery, he was supposed to be walking as much as possible in order to get used to his new prosthesis, but instead she found him sitting on a comfy lounge chair. A cat lay curled on his lap, and both his real and metal foot were propped on an ottoman in front of him. His eyes were closed and he looked completely content—far more comfortable than he'd looked in days.

Unable to help herself, she paused in front of him and took the opportune moment to simply stare. He really was such a handsome man. But now, in repose, he seemed different. She realized it was really his personality that drew her to him. When he was nearby, everybody else in the world ceased to exist.

Just as she'd decided to let him rest, those attractive hazel eyes of his opened.

"Penny," he said. "Hey."

"Hi. Sorry to interrupt," she said, then jumped back as the cat leapt off Michael's lap, hissed at Penny, then lazily sauntered away. "Looks like I upset that cat, too."

"Oh, that was just Serena. She's Winnie Sadler's cat—Beverly told me that she has a regrettable tendency to roam the streets of Pinecraft."

"She seemed to like you."

He grinned at her. "I've been told I have a way with birds as well."

She couldn't resist rolling her eyes. "Obviously. Well, um, I'll just let you go . . ."

"Please don't. I was just thinking about you."

"I hope they were good thoughts."

"Of course." He smiled and gestured for her to come sit near him.

"I finished cleaning rooms, so I'll be going home soon." But as she walked to his side, she noticed that his expression was strained.

"Before you go, I need to tell you something." His chin lifted then, as if he was focusing on a spot just above her head instead of looking her in the eyes. "I've decided to leave at the end of the month. Probably on the twenty-ninth or so."

She didn't even try to hide her dismay. "But that's so soon."

"I know."

"You won't have even stayed here a month!"

"I don't have much of a choice. I talked to my *bruder* and he needs me."

"But . . . but what of everything we talked about? About you taking a step back? About you doing what you wanted?" Of course, what she wanted to ask was *What about me?*

"I meant what I said, Penny, but I can't live with my head in the sand at Siesta Key. I need to do what is expected of me."

"What about us?" she blurted before thinking better of it.

"Us?" Pain filled his eyes before he deliberately pulled himself together again. "We can still be friends, of course."

She realized then that he was determined to gloss over his wants in order to save them both further pain. But what he might not realize was that their separation was going to hurt no matter what they said or how they acted. Therefore, wouldn't it be better for them to at least be honest? One of them was going to have to be brave enough to mention what was obviously occurring between them.

"Michael, I may be shy and a little unworldly, but even I know that what we have is more than just friendship."

"You know what? You're exactly right." Meeting her gaze again, he stared hard. "Why don't you come with me?"

That was the last thing she'd expected him to say. "I couldn't."

"Why not? It would be perfectly fine." His voice turning more enthusiastic, he added, "I don't know why we haven't thought about this before. You can share a room with Molly. It will be great. She'd love the company."

For a split second, his eagerness infected her. It would be so exciting! She'd be traveling the world, meeting crowds of people out to see the Knoxx Family. She could make friends with his sister and brother and his parents. But best of all, she'd get to be near Michael all the time.

It would be everything she had imagined when she'd daydreamed about him.

It would be everything she'd been yearning for when she'd wished to live life to the fullest. No, it would be *more* than anything she'd ever imagined. It would be fantastic.

But it would also . . . absolutely scare her to death.

After all, she was just now learning how to have a job and do things with friends. No matter how much she might want to travel or experience new things this was just too much.

"Michael, thank you for the offer. It's *wunderbaar*. Truly. But, well, I simply can't."

His frown deepened. "Why not?"

She picked the easiest excuse. "I can't leave my parents."

He frowned. "You're not a child. And they'd get used to you being gone."

"I don't think they would. Actually, I fear it might break them."

"Penny," he said gently, "they'll get used to it. People adapt and change. After all, look at my family. Until I lost my leg, we were just a normal Amish family."

She wondered if that was ever really the case. Michael, at least, had such a magnetic personality, she couldn't imagine him ever being "normal"—at least not in the way she thought of the word.

Definitely not in the way she was normal.

Or maybe she'd just stumbled onto the truth. He was "normal," but she wasn't. She would never look at crowds or strangers the same way everyone else did. She couldn't; she'd lived for over a decade being afraid to even step outside of her house alone. She was too scarred by Lissy's abduction and death to ever be *completely* like everyone else.

In many ways she was still learning to cope with this reality by working at the Orange Blossom Inn, and here she had Miss Beverly, Mr. Eric, and even Tricia for support. How would she ever overcome those limitations when she was out on tour with the Knoxx Family?

Choosing her words carefully, she ventured, "Michael, I'm not ready for your life, either. I wish I was. But it's a big world out there and I'm still learning to do things here in Pinecraft by myself." She tried to smile in order to hide her embarrassment. Unfortunately, her lip was quivering so much, she was very likely making a parody of it.

"You wouldn't be figuring it out alone. I'd be with you and so would my family."

"But I don't know them. And we've known each other less than a month. Barely that."

He flinched. "That might be how long it's been on the calendar, but I think we both know that what we've shared has made our relationship far stronger than the date reflects."

She agreed and she knew he was right. However, she still didn't want to risk disappointing him when he saw just how awkward and weak she might very well be. "Perhaps, but I still must say no."

"I see."

"You can't blame me, Michael. You're the one who is rushing off."

"I don't have a choice. My family depends on me."

"Well, my parents depend on me to be there for them."

His expression turned carefully blank. "It seems there is nothing left to say, then."

Feeling as if he'd just pushed her away from him, she jumped to her feet. Yet still, like a desperate, love-sick fool, she paused, hoping against hope that he would change his mind and ask her again. Push a little harder. If he did that, she might even give in and say she'd try touring with him.

But he didn't.

So she rushed back inside the inn. With any luck, she would be able to tell Beverly good-bye and be on her way home in mere minutes. Then, and only then, would she be able to let herself dwell on what she needed to do.

And what she'd just given up.

MICHAEL SAT STIFFLY UNTIL Penny was out of sight. Then he hung his head and called himself the world's biggest jerk.

He'd known her past.

He'd known how timid she was and how each step forward into independence took tremendous courage. Yet with his demands, he'd made her accomplishments seem completely inconsequential.

The crux of it was that her viewpoint made perfect sense, too. No gently bred Amish girl was going to go travel around the world with a man who'd made her no promises and a family who were virtual strangers. Why had he been so eager to ignore that?

"Because you're a selfish fool," he told himself. "Because, yet again, you were putting yourself first. Thinking only of what you wanted."

"That sounds pretty serious."

He gritted his teeth as he recognized the voice behind him. This hour kept getting worse and worse. Turning her way, he said, "How much did you see and hear, Tricia?"

She stumbled. "I saw Penny leaving, then heard you mumbling to yourself. Sorry. I was only coming out here because my aunt wondered if you'd like any pie or cake left over from afternoon tea."

"*Danke*, but I'm not hungry."

She backed up a step. "All right . . ."

"Look, I'm sorry for snapping at you," he said quickly, before he managed to act like a jerk to two women in two minutes. "I, uh, just had a difficult conversation with Penny."

After gazing at him a moment, she stepped forward. "Did you two get in a fight?"

"Not that, exactly. I had to tell her that I'm leaving pretty soon."

She glanced at his leg and frowned. "Really?"

"It's time." The right decision was probably to stop talking, but he continued. It seemed he was destined to be a regular chatterbox this afternoon. "I was hoping she would come with me. You know, stay with my sister and travel with us."

"Why?" she asked as she sat down.

"Why?" He'd thought it was obvious.

She shrugged, as if she was making perfect sense, and he was not. "Well, *jah*. Why, exactly, do you want her to go on tour with you?" Looking at his prosthesis, she said, "Do you want her there to take care of you?"

"Of course not." He'd been hoping to take care of her for a change. To show her that she could do anything because he'd be there to make sure she was safe.

"Then why do you want her to be there?"

"Because I care about her." And because, otherwise, he felt like he would be leaving part of himself behind in Pinecraft.

She met his gaze. "Do you love her?"

Her question caught him off guard. "You're being awfully personal," he chided, mainly to give himself an extra minute or two to regain his composure. Did he love her? Or did he simply admire her very much?

"You don't have to answer. I was only asking."

"Well, I know that I'm going to miss her." And that he liked her a lot.

"That's it?"

He supposed she had a point. "I am developing strong feelings for her, too," he added, inwardly wincing at how, well, full of himself he sounded.

"I'm so glad we got that straight," she teased. "I'm sure she'll be glad to hear that you're developing those strong feelings."

"Fine. I like her. A lot." And the moment he heard those words, he felt better. Lighter. Amazing how being honest with oneself did that.

Seeing that Tricia was now smiling, too, he said, "Enough about me. How are you doing?"

"I'm actually doing a lot better. I like working for Aunt Beverly, and my family has forgiven me for not doing what they wanted."

Her words struck something in him. "They did?"

"Yep. I didn't think it was going to happen at first, but when I started telling them how unhappy I was and how I needed to do something for me, they understood. I'm relieved."

"*Jah*. I bet so." He got to his feet. "You know what? A slice of pie sounds mighty *gut* after all. What kind did Beverly serve today?"

"Butterscotch."

"Oh, yum."

She chuckled. "Beverly's pies would make anyone reconsider ever leaving this place."

"I hope there's some left," he murmured, though he knew there was something far more tempting than pie calling him back to Pinecraft.

Chapter 25

She's gone," Eric announced after he shut the inn's front door and came into the kitchen.

Amy had just stormed out in a fit of tears and a clattering of suitcases. Then, just to make things worse, she'd declared to everyone on the sidewalk that she was going to go check in at the Best Western down the street.

Even Wilma next door had heard—and she had hearing aids!

It was pandemonium. So much of it was transpiring at her inn, Beverly was tempted to climb on one of those giant Pioneer Trails buses parked by the post office and happily let it take her wherever it was going. At least then she might be able to get a whole two hours of peace and quiet.

But for now, Beverly and Tricia stared at each other in shock.

"We got that," Tricia murmured in response. "I think the whole street knows it, too."

He winced. "Sorry about that. Amy is rather dramatic."

Beverly thought the girl was a lot of things but held her tongue. "Was something wrong with her room?"

"Wrong? Oh, not at all," he murmured, completely oblivious

to the fact that Tricia was practically rolling her eyes. "She was mad at me."

Remembering the embrace that she'd walked in on, Beverly shrugged. "I'm sure it will pass."

"No, I don't think so."

"What was she mad about?" Tricia asked.

"You don't have to tell us," Beverly said quickly.

"No, it's not a secret." Looking reflective, he said, "When I told her that she should come visit me, she thought it was some kind of cryptic code that I was about to propose. Tonight, I told her that wasn't going to happen—at least not anytime soon—and it didn't go over real well."

"Wow!" Tricia exclaimed.

Beverly made sure to keep her response far more tempered. "I'm sorry she got so upset."

"Me, too," he said.

"You seemed close," Beverly said, though that was pretty much an understatement.

"We were. But maybe not in the ways that mattered," he mused, sending a wry look Tricia's way. "I didn't want to break up with her, but I wasn't ready to propose." He frowned. "Especially not when she was acting like she expected it."

"Relationships are so hard," Tricia said as she opened the freezer and pulled out a pint of ice cream.

Beverly walked over and pulled down three bowls. "What are you going to do about Amy?"

He smiled. "I'm going to let her cool her heels, then take her to the airport when she feels like answering my phone calls."

"That's it?"

"Yep. She's not going to forgive me anytime soon. Amy is a rather excitable girl. She doesn't do things in half measures."

Grabbing the ice cream scoop, Tricia said, "I didn't get that impression, either."

"What?"

Tricia flushed. "Oh, um, I just meant that she talks a lot."

Eric laughed. "That she does." Walking to the drawer, he pulled out three spoons. "I'm sorry for the commotion, but her visit will be over soon. Her flight leaves in a few hours."

"At least you won't be taking Michael, too," Tricia said. "I'm really going to miss him."

"Me, too," Eric replied. "He and I have shared some great conversations. He's got a way about him, don't you agree, Bev?"

"Yes." After glancing at the kitchen door, Beverly lowered her voice. "I don't know how Penny is going to take his leaving. They've gotten really close."

"Really close," Tricia whispered as she gathered up the pint and deposited it back in the freezer.

Glancing at the swinging door, Beverly said, "I heard them talking in the dining room just now. I'm not sure, but I think Michael just told her exactly what date he's leaving."

"Poor Penny," Tricia said.

"Maybe it won't go too badly," Eric offered.

"I don't think there's any doubt that they're going to be really sorry to tell each other good-bye," Tricia said as she grabbed a bowl and carried it to the kitchen table. "If I were Penny, I'd even find these next couple of days hard."

"At least we have ice cream to eat," Eric said with a grin. "I vote we stay in here for a while and let them have their privacy."

Grabbing her own spoon and bowl, Beverly joined him and Tricia. "I think that's a good idea. I don't want to interrupt their conversation." *Or anything more romantic than that.*

After taking a couple of spoonfuls, Tricia quipped, "The good news is that we're not gonna have to brace ourselves for Penny to yell and scream. Penny is a much quieter girl than Amy," she added, then looked immediately shame-faced. "Sorry, Eric."

He shrugged. "Don't worry about it. I'm disappointed, but, seeing how she acted here, I was beginning to realize she wouldn't ever fit in with us here at the inn."

Beverly almost choked on her bite of strawberry ice cream. That had sounded exactly like he was planning to stay with *her* in Pinecraft.

It was a relief when Tricia started giggling. "Sorry again, Eric, but you've got to admit that she really, really tried to like it here. Especially the *incredible, sugary* sand."

"And the *fantastic, warm* weather and *beautiful, flowery* foliage," Beverly murmured, reciting two of her least favorite Amy phrases.

"I liked her description of you the best, Bev," he said as he spooned up a bite of chocolate chip.

"Oh? How did she describe me?"

His lips twitched. "As a 'green-eyed goddess of the kitchen.'"

One by one, they each burst into laughter. But Beverly couldn't help but feel a little sad at the same time. Eric, too, would be leaving soon. And Beverly was surprised to realize that she was going to miss him. She was going to miss him a lot.

FOR PENNY, THE LAST week had gone by far too quickly. Seeing Michael had been the highlight of each day. They'd played cards, sat outside on the back patio together, laughed with Tricia, and simply enjoyed each other's company.

Michael had also healed. His color returned, he gained a few pounds, and he worked hard when the physical therapist came by to help him adjust to his fancy new prosthesis. His return to health would have been a true celebration . . . if it hadn't meant that it was also time to leave her.

Now, gripping the folded note that Michael had just placed in her hand, Penny attempted to maintain her composure. *"Danke."* After meeting his gaze, she allowed her eyes to drift around the dining room. But she might have had her eyes closed. She didn't see the watercolors of Sarasota, the Battenberg lace curtains, the silky sheen of the recently polished furniture.

"It's not a gift, Pen. It's my schedule for the month and all my contact information. You know, so we can stay in touch."

"You know my parents aren't going to want me to start writing you on the computer."

"That email address is only if you need it," he said patiently, "but I know you can call me from the kitchen here."

She didn't want to call him. She didn't even want to think about him being gone . . . and that he'd asked her to go but she had refused. "It will be long-distance."

"You could call me and leave a message and then I'll call you back. You could do that, right?"

Reluctantly, she nodded. "Of course I can. I mean, *jah*, I can do that."

His expression softened as he leaned closer. "Please don't forget about me, Penny. I'll be looking forward to your calls. And like I said, I'll write to you, too."

This was something that they'd been talking about ever since he'd told her that he was going to be leaving. Over and over he'd told her how important she was to him. How much he wanted to stay in her life, even if he was living far away from her.

"I'll write." Her bottom lip trembled. Mad at herself, she pressed one of the linen breakfast napkins over her lips. It was a futile attempt to conceal her pain.

"Penny, please. Don't do that. Don't pretend you don't care."

"I care. I just don't want you to see me cry."

Reaching out, he pulled her hands away from her face, then enfolded her in his arms and held her close. Immediately, she relaxed against him, feeling the smooth cotton of his shirt against her cheek, savoring how secure and safe she felt in his arms.

"This isn't over, Penny," he whispered over the top of her head. "I'm going to go on this tour and we're going to write and talk and make plans to see each other soon. Even if I have to come here every other month."

Every other month. Every sixty days. It sounded like both a blessing and an insurmountable period of time. Lying through her teeth, she said, "That won't be so bad."

"Not at all," he murmured as he ran a hand along the lines of her shoulder blades. "Who knows? Maybe over time you'll feel more comfortable with my family and you'll even want to join us for a short trip someplace nearby."

Maybe, in time, she could do that. After all, if he was willing to do so much, surely she could, too? "I'd like that," she whispered.

He pulled away but kept his arms loosely wrapped around her waist. "Penny, no matter what, promise me that you'll keep true to our proposal at the beach. Don't forget to keep moving forward and staying positive."

"I won't." She wasn't going to forget one single moment between them. "Will you try to remember it, too?"

"I won't ever forget." With a look of regret, he dropped his hands and stepped away. "It's getting late. The sun will set within the hour. Now, do me a favor and say good-bye."

"Already? But you aren't leaving for the airport until tomorrow morning."

"I'm leaving too early in the morning to see you. And I don't want you walking home in the dark."

"I'll be okay."

"I have other things to do, too," he continued, though Penny was pretty sure he was lying. "I still have to finish getting packed, pay Beverly, and get myself mentally prepared to go out on the road. I won't be able to do any of that if I'm only thinking about you."

She was in no hurry to leave his side, but she knew what he was saying had merit. It wasn't going to be any easier to tell him good-bye in an hour or two. After taking a fortifying breath, she did what she had to do. "Well, then, good-bye, Michael Knoxx."

"Good-bye." His voice sounded thick. Husky. "I promise I won't forget."

"I won't forget, either. Good-bye. And God bless you."

For a moment his eyes drifted to her lips and she was sure he was going to kiss her.

And she knew she would let him. Suddenly, Penny knew she needed that kiss, needed that memory to hold close to her heart when she lay in bed at night and thought about him being surrounded by scores of adoring fans.

But instead of pressing his lips to hers, he resolutely took another step away. "Go, now, Penny," he said softly. "And may the Lord bless you each day with His warm rays of light."

His words were beautiful, his expression was tender.

But her heart was breaking.

So she did as she was asked and left.

Chapter 26

Two weeks later, Michael was beginning to feel as if he'd never left the tour. After meeting his family in Brownsville, they'd flown to Denver, then St. Louis, and now had been in Canton, Ohio, for twenty-four hours.

He was exhausted and already tired of heavy meals and talking to strangers. He was also becoming increasingly frustrated with their packed days. A part of his mind was always aware of the time, and he spent much of his day wondering how he was going to be able to sneak away to call Penny.

In fact, the only good part about being back on tour—besides reuniting with his family, of course—was that his new prosthesis fit well and his stump was completely healed. Except for the occasional phantom pain, he often forgot he wasn't walking around on two perfectly good legs.

Now, as he stood on stage, waiting for his sister to finish her hymn, he resolved to remember his promise to Penny and stay in the present. To try to appreciate each hour of each day.

Even if it wasn't what he wanted to be doing.

As the clapping died down, he stepped forward and lifted an

arm. "And so, my friends, I hope you will walk with me through this life, giving thanks for our comforts and gaining strength from the One who knows our greatest fears."

When several people in the audience called out their prayers, Michael closed his eyes, led the crowd in prayer, then at last stepped away from the microphone.

The standing-room-only crowd surged to their feet.

As the crowd erupted in cheers and the clapping grew louder, he waved his hand again, then stepped to his brother's side as Molly led everyone in one last stanza of "Amazing Grace."

It had been a successful event. Everyone had been united, and the tangible feeling in the auditorium had been euphoric. The Lord had truly been with them tonight.

"You in pain?" Evan murmured into his ear as Molly finished and their father thanked everyone for coming.

"*Nee*. Why?"

"You look uncomfortable."

He was uncomfortable, but it had nothing to do with his leg and everything to do with his heart. "I'm fine."

"Sure you are," Evan replied sarcastically before walking down the three steps at the front of the stage and beginning to greet the folks who had crowded close, hoping for a private word.

Michael ignored him and moved forward to join everyone. His new prosthesis really did fit like a charm. He felt as whole as ever, was sleeping well, and his appetite was back. In short, he was as good as he'd ever been. He had much to be thankful for.

All he needed was to try harder. Surely, if he tried to be happy, he'd start to feel that way?

Seeing his father talking with their organizers a few feet away, Michael prepared himself to join the conversation and say the right things. Just as he silently asked the Lord for some assistance, a man with a military haircut stepped forward.

Michael immediately noticed that his gait was uneven. Holding out his hand, he said, "Hi. I'm Michael Knoxx."

"Drew Shelton." The man's handshake was firm. Solid. But it was the intense look on his face that drew Michael's attention. "Do you have a minute?"

"Of course."

He looked like he was debating with himself, then finally blurted out, "I don't usually go to things like this. My mom does. I only came because she didn't want to go alone."

"I hope you didn't find it too bad."

"What I'm trying to say is that I'm glad I did." He ran a hand through his buzz cut. "I was just discharged."

Hoping to set him at ease, Michael nodded. "You were in the military."

"Yeah. Army." He grimaced. "I thought I'd be a soldier my whole life." Pointing down at his right leg. "But I guess God had other plans."

"You lose your whole leg?"

"No. Just below the knee. People say I'm lucky to still have my knee."

"You are. Rehabilitation with a mechanical knee ain't easy." Michael smiled. They both knew that was a doozy of an understatement.

"It's been hard," Drew said. "You know, getting used to this new me."

"I know. But you will. There's not much choice, is there?"

The other man shook his head. "Sometimes I get so angry about what happened. Then other times, I'm incredibly guilty for feeling sorry for myself when so many other men didn't make it home." His gaze skittered across Michael's face. "How do you do it? Why do you put yourself up there and talk about what happened to you?"

"I go up there for a lot of reasons," Michael said honestly, realizing that maybe he was finally being honest with himself, too. "But I guess I've always done it because I've thought I had a story to share."

"I'm glad I heard it today." Drew flexed one of his hands. "My docs say I need to do some more physical therapy. I've been putting it off. You got me thinking, though. I think I'm going to go back."

"I hope you do. I've just had surgery to repair some damage I caused by not taking care of myself."

More people were crowding closer. Most were staying a respectful distance away, but Michael knew they were also waiting to talk to him. Holding out his hand for Drew to shake, he said, "Thank you for coming over to talk to me. It means a lot. Walk with God."

Drew clasped his hand. "I will. Hey, have you ever thought about writing a book?"

"Not really."

"Think about it, yeah? I know a lot of guys who would benefit from reading your story." Looking sheepish, he added, "Probably a lot more than would ever come to a thing like this. No offense."

Michael laughed. "None taken. Thanks, Drew. Thanks for your service, and thanks for what you said."

After Drew left, Michael turned to the other people who had been waiting so patiently for him. He smiled and listened to their kind words and stories as best he could. However, his mind kept drifting back to Drew's mention of the book.

He didn't know if he was capable of writing about his experiences in a meaningful way. But if he was and if it resonated with people like Drew, Michael realized that it could be the answer to his prayers. He could continue with his life's work but on his terms.

He wouldn't have to travel.

He'd finally get to have a home.

And, maybe, he'd even get to have Penny after all.

Two hours later, he was back in the spacious cabin his family had rented for their two nights in town. As soon as he got out of the shower and threw on some sweats, Michael joined Evan and Molly. Both were lounging on the leather sectional, Evan in old pajamas and Molly in a plain white nightgown and thick terry-cloth robe.

Michael had the beginnings of a headache that was no doubt caused by the war he'd been waging with his conscience. He now knew that he was ready to move forward with his life, to finally seek everything he'd been preaching about for so long. He wanted a regular, normal life.

He wanted to ask Penny to marry him and buy a home in Pinecraft. He wanted to spend his days writing about his experiences, taking care of Penny, and walking by her side on the beach. He wanted to have children and worry about them tracking dirt on the floor and whether or not they'd gotten all their homework done. He wanted all sorts of things that most people took for granted but sounded to him like precious gifts.

But in order to do all of that, he needed to be completely honest with his family.

When his parents joined them on the couch, his mother holding a calendar in her hands, obviously planning for their next stop, Michael knew it was time. Gathering his courage, he blurted his news in the worst possible way. "Mamm, I don't want to do this anymore."

She glanced his way. "You don't want to do what?"

"I don't want to tour anymore. I want to be settled. Live in a home not a hotel room. I want to stop getting on a stage and telling strangers how I overcame a frightening moment in the past."

Four pairs of eyes stared at him in shock.

His heart beating fast, Michael turned away. How was he ever going to apologize enough for that little speech?

His father frowned. "When did you decide this?"

"I've been thinking it for a while, but I made up my mind tonight."

Molly jumped to her feet and scampered to his side. "Michael," she said, tugging on his sleeve. "Why in the world didn't you ever say anything?"

As he gazed up at his sister, he realized that she did not look horrified. Instead, she was looking almost amused. It was definitely not the reaction he'd been preparing for! "What?"

She rolled her eyes. "I wish I would have known. I would've been mighty happy to stop touring for a while."

He could hardly believe what he was hearing. "What?" he repeated.

"You heard me. Constantly flitting around from one place to another is no way to find a husband, you know."

Michael turned to his brother. "Did you know about this?"

Evan had the grace to look guilty. "No."

"I didn't tell anyone," Molly said. "How could I?"

"Easily," Michael retorted. "You should have told me."

"I couldn't! I would have been too ashamed for you to know."

"Why would you be ashamed?"

"Michael, you were touring and traveling even when you needed to rest. Even when you needed surgery. How could I say anything when you were giving this family your all?"

"What about you, Evan?" their mother asked. "What do you think about this constant touring?"

"I don't know what there is to think about. It's our job."

"*Nee*, it's our calling," their mother gently corrected. "But our calling doesn't mean the only options we have are traveling and speaking to crowds for the rest of our lives."

Evan frowned. "But what choices do we have?"

"Plenty," their mother said. "Molly could concentrate on her singing and doing the things most women her age do—making friends, courting, helping others. You, Evan, could at last follow your dreams and do some woodworking. Or even offer your services to another group and be their manager. You're the most organized of any of us."

"We wouldn't have to stop cold turkey, either," their father mused. "We could simply cut back. Maybe only tour a few weeks a year." Turning to their mother, Daed smiled. "We could start sleeping in."

Evan still looked skeptical. "But how would we earn a living?"

"We have money saved. And God will provide," their father said.

Their mother got to her feet and walked to Michael's side. "What we need to remember is that our family's happiness is what is important. That includes you, son. We want you to be happy, not just to be the illustrious Michael Knoxx," she added with a smile.

"Are you sure about this, Michael?" Evan asked. "Are you sure you're not just feeling overwhelmed after your recovery?"

"I'm sure." He now realized that his brother had pushed his

own agenda on Michael when they'd talked on the phone about Brownsville.

"I guess the decision is made," his mother said. "Let's finish out our tour dates, then take a break."

"Which means I'll be heading to Pinecraft sooner than later. And as soon as I get there, I'm going to start making plans with Penny."

"*Jah,*" his mother said with a happy smile. "Michael, you should go call Penny soon and tell her the news."

"I don't know what she's going to say about me coming back." Suddenly Michael wondered if maybe she'd liked him being relatively famous. Maybe she wouldn't still love him if he was just another man living in Pinecraft.

"Which is why you need to call her," his father said again, as if completely changing his life was the easiest thing in the world to do.

But as Evan quietly handed him his cell phone with only understanding in his eyes, Michael realized his father was absolutely right. He simply needed to call Penny and be honest with her. He needed to tell her what was in his heart.

$\mathcal{M}$ichael's decision to leave Pinecraft had been a very good thing, Penny decided as she dipped a cloth in hot soapy water before running it along the insides of another kitchen cabinet.

It had been a very good thing, indeed.

After noticing that her mother was quietly humming to herself as she organized the silverware, Penny let herself dwell on all the changes that had taken place in the last month.

Watching Michael push himself to do what he felt was right had encouraged her to do the same. She knew God had given her all the tools she needed to come out of her shell and become even more independent. Penny simply wasn't sure that she would have tried as hard if she'd had Michael's comforting presence to rely on.

Since he'd left, she'd made a pact with herself to talk to one new person every day. She was getting the hang of looking people in the eye when she shopped now and of chatting with people at the Orange Blossom Inn. She'd also spent time with Violet and her family. Actually, she was gathering a whole group of friends right here in Pinecraft.

Her friendship with Tricia had grown as well. As Penny learned more about Tricia's past, she realized how pretty much everyone had something in their lives to overcome. It made Penny feel as if she and Tricia had a lot in common besides working for Beverly and trying to do a good job at the inn.

Her relationship with her parents was better than ever, too. They'd stopped asking her to account for each minute of her day. Instead, they asked her opinion about things. They were interested in hearing about her new friends and seemed to love her stories about things that happened at the inn. Her parents were reaching out more, too. They had even made friends with some other folks who loved pizza as much as they did and often went out with their new friends.

But above all, the three of them had at last moved forward. Though Lissy's memory was always present, none of them felt the need to dwell on the pain and heartache any longer.

These small steps forward made Penny feel like her family was much like flowers opening to the sun: growing and prospering because they were finally getting what they needed.

In the end, she'd never been happier.

Except when she went to sleep at night. Only then did she let her mind dwell on the one person who would have made her life even better.

Every time she closed her eyes, she thought about Michael. She'd remember snippets of their past conversations, which would lead her to pulling out his letters and reading each one again and again. That would lead her, unfortunately, to staying up far too late and reliving the one time he'd enfolded her in his arms. It had been bliss.

"Penny, do you think Michael will be calling you today?" her mother asked while Penny scrubbed the inside of another kitchen cabinet. Nearby, her mother was carefully wiping down everything that had been inside.

"Maybe. It's been two days."

Glancing at the shiny white telephone now mounted on the wall, her mother said, "I'm glad your father installed that phone."

"I still can't believe it." Even though they were New Order Amish, and therefore allowed to have a single landline in their home, her parents had always elected to shun as many outside methods of communication as possible. But now that her parents were getting out and making more plans, they seemed to appreciate the convenience the way a pair of giddy teenagers would.

Or, as much as Penny herself did.

"It's been so nice to not worry about Michael finding time to call me while I have a break at work."

"It's a small thing. I'm glad you have the phone so you can receive his calls."

"I can't believe how differently you feel about him now."

"I've seen how he's treated you, dear. He obviously cares about you a great deal. And he's been nice to me on the phone whenever he calls," she added with a smile.

Yes, it was true. Michael had gone out of his way to get to know her parents when he called. They appreciated his efforts. And, Penny secretly thought, they enjoyed knowing a celebrity, too.

"When will you see him again?"

"I don't know. He hasn't mentioned when he might get a break. But, of course, it's only been a few weeks since he left."

"But he wants to take a break and come back to Pinecraft?"

"*Jah*. We miss each other," she said.

"Do you regret not accepting his offer?"

"Not at all, Mamm. You know I wasn't ready for that."

"I'm glad to hear you feel that way." She inhaled, obviously gearing up to say something more, when, as if on cue, the phone rang. "You'd better get that, Penny," her mother said as she jumped to her feet. "I think we both know who it is."

As the phone rang again, Penny teased, "Are you sure you don't want to say hello to Michael first?"

Tossing her dishrag on the counter, she made a shooing motion at Penny. "Hurry, child. Get it before he hangs up."

Thinking her mother made a very good suggestion, Penny rushed across the room and picked up the receiver. "Hello?"

"Penny, hey," Michael said.

Smiling at her mother, she said, "Hey to you, too. My *mamm* and I were just saying that we thought it was you calling."

"I need to talk to you about something important. Are you alone?"

"*Nee*. My *mamm* is in the kitchen." She shared a look with her mother, who widened her eyes before sneaking out of the room. "Now I'm alone."

"*Gut.*"

All sorts of terrible situations started forming in her head. "What's going on? Are you hurt again?"

"Not at all. Oh, Penny, you wouldn't believe it. Yesterday I met a former soldier after one of our appearances, and something he said made everything so clear. Last night my family and I talked about touring."

"Oh?"

"I told them my feelings." After a pause, he said, "Penny, I told them I didn't want to tour anymore."

If she wasn't leaning up against the wall, Penny thought she might have fallen down. "Really?"

"I said that I loved God and them but I thought it was time for me to have a normal life. I told them how I wanted to stay in one place. And guess what? Molly was tired of it, too."

She could practically feel his happiness over the phone. It mixed with her own feelings of euphoria and lifted her heart. "You sound happy."

"I am. Because guess what?"

"What?" She was smiling so hard now she was sure she looked like a crazy person.

"Listen, we have to uphold our commitments, but then my family is going to take a long break. Maybe even scale back so we only tour a couple of weeks a year."

"What would you do instead?"

"My father said he thinks I should write about my experiences. I think I am going to give it a try."

"Oh, Michael. Yay."

"Yeah, yay," he said around a chuckle. "Penny, you know I care for you, right?"

She nodded, then made her lips move. "Right. I care for you, too."

"*Verra* much."

"Me, too." Grabbing the telephone cord, she twirled it around her finger. Her pulse was racing so fast, she needed to do something to try to settle herself!

"When I know more I'll tell you, but right now, just know that I'm planning to come see you as soon as possible. We've got a couple more appearances scheduled over the next few weeks, but once those are done, I'll be on a plane to you."

She loved how that sounded. "I can't wait."

"Me, neither. I'm going to get off the phone now, but I'll write you later."

"I'll write you, too."

"Bye, Penny."

"Good-bye."

When she hung up the phone, she hugged herself tightly. She wasn't sure what the Lord had in store for her but she was starting to believe that it was going to be very, very good.

Wunderbaar.

Chapter 28

It was only eleven in the morning, but already the early July sun was beating down on everyone in Sarasota, Florida. Penny was hardly aware of it, however. There was only one thing she was able to concentrate on, and that was the man holding her hand right there in the middle of Pinecraft.

Ever since he'd arrived at the Orange Blossom Inn two days ago, Michael had been a man on a secret mission. He'd spent at least four hours with Eric before Eric had left to catch a plane back to Pennsylvania. Later, Michael had been on the phone with his family, and Penny had even seen him and Tricia going over a bunch of notes last night before she'd headed home. To make matters worse, every time she asked him what, exactly, he was so busy doing, he simply smiled and asked her to be patient.

Now, as she struggled to keep up with him on the sidewalk, she was simply hoping he would let her catch her breath.

"Wait a minute, Michael," Penny gasped. "Slow down, why don'tcha?" When he continued as if the ground would burn his toes if he slowed, she added another word for good measure. "Please?"

But instead of bowing to her wishes, he continued, unabated.

It seemed that "please" *wasn't* the golden word in this instance. Perhaps it was time to use some sweet words and gentle reminders.

"Michael, I'd like us to slow down. I'm worried about your leg, you see."

"My leg is fine. Don't worry."

"I know it feels fine now, but what if something happens?" she asked, practically panting as he increased their pace. "I mean, you did just get on your, uh, feet."

"My foot is good, and my prosthesis is, too. That isn't an issue anymore."

"I know that." Well, she kind of knew that. "But since we're not in a hurry to go anywhere—"

"We *are* in a hurry," he interrupted as they came to a sudden and abrupt halt at the SCAT stop. "We've got a shuttle to catch."

"To where?" She wasn't even sure how he knew the SCAT schedule.

"You know."

"We're going to Siesta Key?"

"Absolutely." Looking down, he grinned.

Absolutely. Her body warmed at his use of that now familiar word. The way he loved to say it and how she loved to hear it. That one definitive word symbolized everything that he was: confident and sure. Positive. Maybe even seductive. That one word encompassed everything that was Michael Knoxx, and everything she'd ever hoped would happen between the two of them.

"Ah, here we go," he said as the shuttle approached. "Right on time."

She followed him onto the shuttle, took a seat next to him,

and decided to keep the rest of her thoughts to herself as the bus zipped down Bahia Vista and continued past Conrad Avenue. Less than fifteen minutes later, they stopped at Siesta Key.

Michael carefully escorted her from the bus and across the parking lot as if she were a fragile thing.

"Hey, are you going to be okay out here, Pen?" he asked. "I wanted to surprise you, you see. But now I'm thinking that I should have brought sunscreen."

"I'll be just fine." She put sunscreen on her face every morning.

"Do you want something to drink?" With a frown, he said, "I should have thought about water, too."

"I'm not thirsty," she replied, bemused.

Looking satisfied, they continued their way toward the beach. His confident stride was in direct contrast to their previous walk, when he had been in pain and she'd been scared their trip to the beach was going to injure him further.

Now, as Penny eyed Michael, she was still slightly in awe of him. Oh, not the famous celebrity—rather, she was in awe of the tender, compassionate man she knew him to be. The private man who put his family before his own needs. The strong Michael, who never complained about his pain or discomfort, or even the hand the Lord had dealt him. Instead, he'd simply shouldered his burdens and continued on with his life.

But most of all, she admired the man she'd grown to love, the man who cared so much about her that he'd come back to Pinecraft.

Now, all she needed was for him to finally share what was on his mind. "Michael, I think we need to talk about your plans sometime today."

He flashed her a smile. "Sure we do. But not yet." With hardly the smallest of hesitations, he climbed down the steps from the parking lot toward the wide expanse of beach, taking her with him. Then, as she slipped off her rubber flipflops and picked them up, he rolled up one pant leg, then the other, and pulled his one loafer off.

She looked down and saw that his prosthesis had its own kind of shoe. "Will your leg be okay in the sand?"

"It's good on any kind of surface."

"But if it gets sand in it . . ."

"If it gets sand in it, I'll wash it off."

Of course. He made it all sound so simple. And maybe it was. Maybe she was the one making things complicated. Maybe she needed to simply enjoy his company instead of wondering why he'd come back, when he was going to leave, and if he was in pain or feeling any discomfort.

After they walked a bit on the warm sand, the sun nearly over their heads now, he grinned. "What? You're not going to say a word now?"

She shrugged. "How can I? You seem to have all the answers."

"Not all the answers, Penny. Sometimes I have questions, too."

Well, that sounded very cryptic, indeed. Sharing an awkward smile with him, she stayed by his side as they reached the water's edge. With pleasure, she dipped her toes in, squealing under her breath at the water's temperature.

"I would have thought it would be warmer by now," he said.

"It is warmer, to be sure. But it's also only the beginning of July, Michael. Give it time."

He nodded, then reached out and linked her hand in his. "Let's go sit down," he said as he led her to a sand dune. It was a little off to the side, well away from the rest of the crowd. When she sat down next to him, enjoying the feel of the warm sand on her legs and toes, he turned to her.

"So," he began. "I guess you're wondering why I dragged you out here."

"I'm wondering a lot of things. I've been wondering what you've been doing for two days." Before he could reply, she added, "We've hardly even talked about your last night with your family. You all were in Mississippi, right?"

"*Jah*. We were there." For the first time that afternoon, he looked uncertain about how to respond. He paused, then blurted, "It went all right."

"That's it? What about your family? Were they sad to see you go? Were you sad that it was your last event for six months?"

"It was hard," he admitted. "As eager as I was to see you and move forward, it was bittersweet, too. I love my family but I genuinely like them, too. Even though I am looking forward to doing my own thing, I'm going to miss seeing them all the time."

"That makes sense. Maybe you can still see them from time to time, but the way others see their parents and siblings— for fun."

"Fun, hmm?" He smiled. "*Jah*, that does have a nice ring to it." He paused, then continued. "Anyway, our last performance went just fine. Better than most, I think. My sister's voice sounded beautiful, my parents' testimonies were moving, and when I got up and told my story—the story I must have told a hundred times—I got tears in my eyes."

"You ended on a high note."

He blinked, then the faint cloud of worry that had settled over his expression slowly faded away. "That's right. We did."

Gazing out over the horizon, above the spot where the waves crashed against the shore, he seemed to weigh his words. Finally, he said, "But here's the thing, Penny. For the first time in years,

I felt as if Got was pleased with me. As if He knew that I was finally going to follow His will and do something more with myself."

"What do you think that something is?"

"I think it's to write that book I told you about. I think when I start this new project, I'm going to at last be doing what I'm supposed to do—living my life *while* sharing my story."

"I like that." She was so proud of him. She knew he was giving up a lot to take this leap of faith, but she also felt that this leap was the right thing for him to do.

He grinned. "I'm glad you approve. I'm really glad I've made these decisions and am moving forward at last."

"Just like me," she murmured, thinking of the many times she'd wished she could break away from her parents' confines in order to actually live—something that Lissy had never had the chance to do. Now that she'd gotten the courage to do just that, the possibilities for her future seemed endless.

"Yes," he said with a small smile. "I want to be just like you. Penny, ever since we visited this beach, I've been taking our proposal to heart. I've tried my best to live each day. I've tried my best to enjoy each moment we have on this earth. I've committed myself to appreciating this life and this body—and all its imperfections—and my heart, and all its needs. And because of that, everything that's happened has been nothing short of miraculous."

His words meant so much to her. So much that she merely nodded and attempted to keep her tears at bay.

Michael noticed. Leaning closer, he gently brushed a tear away. "I've fallen in love with you, Penny. I want to be with you. I want to start each morning by your side and end each day giving thanks for the blessings that you bring to me."

As she gazed at him, Penny wished she could think of even half as many beautiful words to express herself. But all she could do was speak from her heart. "I've fallen in love with you, too."

His eyes lit with happiness. "I'd get on one knee if I could. But since that is beyond even this fancy, new prosthesis, I hope you'll know that I'm laying myself at your mercy. Will you do me the honor of becoming my wife? Will you be mine?"

She felt like she was on the verge of laughing and crying at the same time. Wasn't that just like Michael? He could say the sweetest things even while somehow still managing to make her grin.

"Oh, Michael, yes," she replied, not even caring about the tears that were falling down her cheeks far too quickly to be brushed away. "Yes, of course. I love you, too."

His grin widened so much, his dimple appeared.

She smiled back, then held out her other hand and linked hers with his. And then there they sat. Linked by hands. Linked by hearts.

It was the happiest moment of her life.

It was the happiest moment of her dreams, and the best part was that she knew there were so many more of those happy moments to come.

Epilogue

Three months later

It was humid in the way only Florida in early October could be—sunny and hot and bordering on oppressive. Most people took care of their errands in the early morning, happy to spend the majority of the day inside.

Penny Knoxx was no different. After she parked her bicycle under the carport along the side of the house, she grabbed her two canvas bags filled with fresh fruits from Yoder's produce, and a box of muffins that she'd picked up from the basket in Beverly Overholt's kitchen at the Orange Blossom Inn. Then, seeing that everything in their yard looked in good order, she quietly opened the back door.

As she expected, the house was quiet. After absently patting their new kitten—it seemed Mrs. Sadler's cat, Serena, had been escaping a few months ago for a very good reason—Penny washed and sliced the fruit, arranged it on a plate next to one banana-nut muffin, and then poured a mug of coffee. When everything was arranged just so on a pretty tray, she walked down the hall to her husband's office where she edged open the door with her hip. The kitten scampered through the opening with a meow.

"Knock, knock," she said as she entered the room. "It's time for a *kaffi* break."

Michael glanced up from his computer with a smile. "Looks like you've brought me more than a simple cup of *kaffi*."

"I did. When I was walking by Yoder's, I noticed they had fresh strawberries on sale," she said as she set the tray on the corner of his desk. "They looked so good, I couldn't resist picking up some for you."

He popped one in his mouth. "They're delicious," he said with a pleased expression. "You know me well."

Taking a seat in the big, comfy easy chair next to his window, Penny reflected that his words couldn't be truer. She did know Michael well. After he'd come back to her and they'd both become brave enough to share what they each truly wanted, it had been only a few days before they began with wedding plans and looking for a house to make into their home.

They'd agreed to have a simple, quiet wedding with just their immediate family and friends. Penny was still uneasy around large crowds of people, and Michael had feared that if they had a big wedding he and his family would have felt obligated to invite the many friends they'd made around the country. That had been the last thing he'd wanted.

Therefore, they'd had their ceremony in the Kauffmans' backyard. The Kauffmans had a big house and lovely backyard, easily twice the size of Penny's parents'. There, a group of about thirty had gathered one Wednesday morning in August and quietly helped them celebrate their special day. Penny had felt radiant in her blue dress. Michael still said he'd been the happiest man in the state of Florida.

Since the wedding, they'd spent a lot of time simply enjoying being around each other and sharing dreams for the future. Michael had begun his book. Amazingly, word had gotten to a publisher and an editor had visited him right there in Pinecraft. A few hours later, Michael had invited Penny to join them, and shared his news: Michael had been contracted to write his memoir and share some of the things he'd learned since his accident in the ravine.

Penny was glad for his new venture, but when she saw the look of peace in his eyes combined with the sense of satisfaction he'd been wearing since, she was even more pleased. Finally, Michael was done wandering and searching. He'd found a center for himself and a way to share his story and his vision without compromising his goals.

Later, when he'd asked her what she hoped to achieve, her answer had been very simple, especially since she'd realized that her dreams had already come true: she'd wanted a happy life, a husband to love, a home to care for, and a future filled with children.

With the Lord's help and Michael's love, she knew those things were coming true.

Which made her smile, because today she had something special planned for Michael, and she could hardly wait to set things in motion.

"Penny, aren't you eating?" Michael asked as he pulled off a chunk of his muffin.

"I already did. Miss Beverly invited me in for breakfast."

"Do you miss working at the inn?"

She sighed dramatically. "Oh, Michael, you ask me that at least once a week."

"I simply don't want you to feel like you're giving up too much."

"I'm not. And I'm glad I'm not working there now, if you want to know the truth. Miss Beverly and Mr. Eric seem to be at odds with each other all the time. Plus, Tricia is working full-time, too. They don't need me anymore."

He smiled. "And how is Tricia doing in your place?"

"About how you'd expect," she said, thinking of Miss Beverly's complaints about Tricia's spills and disasters. "I don't think the Lord ever intended for Tricia to be a maid." She thought some more. "Or a cook."

Michael's smile broadened into a full-fledged grin. "Or to ever touch an iron."

"Jah." Remembering the pots on the back porch filled with scrawny snapdragons, Penny added, "Tricia ain't too *gut* with gardening, either."

"I hope she figures out what she *is* good at pretty soon."

As Penny watched Michael bite into another strawberry, she gestured to his computer monitor. "How is your writing coming along today?"

Immediately, his expression changed. "It could be going better, I'll tell you that. I don't understand how it is so hard to put my experiences into words."

"Remember what that editor told you? First get the words out, then we can think about making some sense of them."

"I'll do that. When Evan and Molly come out to visit, they both said they'd give me a hand, too."

"I hope you will take them up on it."

"With you here to remind me? I'm sure I will. So, what are your plans for the day?"

Doing her best to keep her voice sounding especially nonchalant, she said, "Well, at first I thought I'd wash the kitchen floors, then maybe visit my mother later this afternoon, but then I decided we should do something else."

Taking hold of her hands, he pulled her to him. "And what is that?"

"What do you think about going to the beach today?"

"You want to go to Siesta Key?" He glanced at his computer screen. "I was kind of thinking I'd try to tackle another chapter today."

She knew his work was important, but the news she had to share was important, too. "Oh, Michael, everything you're writing in your book has already happened," she teased. "Can't you write about it tonight or tomorrow?"

"I suppose I could."

"Maybe the words will even come easier if you get a tiny break."

He squeezed her hands as he looked at her more closely. "You really want to go, don't you?"

"I do. It's our special place."

He stood up. "In that case, I think I'd better head to the beach today with my wife." After picking up the tray in his hands, he led the way to the kitchen. "How long is it going to take you to get ready?"

"Five minutes?"

In the kitchen, he laughed when he saw their beach bag already sitting by the door. It was overflowing with towels and snacks. "It looks like you were planning on me saying yes."

"Maybe I was."

"You are up to something, Mrs. Knoxx."

She didn't even try to deny it. Smiling, she nodded. "I am."

"Care to give me another hint?"

"All right. It has to do with another proposal."

His expression darkened as his gaze skimmed over her body. "Another proposal? Is it a good one?"

"Absolutely," she said, teasing him by using his favorite word. "Michael, it's absolutely the best news ever. Well, besides you asking me to marry you."

"I can hardly wait to hear what you have to say," he murmured as he wrapped his arms around her middle and tugged her to him. "Are you sure you have to be standing on the beach to tell me?"

No, she didn't have to be standing on the beach in order to tell him that they were going to have a baby in nine months' time.

But that's *where* she wanted to tell him. She wanted to stand on the beach, feel the ocean breeze on her cheeks, the warm, silky sand under her toes, and to gaze into his eyes and then— and only then—give him her news.

"I'm positive, Michael. Go get ready so we can catch the shuttle."

He brushed his lips against her cheek before releasing her. "All right. I'll be ready in five minutes. I can't wait to hear your news while I'm standing on the beach at Siesta Key. But first, wife, I think you had better kiss me."

Before she could respond to that, he bent his head and lightly kissed her lips. Then he kissed her again.

And as Penny wrapped her arms around his neck, she decided she wouldn't change this moment. Or their past. Or anything in their future. Not a single, solitary thing.

Everything was right in her world. Everything was wonderful. Absolutely.

Insights,
Interviews
& More ...

Meet Shelley Shepard Gray

The New Studio

PEOPLE OFTEN ASK how I started writing. Some believe I've been a writer all my life; others ask if I've always felt I had a story I needed to tell. I'm afraid my reasons couldn't be more different. See, I started writing one day because I didn't have anything to read.

I've always loved to read. I was the girl in the back of the classroom with her nose in a book, the mom who kept a couple of novels in her car to read during soccer practice, the person who made weekly visits to the bookstore and the library.

Back when I taught elementary school, I used to read during my lunch breaks. One day, when I realized I'd forgotten to bring something to read, I turned on my computer and took a leap of faith. Feeling a little like I was doing something wrong, I typed those first words: *Chapter One.*

I didn't start writing with the intention of publishing a book. Actually, I just wrote for myself.

For the most part, I still write for myself, which is why, I think, I'm able to write so much. I write books that I'd like to read. Books that I would have liked to have had in my old teacher tote bag. I'm always relieved and surprised and so happy when other people want to read my books, too!

Another question I'm often asked is why I choose to write inspirational fiction. Maybe at first glance, it does seem surprising. I'm not the type of person who usually talks about my faith in the line at the grocery store or when I'm out to lunch with friends. For me, my faith has always felt like more of a private thing. I feel that I'm still on my faith journey—still learning and studying God's word.

And that, I think, is why writing inspirational fiction is such a good fit for me. I enjoy writing about characters who happen to be in the middle of their faith journeys, too. They're not perfect, and they don't always make the right decisions. Sometimes they make mistakes, and sometimes they do something they're proud of. They're characters who are a lot like me.

Only God knows what else He has in store for me. He's given me the will and the ability to write stories to glorify Him. He's put many people in my life who are supportive and caring. I feel blessed and thankful . . . and excited to see what will happen next! ∾

Letter from the Author

Dear Reader,

Last February when Tom and I visited Sarasota, Florida, we ended up at Pinecraft Park around five that evening. My Amish friend walked us over, and the three of us stood on one side of the chain-link fence chatting with everyone on the other side who were playing shuffleboard. In the distance, some boys were playing basketball, while a group of young children were playing tag. The street nearby was filled with parked bicycles and a couple of scooters and a whole lot of people of all ages. Everyone was simply visiting and passing time.

Then I noticed that under the nearby pavilion, a crowd had gathered. A sense of anticipation filled the air. Soon, the benches were becoming filled and others crowded around the stage. I was kind of confused, and asked my friend what was going on. With a smile, she said a missionary group had come to talk. Tom and I were just as intrigued by the event as everyone else, so we walked over and stood on the outskirts.

After a brief introduction, a whole family took the stage, which was basically just a raised platform on one side of the pavilion. Then, the father spoke. And as he told his story, the crowd hushed. He told all of us about some trials his family had gone through, and how prayer and God's light had gotten them through that difficult time.

It was a beautiful testimony.

And then, very sweetly, his daughters started singing "Amazing Grace." Soon, almost everyone present was singing along.

I squeezed Tom's arm, knowing that I would never forget that moment. It was absolutely beautiful!

That evening was one of the highlights of my time in Pinecraft. I also knew by the time I went to sleep that night that I wanted to write about a family like the one I'd heard. I hope I did them justice.

I hope you are enjoying this series as much as I am enjoying writing it! Next up is *A Wedding at the Orange Blossom Inn*. The romance features two people who have been widowed, their many children, and a beagle named Frankie. I can't wait to share more of Pinecraft with you!

With blessings,
Shelley

P.S. I love to hear from readers, either on Facebook, through my website, or through the postal system! If you'd care to write and tell me what you thought of the book, please do!

Shelley Shepard Gray
10663 Loveland Madeira Rd. #167
Loveland, OH 45140 ∾

Questions for Discussion

1. At the beginning of the book, it's obvious that both Penny and Michael need to make some changes in their lives after spending years of keeping everything the same. Can you remember a time in your life when you needed a change? What led you to make the change?

2. Both Penny and Michael have overcome traumatic incidents in their past. Though their situations were extreme, most people can point to difficult situations that they've had to overcome. How have you moved forward after a trying time in your life?

3. Showing Penny's growth through her new job at the Orange Blossom Inn was gratifying for me to write about. Do you think she could have become as confident and self-assured if she'd been working at a different place? Why do you think her parents needed her to be the one to move forward first?

4. Michael's conversation with Drew was a turning point for him. Who in your life has provided some desperately needed wisdom?

5. Beverly and Eric's relationship continues to evolve in *The Proposal at Siesta Key*. They have begun to trust each other and now have slowly begun to form a friendship. Is there

anyone in your life who became a friend over time?

6. Why do you think Beverly needs Tricia in her life?

7. The idea that bad things can happen to good people is one of the mysteries of faith. In the novel, Penny's family certainly grapples with it. How have you come to terms with this idea?

8. I used the following Scripture verse to guide me while writing this book: *Open my eyes to see the wonderful truths in your instructions* (Psalm 119:18). What wonderful truths has the Lord asked you to open your eyes to see?

9. I felt the following Amish proverb was particularly meaningful to many of the characters in the book: *Growing old is easy—the hard part is growing up.* What does it mean to you?

Chocolate Pecan Pie

2 tablespoons margarine
½ cup chocolate chips
3 eggs (beaten)
½ cup white sugar
1 cup light or dark corn syrup
1 teaspoon vanilla
1½ cups chopped pecans
1 unbaked pie shell

Melt margarine, then add chocolate chips and stir until melted. Set aside. Beat together eggs, sugar, syrup, and vanilla in a medium bowl until creamy. Add melted chocolate chips. Stir in pecans and pour into unbaked pie shell. Bake at 400°F until done, about 50 minutes. Cool on wire rack. ∿

Taken from *Our Family's Favorite Recipes* by Clara Coblentz. Used by permission of the Shrock's Homestead, 9943 Copperhead Rd. N.W., Sugarcreek, OH 44681.

Shelley's Top Five Must-See Spots in Pinecraft

HONESTLY, I FELL IN LOVE with everything about the tiny village of Pinecraft, nestled in the heart of Sarasota and nearby Siesta Key! Here are five places to start your journey:

1. *Yoder's Restaurant.* I've been to a lot of Amish restaurants. I've eaten a lot of coconut cream pie at each one. But nothing has compared to this well-known restaurant. The line to get in is always long, usually at least a thirty-minute wait. But the long lines allow everyone to chat and make friends.

2. *The Produce Market at Yoder's.* The market next to Yoder's is full of beautiful Florida-fresh produce. We couldn't resist picking up two pints of strawberries and five oranges. Just to snack on—in between servings of pie, of course!

3. *Pinecraft Park.* It's the social center of the community! The night we were there, kids were playing basketball, men and women were playing shuffleboard (women have their own lane), and there were at least another forty or fifty people standing around and visiting.

4. *The Bus Parking Lot.* Behind the post office is a large parking lot where everyone meets to either board one of the Pioneer Trails buses or to watch who is arriving and leaving. ▶

Shelley's Top Five Must-See Spots in Pinecraft *(continued)*

5. *Village Pizza*. It's located right behind Olaf's Creamery. You can order a pie and take it right over to one of the picnic tables outside. The pizza is delicious. Eating pizza outside in the sunshine in February in the Florida sun? Priceless. ⌒

Scenes from Pinecraft

Photographs courtesy of Katie Troyer, Sarasota, Florida

The Pioneer Trails bus arrives in Pinecraft.

Siblings and friends at Big Olaf in Pinecraft.

Scenes from Pinecraft *(continued)*

Enjoying a Song Fest at Pinecraft Park.

Playing bocce in Pinecraft Park.

A Sneak Peek of Shelley Shepard Gray's Next Book, *A Wedding at the Orange Blossom Inn*

Coming Fall 2015 from Avon Inspire

FRANKIE WAS ON THE LOOSE. Again. "Mandy, dear, are you sure you didn't see where he went off to?" Emma asked her six-year-old daughter.

Mandy shook her head, the long white ties of her *kapp* swinging with the movement. "I was talking to Frankie about my daisies, but I guess he weren't too interested in them."

"I fear his actions have less to do with your daisies and more to do with the scent of pizza," Emma said around a frown. "He has never met a pizza he didn't want his stomach to know well."

"I'm sorry, Mamm. I thought the gate was closed."

Walking to the freshly painted white fence that surrounded their house like pretty white icing on a cake, Emma examined the gate. The latch was in place. Then she noticed the beagle-sized hold underneath it.

"Looks like Frankie dug his way out this morning."

"Oh, brother." Mandy let out an exasperated lungful of air. "Frankie can sure be a bad beagle, Mamm."

"Indeed." Ever since Frankie had been a puppy, he'd had an inordinate fondness for pizza. But now that he'd reached ▶

the ripe old age of ten, he seemed to have developed a real problem with wandering off in search of his favorite snack. Honestly, one would think he was too old for such nonsense.

Emma knew *she* was. She had three girls to take care of by herself, as well as her home and part-time job. She had no time to track down wayward beagles.

"One day I'm going to have had enough of his foolishness," she muttered.

"Frankie don't mean to be bad, Mamm," Mandy protested as she grabbed Emma's arm. "Don't be mad. He's simply a really hungry beagle." She brightened. "Like the caterpillar in that picture book!"

"I know, child." Gently, she rubbed her thumb over the little line that had formed between her middle child's brows. "You know I would never do anything to hurt Frankie. Go get your sisters, and hurry, please. We're going to have to look for him."

While Mandy ran back inside, Emma put her hands on her hips and looked left and right. Then she did it again, valiantly hoping that Frankie would suddenly appear trotting down the street toward them.

But that was unlikely to happen. If her silly dog had managed to sneak a slice of pizza, he wouldn't still be wandering around. Instead, he would be looking for a shady place to take a nap.

And because he was a very deep sleeper, he would likely not even hear the four of them calling his name.

Behind her, the screen door squeaked open with a sprinkle of giggles. Looking at her three angels, Emma did a quick inspection. All three were dressed for the day. Their three different shades of violet dresses neatly in place, rubber flipflops on clean feet, and white *kapps* on just so.

They were her heart, for sure and for certain. After Sanford had passed away three years ago, Emma had wondered if she'd ever smile again. But then she'd looked into her sweet girls' faces and knew that the Lord was good, indeed. He might have taken Emma's husband away far too early but He'd also given her three *wonderful-gut* reasons to live.

All she needed was for Frankie to stop escaping and her life would be fine.

"Where do you think Frankie went this time, Mamm?" little Annie asked.

"Wherever he smelled pizza." Feeling vaguely like a bit of a canine herself, she breathed deeply through her nose. "Do you girls happen to smell any?"

"We never do," Lena said. As the eldest daughter, all of eight years, she currently had an answer for everything. "But I think we should go to the right today when we start looking."

"How come?" Mandy asked. "The Kaufmanns live to the left and they always are eating pizza."

Lena shrugged. "Frankie went left last time. Plus, it's kind of early for them to be eating pizza. They're usually all at work or school this time of day."

That was as good a reason as any. Holding out her hands for Mandy and Annie, Emma turned left and let Lena lead the way.

"Frankie? Frankie!" Lena called out. "Frankie, you silly beagle. Where are ya?"

"Frankie, come home! You, you hound!" Emma yelled in her best no-nonsense "mom" voice.

"I don't think Frankie likes being called a hound, Mamm," Mandy said.

"Let's just hope he comes when one of us calls."

Taking that as an invitation to bellow, Lena took a deep breath. "Frankie!"

Emma winced. "Lena, not quite so loud."

"But if he's sleeping he won't wake up."

"I know, but—"

"Who's Frankie?" A boy sitting on the front steps of the Orange Blossom Inn said as they approached. He looked to be a year or so older than Lena. He was also dressed in long trousers, a light blue shirt, suspenders, and wore a straw hat. He was surely Amish, but his attitude told Emma all she needed to know . . . he, too, was blessed with the know-it-all syndrome.

Lena marched right up to him. "Frankie is our beagle. Have you seen him?"

"Nope. Why's he called Frankie?"

" 'Cause that's his name, that's why." ▶

"Well, I wouldn't come if I was a dog named Frankie. That's a silly name for a dog."

Lena planted her hands on her hips. "Frankie likes his name. A lot."

"Then why doesn't he come when you call?"

"He likes pizza," Annie said as she scampered over to him. "Do you?"

Emma braced herself to step in. Surely he was going to say something snarky, Lena was going to blurt something inappropriate, or Annie was going to start crying.

But instead, the young man stared at little Annie for a moment, stood up, and smiled. "Did you say he likes pizza?"

"Oh, *jah*. He loves it!"

"My family does, too. And they just happen to be eating it out on the back patio. Come on."

Next thing Emma knew, all three of her girls were following the boy into the inn. Though Emma wasn't afraid for them—she'd known Beverly Overholt, the proprietor for several years now—Emma wasn't especially certain that either the boys' family or Beverly would want three little girls to be traipsing through her inn.

But since they were inside, she followed, looking for Beverly as she stepped into the lovely entryway. When Emma spied Beverly standing by the stairs, her arms folded across her chest and grinning, she grimaced. "Sorry about the interruption. I'm afraid we're searching for Frankie again."

"When I heard you calling for him down the street, I thought that might be the case," she replied. Pointing toward the kitchen, she said, "They went that way."

"*Danke*." Emma hurried on. There would be plenty of time to apologize better later. For now, she had to keep track of her busy girls before they managed to get into as much trouble as one missing beagle.

The moment she passed through the swinging kitchen door, a pretty blond girl about eighteen or nineteen smiled at her. "They just went out the back door," she said, opening the door helpfully.

"*Danke*."

Then, as she finally stepped out onto the back cement patio, six—no seven—pairs of eyes turned her way. Three were her girls. The other four belonged to three boys and one man. One very handsome, very perplexed-looking man with dark blond hair and very light blue eyes. "Hi," she said weakly.

"Hi," he said right back. "I hear you're looking for Frankie the beagle?"

She nodded. She was embarrassed, but this was no time to wish for better behaved beagles or less trusting little girls. "He wandered off." Feeling more than a little foolish, she asked, "Have you seen him, by any chance? He's tricolored and has white feet and a white-tipped tail."

"Just as if he stepped in paint and got his tail dirty, too!" Mandy supplied. "He really likes pizza."

"I think we just met a dog with that very description," the man murmured.

Almost a little too mildly.

Emma just now noticed that he was staring at his pizza box. Then she noticed that the paper plates next to the box hadn't been passed out.

And a slow, sinking feeling settled in.

"Did, um, Frankie find *your* pizza?"

"He did." When he opened the lid, Emma groaned. At least half the pizza was gone. And the pieces that remained were decorated with paw prints.

Frankie had struck again.

"I'm so sorry. I'll go buy you a fresh pizza."

His lips twitched. "I'd take you up on it if I didn't feel so sorry for you."

"Why?"

That's when the boy they'd been talking to silently pointed one finger down below him.

Both Emma and her girls leaned down to see what he pointed to. There was Frankie. Lying on his side, stomach distended, eyes closed.

He was breathing deeply and kind of snoring, too. Orange pizza sauce dotted the white patch of fur on his chest. It was obvious that Frankie was going to have a pizza hangover for most of the day.

While the girls groaned, Emma fought against taking a seat ▸

at the table and silently hoping for some stranger to come along and take over her life for the next four hours. If they attempted to move him, he was liable to throw up. Unfortunately, she knew this from experience.

The man looked like he was trying hard not to laugh. "I'm starting to get the sense that he's done this before."

"All the time," Lena whispered. "He can't help himself, though. It's his weakness."

"I really am sorry," Emma said, looking at all of the boys and the man. "I don't know what to say."

"Why don't you tell me your name instead?" he murmured.

Suddenly, a whole other feeling came over her, and this one had much more to do with noticing that he was handsome.

"My name is Emma. Emma Keim. And these are my daughters, Lena, Mandy, and Annie."

"Where do you live?" the oldest boy asked, who she now realized wasn't actually a boy. No, he was more a young adult.

"Just down the way," she said evasively.

"We have a white house and lots and lots of orange and cherry trees," Mandy said.

"We're living here at the inn while my *daed* gets our new *haus* fixed up," the middle boy said.

"Oh?"

"I'm Jay. And these are my sons Ben, Mark, and William."

She smiled at them all. "Pleased to meet you. I am sorry about the pizza. If you could wait a minute, I'll run home and get my purse and give you some money to pay for a new one."

"That's not necessary."

"But I'm sure your wife won't like your boys missing a meal." The moment she said that, Emma wished she could have taken back every single word. Now she not only sounded rude but more than a little intrusive.

All four men looked mighty uncomfortable.

"We don't got a *mamm*," William said quietly. "She's up in heaven."

"I am mighty sorry to hear that," Emma said. "It's hard to lose a parent."

William looked at her curiously. "How do you know? Is your *mamm* up in heaven, too?"

"No, but, um, my husband is."

A new awareness crackled in the air. The man—Jay—lost his smile but he seemed to be examining her more closely. "I'm sorry for your loss, too."

"*Daed*, how about me and Tricia take William and Mark to Village Pizza?" the oldest boy asked.

"Tricia?"

"She's the girl who works here, remember? You met her yesterday."

"Oh. Well . . ."

"They need to eat, *Daed*."

After giving him a long look, he nodded. "*Jah*, sure. Go ahead."

"Can the girls come, too?"

"*Nee*. We don't really know them," Jay said before Emma could say the same thing.

Ben looked tempted to argue, then shrugged. "Let's go," he said to his brothers.

"Ben. Manners."

"What? Oh, sorry. Nice to meet you," he murmured before shuttling his brothers back inside.

Emma noticed all three of her girls staring in the boys' wake. She wondered if it was because they were new or because they were boys.

She stood up. "Well, um, I think it's time to grab my beagle and be on our way."

"How will you get him home?"

"I'll carry him."

He looked extremely doubtful. "Is it far?"

"*Nee*, just a couple of houses down."

Lena lifted two hands and showed off eight fingers. "Eight of 'em."

"That's too far for you to carry a heavy dog. I'll carry Frankie."

"I couldn't let you do that."

Before she could protest any more, he bent down, contorted himself to slide two arms around a snoring beagle, and with a grunt lifted him in his arms. "He's pretty hefty. Ain't so?" ▸

"He's chubby. Sometimes I think he needs to go on these pizza journeys," she said as she led him through a back gate and up the side yard to the street. "They're the only exercise he likes."

"We'll need to change that, I think."

"We?" she asked as they walked down the street, her girls scampering in front of them.

Looking down at her, he smiled. "I have a feeling between your three girls and my three boys and one beagle with a penchant for pizza that we're going to be seeing a lot more of each other."

She thought that was a pretty cheeky thing to say. But since he was carrying Frankie, she supposed he had that right. "We do have a lot in common, I suppose."

"We're a regular widows' club, I think," he said as they passed yet another home.

That had never been a club she'd imagined she'd be in. "Maybe we could simply be friends. That is, if you're intending to stay in Pinecraft."

"We are." Turning, he gazed at her over Frankie's head. "We're here for good. And until this very moment, I wasn't sure why the Lord had called us to move."

"But now?"

He smiled at her before looking straight ahead again. "Now I'm coming to see that yet again, the Lord works in mysterious ways."

She had no idea how to reply to that. Therefore she decided to say nothing at all. ∽